A GRAVE MUST BE DEEP!

Theodore Roscoe

A GRAVE MUST BE DEEP!

THEODORE ROSCOE

ILLUSTRATED BY

V.E. PYLES

STEEGER BOOKS • 2019

PUBLISHING HISTORY

"A Grave Must Be Deep!" originally appeared in the December 1, 8, 15, 22, 29, 1934, and January 5, 1935 issues of *Argosy* magazine (Vol. 251, No. 5–Vol. 252, No. 4). Copyright © 1934, 1935 by The Frank A. Munsey Company. Copyright renewed © 1962 and assigned to Steeger Properties, LLC. All rights reserved.

Visit steegerbooks.com for more books like this.

TABLE OF CONTENTS

CHAPTER I

UNCLE ELI

I Met Murder On The Way
He Had A Masque Like Castlereigh
Very Smooth He Looked, Yet Grim
Seven Bloodhounds Followed Him—

Masque of Anarchy

TAKE AWAY THOSE candles! It was that kind of light the first time I saw Uncle Eli; and the last. Glittery, windish light; the sort of glim to cast moving shadows and make the darkness darker than it is. None of that pallid glow for me. I like brighter hues. Reds and indigos, chromes and autumn brown; the colors of daylight and of Patricia's cheeks and eyes and nose (with freckles on it) and hair. Nothing to remind me of wax or dusk-gray or frogbelly green. I hate black, too, but let's not dispel it with candles. They make me think of Uncle Eli.

Uncle Eli was not my uncle. He was not Pete's uncle, either, by relationship. I'd never heard or imagined such a relative in all those weeks I'd been struggling at her portrait (full length, life size, Pete in a summer frock with a big straw hat swinging in her hand—"Southern Hospitality, by E. E. Cartershall, '34") and trying not to write valentines to her between poses on the side. I'd been that way about the girl for two years, but Pete was an expert at scorning me, saying love and paints didn't mix.

"None of this artists and models romance for me," she would

chill me with a smile. "You've fallen for the portrait, not me. And it flatters my Roman nose."

"Compared with you this daub is a cartoon," I'd groan. "Honest, Pete, I don't think it has a chance. I still think the background's too dark and that left hand—my old trouble, painting hands that look like clubbed feet—ah, I'll never finish in time, anyway."

Pete's eyes had a way of blazing. "You won't if you sit there in front of it like an ossified edition of The Thinker. For six week I've worked along with you—"

"That's just it," I had to protest. "You stick with me in this garret and you'll starve. When you could work for Jeff Galata and—"

"Magazine covers! Look here, you! I've stuck so you could do something real. If you finish this for the Academy showing—"

"You've been a princess," I told her unhappily, "and I've turned out another piece of junk. I'll never finish it—"

That would bring her down off the platform to grab me by an

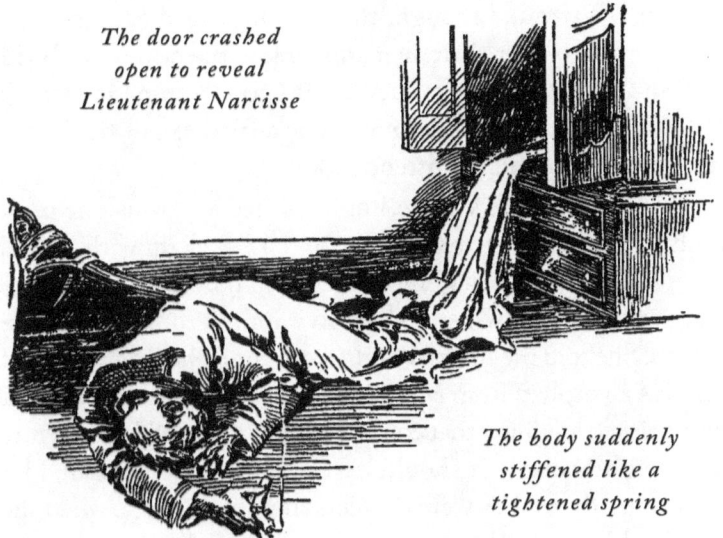

The door crashed open to reveal Lieutenant Narcisse

The body suddenly stiffened like a tightened spring

ear. "I'm a model, not a critic, and I don't think this canvas is a masterpiece, but just as truly I think it has a chance. You know you can paint."

"If you hadn't kept telling me that, I'd be making an honest living, house to house, selling vacuum cleaners," I would complain.

"Cart, you've got to finish it! I've put my faith in you, and I'm banking on you to win the prize. Listen—it's a business proposition with me. If you win the five thousand you can pay me back for all the times I've modeled for nothing. You've *got* to finish it."

Which would sting me into furious self-reproach, and I'd start over again and paint like a fool until the next argument. Away down under, I didn't think my canvas had a prayer at this showing—one of those free-for-alls sponsored by a fat dilettante with two stomachs and a hatful of coin. Five thousand prize money, and just the sort of rainbow's-end contest to make a lot of hopefuls quit errand boy jobs and waste enough canvas to have rigged the Spanish Armada. My picture wasn't too sour—in that crisp organdie frock with her Leghorn hat and a suggestion of blue dusk behind her, Pete's portrait might suggest a Watteau. I thought the tilt of the head gave it an air, and the pose wasn't entirely mannered, as the critics say. But I was almost certain the money would go to some Greenwich Village painting of a nude sunset like a fried egg or the Leaning Tower at midnight with no moon.

I didn't live in the Village, but inhabited a brownstone front on East Forty-fifth, five stories up under a skylight with a smell from an East River slaughter house when the wind was unkind. Pete washed her own stockings in a rented room on Thirty-eighth. She told me the first night I ran across her in Zoro's that she was an orphan from Miami, Florida, and I knew at once if I ever painted anything that could win a prize it would be a picture of Patricia Dale. As it should have been painted, I mean. Her eyes. Sometimes they were purple, sometimes indigo, when she wrinkled her nose they were blue with sunlight and when she was angry they were coral green. How can you paint eyes like that in a portrait, with only three weeks left to put them across?

"Stop the whining and work on it!" she reproached me, green-eyed, the night the showing was just ten days away. March thirty-first, it was, and in a couple of hours it would be April first (I have every bad reason to remember the peculiar date) and I hadn't touched the portrait for two days. A sour rain was chattering on the skylight and a piece of wallpaper was peeling off the ceiling and the attic was chill and shabby as something from a Russian novel. If I hadn't had a sense of humor and Pete hadn't phoned she was coming over I'd have felt an inch above the curb. Matter of fact, I had a German Lüger pistol, relic of the War, in my table drawer, and had gone so low as to wonder if it was loaded.

THE DAY had started on its left foot with a hangover and a batch of bills and a call from the Greek landlord to ask me why the hell, Mr. Cartershall, do I never pay the rent. I paid the rent and was sore because there wasn't enough left for an Easter gardenia for Pete.

Then Pete came over soaked in a coat much too thin for the weather, and sat for a while under the electric glare looking paler than was good for her. I tried to get in a mood to work on the expression about her eyes; fussed for an hour mixing paints; then didn't touch a brush to the dry canvas. We quarreled like panthers; I told her for the tenth time I'd never finish the portrait; she pronounced me lazy; and by then the light was too poor for anything.

At nine o'clock by the old grandfather alarm clock, we pushed the paints away and took it easy in front of the gas log, munching sandwiches and beer and smoking cigarettes and listening to the rain. Pete could look like summer, sitting there in her costume with the straw hat across her knees. But her bright smile did not fool me. I knew she was working Saturday mornings in a department store; and she had no business throwing in her lot with a fellow who should have been painting grocery calendars and couldn't do her justice. I had an unhappy impulse to get up and throw that attempted canvas out of the window.

Lucky I didn't. That portrait of Pete was going to have an amazing destiny.

There was a knock at the door. *Thump, thump, thump* on the panel. Fate was there, but answering the summons I didn't know it. I saw only the unwelcome person of Mr. Diogenes Karkavitsas, janitor, with a card in his hand.

He handed me a greasy, suspicious look and the card.

"Man downstairs, he's asking for Miss Dale. Says she's in your room. I wouldn't let him in, and he give me this."

Pete came over; together we looked at the card. No ordinary calling card, I can tell you, but more like an Easter greeting, engraved with gilt curleycues. Pete made a bewildered shrug at the name.

Maître Pierre Valentin Bonjean Tousellines, LL.B., Comte de Limonade.

"Heavens, what a name. I couldn't possibly know such a man. French, too. Maître means he's a lawyer. And Count of Lemonade!" Her eyes were wide blue, staring at the card. "Sounds like somebody from the court of Louis the Fourteenth or Alice in Wonderland."

"A thousand pardons, *ma'mselle,* but I am neither."

THE GREEK janitor jumped with a start. So did Pete and I. The voice spoke out of nothingness in the dark hall. Then, in the creep of light from the door, we discovered a shadow in the blackness at the head of the stairs. The glimmer of rainwater on dark cloth. White eyeballs and a gleam of shining white teeth.

"Come on in, we know you, and April fool," I said.

The shadow stepped softly into full light, edged the janitor aside with a dignified gesture; and the April fool was on me. Standing in the room in a rainsoaked and ancient redingote, storm rubbers and stovepipe hat, under his arm an enormous umbrella that looked as if it had just been handed him by Mother Goose, was a little Negro, a dwarf of a man, as black and wizened as a raisin.

"Ma'mselle Dale?" He smiled and his face was all teeth. Then when he spoke it was an underslung jaw with a huge, purple lower lip under eyes like eggs. "Ma'amselle Dale, they told me at your lodgings I might find you at the apartment of *m'sieu.* My apologies for intruding uninvited, but there is need of haste. I come from Morne Noir as emissary of your Uncle Eli."

"Uncle Eli!" Pete gasped; and all at once there was a color in her eyes I had never seen there before.

So this is not a story of New York studio life, after all. Instead (if you must have art) it is a story of graveyard birds and gallows birds and the thumping of voodoo drums.

A story of tropic Haiti, and the candlelight that shone on the features of seven murderous myrmidons and on the wan, green face of Uncle Eli.

BUT, OF course, I didn't guess it just then. I fancy I stood staring at this goblin-like visitor and wondering what Aladdin's lamp he had stepped from, and staring again at Patricia, startled by the color in her eyes. For a moment the only sound in the room was the drumming of rain on the skylight, the drip of the umbrella making a puddle at the little black man's feet. Pete frowned.

"Uncle Eli," she repeated. "What is he up to now?"

To my astonishment the little old Negro uncovered a head as blue-black, bald and shiny as an ebony cannonball; crossed himself twice. "Your Uncle Eli, *ma'mselle,* is up to nothing. Your Uncle Eli is dead."

"Dead!" Pete put a hand to her throat.

"Yesterday," said the apparition in the redingote. "The funeral will be day after tomorrow."

"Funeral," Pete whispered; and under her breath to me: "Cart, don't go away."

I wasn't going away. It was that thieving Greek janitor of a landlord who was retiring. At the word "funeral" he had let a squeak out of his throat; and we could hear his carpet slippers on the stairs. The little old Negro clapped on his stovepipe hat, crossing himself again.

"*Oui, ma'mselle.* I fear your Uncle Eli—was murdered!"

Something crawled on the back of my neck, and I came out of the trance. The thing was going too far. "Listen, Harlem," I snapped. "If this is a gag cut it short and get out of here before I boot you five flights to the street. Go back to your shine stand and tell the funny man who hired you to come up here in that costume that scaring ladies isn't as humorous as he thinks it is. And close the door."

He closed the door, but continued on the inside. Apparently Pete had not heard my outburst. "Uncle Eli," she was saying to herself. "Murdered. How awful. I suppose there were a lot of people who didn't like him."

Great Scott, maybe the thing wasn't a wheeze after all. The

gnome ignored me with a blink. The purple lower lip was speaking again.

"Forgive me for startling you, but times flies. Four hours after your uncle's regrettable death, *ma'mselle,* I hurried from Cap Haitien. The fastest plane to Miami; on to New York. If I had not had to spend the early evening seeking your address—"

"How—how did *he* know where I lived?"

"How, *ma'mselle?* That I do not know. Your Uncle Eli came several times in the past few years to this city on business. There were, I believe, agents—"

"Oh—"

"You are unaware, perhaps, of the magnitude of his interests. Morne Noir, *ma'mselle,* is one of the largest estates in our Haitian Republic. There are many acres in cane. There is a sugar mill. *Alors,* there are his fishing interests over in La Gonave, also fifty thousand *gourdes* on deposit at the bank in Petianville and gold bonds in the Banque Nationale. Although sugar is down and the American exchange doing deplorably with many of his securities there, your Uncle Eli died a man of wealth, leaving a noteworthy fortune. The château at Morne Noir and an estate of some hundred thousand dollars."

"I'm not interested in Uncle Eli's estate," Pete said coldly. "If he was killed I'm sorry and hope justice is done. Thank you for bringing the—the news."

"As your Uncle Eli's lawyer and executor I was so commissioned. *Ma'mselle!* It was your uncle's instructions that I was to communicate with you immediately, if, when, and at such time as he should die. Yesterday afternoon it was, when your uncle was discovered seated in the library, dead with a book in his lap. It was his habit to go there during siesta hour and read. He was found by his personal physician, who, coming from the hospital at Cap Haitien, stopped in to call. Shot in the head. *Mon Dieu!* But no one was in the house at the time, *non!* No gun was discovered, no tracks, nothing. His face was covered with blood. I saw it. In fact I followed the doctor into the house, arriving on the scene just after he extracted the bullet. A bullet from a nine millimeter automatic. The body was stiff. Dr. Sevestre said it had been dead one hour, and prepared it at once for burial. The police? *Poof!* The fools know nothing. Suicide, perhaps. Bah! Of that I will speak later. I can only say, *ma'mselle,* that you should feel interest in the estate as you have been named a possible heir."

PETE SHOOK her head. "Not by Uncle Eli."

"In writing, *ma'mselle.* Along with several others."

"I'm not—"

"Pardon me," the lower lip said. The old man set the umbrella against the door; dug wildly in the bosom of the greatcoat, to produce an impressive envelope. A big white envelope sealed with a red rosette of sealing wax. He held it toward Pete. *"Voilà!* Here is the money, *ma'mselle;* more than adequate to take you by express plane to Miami and Cap Haitien. My instructions were to deliver this if you will go. *Bien."*

Pete regarded the envelope with an expression of unbelief. "For me? Uncle Eli left money for me? To go to Haiti?" She threw back her head and laughed. "Pinch me, somebody. A hundred thousand estate! Uncle Eli! Oh, my!" She waved the straw hat at the ceiling. "Whee!"

"You will go to claim your legacy?"

"Will I *go?* Well, if I've been left some money I don't see why I shouldn't—"

"Then you must hurry, *ma'mselle,* for there is barely enough time. There is a plane for Miami early to-morrow which you must take. In Miami you will take a plane to Cap Haitien, and no time can be lost. Myself, I must leave to-night. I will be in Cap Haitien to meet you and will, myself, conduct you to Morne Noir. Attend! You cannot miss to-morrow's plane."

Pete stood very still. "To-morrow's plane?"

The little old Negro nodded. "For if you are not there to hear the reading of the will you forfeit any heritage. Such are the written instructions of the deceased." Another paper came out of the redingote. The white eyes travelled down the document, reading.

" 'The will now on file with Maître Tousellines' (at your service) 'is to be opened and read by said Maître Tousellines just prior to the burial service which is to be held in the library of Morne Noir on the midnight of the third day after the death of testator. The reading shall be made by Maître Tousellines to the heirs or devisees named and in the presence of my personal physician, Dr. Sevestre, as witness, and any other witnesses attendant to the burial service. An heir so named who fails to hear the reading and remain present throughout the funeral is automatically disinherited, with his or her share of the estate, as bequeathed in the will, reverting to the local government.'"

The old man droned the paragraph; yanked another leaf from his coat. "I have here the list of possible inheritors, the devisees, *ma'mselle*. Your name is included."

"And to collect my share I've got to leave for Haiti to-morrow and be there at the funeral."

"As stipulated, *ma'mselle*. I can only advise that the fortune is considerable, and it would be to your interest to go." He handed her the envelope with the money; stowed the papers back into the redingote; adjusted the stovepipe; clutched up the umbrella.

As for me, I was dizzy. The rain was still drumming on the skylight; that was real enough. But I would be disappointed if the darky did not say "Abracadabra!" and vanish.

He opened the door and stood, crow-like, in the frame. "I will await you at the *douane* in Cap Haitien, *ma'mselle*. Permit me to remind you, if you do not go you forfeit your rights to a bequest. *Bon soir, ma'mselle.*"

Pete stood looking at the envelope in her hand. I jumped to the door. "Wait a minute," I called. "Any objection to Miss Dale's fiancé coming with her?"

Eyes looked up the stairs. "There are none so stipulated by the deceased, *m'sieu. Bon soir.*"

"HOLD ON," Pete said, as I closed the door. "Get that—that

African lawyer back here. I'm not going to need this traveling fare because I can't go."

"Can't go? With a crack at this uncle's fortune of yours?" I blattered the King's English. "With this chance at a hundred *thousand!*"

Pete made a face. "He wasn't my uncle, Cart. Not really. Not even a close relative, thank God. I—I hated him."

"Who was he?"

"A fifth cousin of dad's, perhaps. And when father died he left me in the care of this hawk. Eli Proudfoot. He was my guardian. Ugh. Skinny. Big Adam's apple. Must have been fifty, then. Little glassy eyes like camera lenses. Kind of sneaked when he walked."

"But he's leaving you this—"

"I guess he had some money, even then. We lived in a mouldering old Florida house. I can still remember how his lips would sort of purse when he'd kiss me. I was ten. When I was seventeen he tried to make love to me—asked me to marry him. One of those horrible old Romeos. I couldn't stand it. I slapped his face and ran away. He simply boiled with rage, and threatened to have me brought back. I hid. Then I heard he'd gone to this place in Haiti and become sort of a white Emperor Jones or something. I haven't heard of him since. I don't wonder, really, that somebody took a shot at him. Once I saw him jab a lighted cigar into the flank of his saddle horse."

"Sounds sweet," I said. "But just the same he's relented, and cut you in on his will. A hundred thou—"

"I'm not—"

"You bet your sweet life you're not going down there alone. I'm going with you. I've got just time to borrow the fare from a friend and I can pack in a—"

"I'm not going, Cart."

"With that money just dropping in your lap?" I capered. "Don't stand there—" Then I saw where her eyes were. "Lord! Don't tell me you're thinking about that damned painting!"

"Cart," she said firmly, "do you think I'd step out on you just when you're getting it finished? You've got to work every minute of the next few days."

I could have wept. "Do you think I'd see you lose a fortune so I could miss winning that fool prize?"

"Listen," she blazed. "You told that black lawyer you were my fiancé. Well, E.E. Cartershall, you're not my fiancé. You've asked me to marry you often enough, but I'll tell you one thing right now. You'll never get an answer from me until that painting is finished!"

"But we'll take it with us," I hollered. "Look! I'll take it off the frame—it's dry, and won't hurt it a bit—and I'll carry it rolled up and when we get there I'll stick it on another frame and I'll paint while we're there and no time lost at all. I'll work in Haiti, see? Holy mackerel! don't toss any hundred grand for anything as simple as that. I won't let you. You're going, and I'm going with you."

"I won't go," Pete said.

She wouldn't have, either. And to tell you the truth, I was a little blue about all that money, because I knew what it meant. This business of the poor artist and the rich—but I didn't hint any of that in the argument.

CHAPTER II

DEATH WATCH

NOT MANY HOURS after that we were driving in a buggy through the dirtiest black rain I've ever seen, on the darkest road to any place but one. Maître Pierre Valentin Bonjean Tousellines, LL.B., Comte de Limonade, drove what we could see of a horse, and was speaking of murder. Pete sat with her eyes glistening. The more I was seeing of Haiti the less I was liking it, the gladder I was I'd insisted on coming with Pete and the brighter I felt for remembering to stick my Lüger automatic in my Gladstone.

The rain was falling with a swishing sound, and away off in the blackness somewhere there was a faint *tumpy-bum-bum, tumpy-bum-bum*, like the beating of a heart.

When the wind blew the rain sheeting across the road the sound faded, and when the rain swung back in a drizzle the sound grew louder. You couldn't see your hand before your face outside the buggy curtains, but you could hear that sound. It was there like a presence. It had come with nightfall, along with us and the rain and the buggy-ride. I didn't like the sound and I didn't like the buggy-ride. I hadn't wanted to leave the seaplane out in the bay and go ashore in the rowboat to meet the little black lawyer—

The plane had come into the cape at twilight, and there was Haiti with darkness already pooling over the town along the shore. Palm trees and white roofs. A sort of hothouse steam in the air. A smell they told us was Cap Haitien. Jungle-green hills swooping up behind the town and steep mountains scowling high up in the dusk with clouds mumbling among dark cliffs. Pete was on needles and pins to get ashore, and fascinated by a ruin we could dimly see at the top of a distant mountain.

"Yeah," the pilot told her. "That's Christophe's Citadel. La Ferrière. This Christophe was the black king, emperor of Haiti around the time of Napoleon. Built that fort up there. Used to order his soldiers up there for discipline, an' command them to march off the cliff."

Pete nodded, "So that's the place. This Caribbean climate seems to make them grim."

"Yeah. This Christophe shot himself with a gold bullet, and they buried him in a lime pit up there," the pilot chuckled. "They say the hand didn't sink. They say it stuck out and reached at the sky. But you know these black Haitians. Believe anything. Voodoo charms and all that. You'll hear the drums, most likely. Myself," said the pilot, "I don't like it here. Well—have a nice honeymoon."

"You're not even close," Pete told him crisply. "We're going to a funeral."

"I feel a little as if I were going to my own," I had to mutter later on when we were being sculled ashore in a red rowboat by a tan Negro in a pair of violet pants. The scene was done in shades of blue, blue-gray and green. The headlands of the cape were shadows; the purple mountains looming taller and darker as we neared the foreshore; the boat burbled in a bay like dark wine. In the dusk I could make out our Senegambian attorney in the stovepipe hat, a silhouette on the dock. We were Charon's customers going to the Land of Shades, and there was the mortician waiting for the tickets.

"I DON'T know about this," I said to Pete.

"About what?" She sat with her feet on the luggage, my paint-box in her lap, the unfinished masterpiece hugged under her gabardine.

"About landing in this Negro republic after dark like this."

"I thought you were all for coming. Not scared, are you?"

"My teeth," I bowed haughtily, "are chattering. All the same, young lady, don't forget I'm—"

"You're not responsible for me, Mr. Cartershall. I'll take care of myself and you'll take care of yourself. All you've got to do is keep your mind on your business and paint."

Cart

Life does have its surprises. One evening you're under a skylight on Forty-fifth Street; two evenings later you're under a mountain range fringed with palm trees. And there was something somber about those hills. I was glad I'd had brains enough to wireless from Miami and ask the authorities about Master Tousellines. I hadn't told Pete; but the reply was in my pocket.

Master Tousellines, as far as the consular service knew, was a barrister in good standing.

He doffed the stovepipe to Pete, and without further greeting hurried us from the dock to an old Buick. We drove past shabby walls, down shabby streets in a darkness that prevented sightseeing. Pete exclaimed over a donkcy cart under a street lamp and a Negress with a rooster perched on her turban. I glimpsed a couple of grille doorways I would have liked to sketch. Then we were on an open highway, and the landscape was gone.

The black boy at the wheel drove like an idiot. The car squealed on the curves. Master Tousellines sat in silence in the front seat beside the chauffeur; and Pete and I were two sparks from cigarettes in the back seat. Three hours through the night at about sixty miles an hour, climbing most of the way. Now and then the headlamps picked out a palm tree, a dim wall or a pig,

not stopping for the pig. At last the car halted in the middle
of Nowhere. There was a huge gray tree bearded with Spanish
moss, a bony horse tethered to a lower limb, a buggy posing for
a case of rickets. Everybody out. The black chauffeur piled our
luggage to the ground. Our guide indicated the buggy.

"We proceed, *ma'mselle,* in the carriage."

Pete appraised the vehicle doubtfully. "If that's an example
of Uncle Eli's estate—"

"It is the only means of travel in this section, *ma'mselle.* By
horse. The roads about Morne Noir are exceedingly difficult."
He mined from his coat a silver watch as old as the buggy, the
night, the tree and himself; snapped open the lid. "*Alors!* We have
a trifle over an hour. Excuse me, but we must hurry."

SOMETHING WET splashed on my face, and away off in
the dark I heard a faint, muted thumping. "It's going to rain," I
growled. "And what's that sound?"

"It is the season of the *avalasse,* the bad weather," was the
intoned response. "I fear we may be caught in the torrent. The
sound, *m'sieu,* is that of a Rada drum."

"I could do without it," I confessed.

"So could I," Pete admitted, edging a little closer on the seat.
"Cart, did you ever see a night as black as this?"

I never had. The buggy lamp was Futility on the dashboard,
hissing in the rain. We were drawn by the steaming hindquarters
of a horse into the blindest midnight that ever congealed under a
waterfall. Maître Tousellines was the Invisible Man. There didn't
seem to be a profile between the shadow of his coat-collar and
the brim of the stovepipe hat. The reins and the whip appeared
to move in midair of their own volition. Eyes and white teeth
were all that remained of his face save when the lampshine
touched with a radium-like luminescence his swollen lower lip.

The lower lip moved. "It is only the Rada drum. The plantation hands, *m'sieu,* are having a dance. It is a custom of the
funeral ceremony in our country. You do not know of the Rada
drum?"

"What's it about?" I asked.

The white eyes rolled, uneasy in their sockets. "There are three of them, you comprehend. *Maman, papa* and *boula*. Mamma drum, papa drum, baby drum. There will be a service in the *houmfort* on the Morne, an invocation to Damballa. The drums are asked to ward off evil spirits from the dead, and you hear them replying, mamma, papa and baby."

"Cute," Pete said.

We drove in the pitch black rain listening to mamma, papa and baby warding off evil spirits. Water flogged the buggy-top, whipped the sidecurtains, spattered in brown showers over the dashboard. The buggy was a frail thing in that downpour, a flimsy trap of wheels and sticks swimming us uphill. I made three attempts to light a fresh cigarette in the wet, and gave it up. I could feel Pete getting mad. There wasn't any road; only the *clop, clop, clop* of our soaked beast and the *thumpy-bum-bum* going on in the blackness.

"Myself," said the Invisible Man beside me, "I do not believe in such things, you comprehend. I am an educated man, *m'sieu,* and have studied law in Paris and New Orleans. Perhaps it is well for me to warn you that the Haitians of the district about Morne Noir are those of a peasant order. I can assure you I have no faith in their primitive beliefs and will do all possible to felici-tate the business of *ma'mselle* at hand."

"You don't expect any troublesome delays?" I snapped.

"Mais non, m'sieu. Only—Haiti is a, I am sad to confess, coun-try the somewhat primitive. In the matter of a homicide, for example."

"You were going to tell me something about Uncle Eli's demise," Pete remembered.

THE WHITE eyes revolved in the blank between the tophat and the collar. "It is only that I do not trust the ability of the local gendarmerie, *ma'mselle.* The inspector from the Garde d'Haiti was working on the case when I left for New York. A clear case of suicide, he reports. But the facts are as I have told you.

M'sieu Proudfoot had gone to the library as was his custom for the afternoon siesta. The house was empty. Dr. Sevestre found *m'sieu* seated in a chair with a book in his lap, his face streaming blood and a bullet in his head. I entered not ten minutes later to see the doctor plucking the bullet from the forehead of the deceased. The doctor covered the face with a handkerchief and together we carried the corpse to a room where the doctor set about preparing it for burial. The body was very stiff."

"Nicy story for a rainy night," I said.

"It doesn't sound like Uncle Eli to commit suicide," Pete suggested.

"He was in excellent health, *ma'mselle*. And then, as I pointed out, where was the gun? *Non!* the doctor had the bullet which was later determined of nine millimeter calibre. But no gun. I made a tour of the library, and later a quick search of the grounds beyond. No gun, no tracks, nothing. I have learned that there was an *enquête* (which corresponds to the inquest of your country, only there was at Morne Noir no coroner) during which the police hinted at Dr. Sevestre. Perhaps the doctor, on entering the library, had fired the shot. But I saw the doctor enter the house, and I stood without on the veranda for some ten minutes. I heard no shot. And then the body was exceedingly stiff with rigor mortis. It was, I assure you, an unhappy sight."

Pete made a little sound in her throat. "I'm sure it was."

"But the police, bah! they are only capable of arresting chicken thieves. That inspector. His decision was of the most pompous. If there are no traces of a murderer found, says he, then who can say there is murder?

"I asked about the gun. *Alors,* is his reply, perhaps one of the servants stole into the library, saw the gun, picked it up and fled in fright."

"Can't say as I'd have much faith in the local constabulary," I said.

"They are blacks, *m'sieu*, of the most thick-headed. I said as much to this inspector. The case is to be closed as suicide, he told me. He said that was the only possible explanation. That and—and—and one other explanation—"

Rain swirled through the buggy, and gave us a dousing. The lamp *sszzzzed* and went out, and everything vanished. "Woosh," Pete spluttered dismally. "And what explanation was that?"

"He said—" the voice beside me lowered, seemed to sink into something hollow, "the inspector said your Uncle Eli might have been murdered by a *zombie!*"

"What's a *zombie?*" Pete questioned him.

"A *zombie*," the hollow voice sank almost below the black rain, "a *zombie, ma'mselle*—but understand that I, Maître Tousellines, am a man of education and do not believe such things. But the Haitians of this district, *ma'mselle*—in a case like this—well, *ma'mselle*, as your Uncle Eli's lawyer it is scarcely—it is scarcely conformant for me to speak so of a client, but *M'sieu* Proudfoot was a hard man. Of a temper, you comprehend me. In matters of discipline. There were several whom he punished most severely, and two, I believe, he killed in self defense—"

"What's a *zombie?*" I demanded.

"A *zombie, m'sieu*," the hollow voice bassooned to a gurgle, "a *zombie* is one who has died but is not dead. A corpse resurrected by witch doctor's magic from the grave. A living dead man who returns as the slave of some master, who may labor in the field or walk unseen with silent steps on errands of revenge. It is the unfortunate belief of the Haitian inspector, *ma'mselle*, that your Uncle Eli—but *I* do not believe such nonsense—that your Uncle Eli may have been murdered by a *zombie*."

There was a tremendous spate of rain during which the buggy seemed to go sweeping up the road; then an abrupt drizzle and the pitch dark filled with the booming of drums.

"But here," said Maître Tousellines, "we are."

I looked up and saw an angel.

IT WAS standing beside the buggy with its head floating high in the mist; a giant of a thing some twenty feet tall, arms folded and chin bowed on chest, wet robes hanging limp to the sandals, wings swooped together at rest, sentinel on a massive cube of granite. Light, sifting watery through a fan of patent leather trees, made to glisten the brook that ran from the angel's nose; touched a shine to the massive sad face. The sightless eyes looked down at me. The thing must have weighed in at six tons. Too heavy for the wings, so the fellow got around on rollers that stuck out from under the granite platform, and, attached to his ankles, a block and tackle.

"Well, hallelujah!" Pete looked out at the angel. "That's not Uncle Eli's ghost?"

The lawyer said no, the angel standing watch in the rain beside the road was not Uncle Eli's ghost. It was, said the lawyer, Uncle Eli's *pierre tumulaire.*

"His tombstone, *ma'mselle.* Some months ago he ordered the marble and had the cutters contrive this monument. Perhaps you know *M'sieu* Proudfoot was given to, one might say, the eccentric. It is my opinion that death, these last several years, had been preying on his mind."

"Not getting religious, was he?"

"Then he ordered a coffin, a rosewood coffin, built by the local carpenter. He locked it in his private store room and often, I am told, would sit alone with the casket, reading the Bible and sometimes other—other books. About the grave and the interment his instructions, in writing, are most explicit. He marked out the spot, himself. On the *morne* a half mile from the house, a place overlooking the sea. Under an ancient silk cotton tree, and the grave must be ten feet deep."

"Cart," Pete whispered to me, "does it strike you this affair is getting a trifle morbid?"

That was how it struck me. The old black lawyer was nodding to himself. "I have instructed the gravediggers."

"Let's get on with it," I snapped. "Do we get out here?"

We got out. I stood up to my shoetops in mud and helped Pete from the buggy, while the wet stone angel looked on. All the time the drums were tubbing louder and not funnier, and, no matter the shine sneaking through the trees, there wasn't enough light to see a match by. I could hear water guttering and draining, and the air was vaporous with smell of woods, dank green. Then a lantern came swimming through the gloom, bringing an old man. A thin, cordovan-leather Negro in a flag-striped suit and a floppy sombrero, with a whisker like a goat's tuft on his chin. He bleated Haitian at Master Tousellines, who promptly snatched the lantern.

"This is Cornelius. Your Uncle Eli's house boy."

"Then he didn't kill Uncle Eli," Pete nudged me. "Servants never turn out to be murderers in mystery plays."

WITH THAT woodsy smell and the stone celestial looming in the gloom, it was like disembarking in a cemetery. The lawyer consulted his timepiece. *"S'il vous-plaît,* it is nearing midnight. If you will follow me."

We followed him while the tufted Cornelius brought up the rear, towing the dilapidated rig. Single file we ascended a soggy path through a bowered corridor of mossy trees flanked by tall, wet ferns.

"Ugh," Pete breathed. "I feel as if I were stepping on frogs."

I didn't breathe anything. That newly-wed couple of drums and their infant were breaking a lease, and I didn't fancy the neighborhood. The path made a wriggle; entered a valley cleared for a broad sweep of compound. The valley was like a great bowl scooped out under the sky, with a crust of jungle timber on its upper rim and its curved sides dim with mist. A row of shabby plaster huts were hugged together near our path; outbuildings, cookhouses, hencoops, servants' quarters. The largest hut in the huddle was agog with sound and lights.

Bonfire yellow streamed from the crooked windows; the boom-thumped air shook a parade of dancing shadows across the bright door. I glimpsed a roomful of blacks, crones and children cavorting around what might have been an altar. Candles winked in smoky fists, black arms grabbed at the ceiling; a white goat stood on the altar and said, "Baaaaaa!" One couldn't spy the drums, but the whole valley vibrated with the racket. The place smelled.

"Voilà!" our guide informed us, revolving his eyes. "It is the *houmfort,* the temple of mystery. I do not, myself, approve of voodoo. But the château, it is not far—"

We hurried through what once had been a garden and was now a ruin of shrubs, muddy cornfields, hodge-podged with hydrangea, breadfruits and flower beds, passing a weedy-smelling pond outlined by a concrete walk. The *bassin* where we could bathe, Tousellines announced. The swimming pool.

"Don't they ever stop drumming?"

"It will continue for a while, *m'sieu.* A ceremony that will last for a day after the burial. But then"—we were crunching up a curving gravel drive—"here is the château. Welcome to Morne Noir."

We couldn't see much of that manse in the darkness, but I had the impression of a ship that had somehow drifted inland on the rain and keeled on its beam against the hillside. Two stories of gargoyles and ramshackle gingerbread, fronted with a tiered veranda that lost itself around either end, the wings blotted out in night. The walls were a sprawl of dim plaster; Spanish moss dripped from the upper gallery; thick vines screened the veranda like weeds on the hull of a sunken vessel. Shrubs clung around the lower part of the house, and to one side I made out a hydrangea bed and a thicket of coconut palms.

A coach dog that had apparently ossified to green iron stood guard on the terrace. The door was lighted by a red globe such as one used to see on fire-boxes. The red glow sifted out through the gloom; and I didn't need to go into the reception hall to know it would take a heap of living to make this house a home.

The hall smelled like an old hotel. There was an impressive stairway swooping down from a mezzanine; a barn-high ceiling and an upper gallery that ran around the hall like the one on the outside of the house. Electric grape chandeliers clustered under the ceiling. Sliding doors closed near the entryway, and a glimpse of more closed doors above and below.

PETE SAID. "Whoo!" taking off her hat and shaking her hair. Cornelius bell-hopped the bags up the stairway, and I tossed my wet hat on a horsehair settee, listening to Tousellines advising us we were to have the two large front rooms in deference to the lady guest.

Pete regarded the paneling. "Mahogany, too. Notice the carving, Cart. That's French. What's that sound?"

It was not the inescapable drumming, but an eld, clicking sound that came from a door down the hall.

Tousellines waved. "It is the billiard room. The other guests are there. I have assigned them to rooms off this lower hall so you may have the upper house to yourselves. *Dieu!* we have but five minutes before the funeral."

"Where—is Uncle Eli?"

"All is ready, *ma'mselle*, in the library. I suggest you and *m'sieu* enter at once while I summon those others. *Bien!*" Shedding the stovepipe, he stepped to open the sliding doors. I took a breath and Pete's arm, and we marched in. Into a long, misty-lit room with tall, blinded windows, walls regimented to the ceiling with dark books, everything exuding a nostril-clogging aroma of decay and fust. A man in a white linen suit stood engloomed at the elbow of a gigantic leather-and-buttons armchair.

Maître Tousellines exclaimed: "Dr. Sevestre!"

The man looked up. His face, in that light, was mulatto-saffron, Aryan-featured. He wore a black toothbrush mustache. His eyes were shoe buttons. He tossed something from hand to hand, gave Pete and me a swift scrutiny, nodded at the lawyer.

"It is time?"

"In a moment. This is *M'sieu* Proudfoot's niece, Miss Dale, and her fiancé."

"You're the doctor who found Uncle Eli?" Pete said.

"He was seated in this very chair, *ma'mselle*. It may have been suicide," the doctor spoke loudly, "but," his voice lowered to a whisper, and I could hear Maître Tousellines' footsteps retreating down the hall, "but such is not my opinion. Your uncle's spirits were good; health excellent. Barring a slight cirrhosis of the liver and a beginning aneurism of the heart, which I disclosed by my autopsy, his condition was sound—"

Pete backed away from the chair. I saw the doctor was tossing a bullet in his hand. Only it wasn't the doctor, capturing my attention right then. It was the scene at the other end of the library; the huge rosewood coffin mounted silent before a half-circle of empty chairs.

It was stark. No flowers. Nothing. Just the coffin and the chairs and the four giant candles that stood, two at the head, two at the foot, of the casket. The candlelight wiggled, and the pale glow fell on the wan, green face of an old man. It was not a nice face, even in death, at a distance. The eyes were shut tight, the blue mouth was a trap, the head was bald but for a few white wisps, the nose was sharp as a blade. The skin was stretched like tinted writing paper over the bony cheeks, and there was a strip of adhesive tape on the prominent forehead.

The coffin dwarfed its occupant; he looked like some unwholesome doll in a box too large for it; his pillowed profile casting a goblin shadow on the wall, like a silhouette scissored from black paper and pasted there. It was too late at night for this sort of thing.

"Poor Uncle Eli," Pete said quietly.

"I told the mourners not to start a game of billiards," the physician scolded.

Drums muttered softly beyond the shuttered windows; and I stared at the dead man's folded hands and wished for a cigarette. Somewhere a clock began to grind and strike; loud voices were moving up the hall. I turned to see Maître Tousellines march through the portals, watch in palm; and herded at his heels such a group of persons as I never hope to see foregathered anywhere again. There were seven of them.

As Pete whispered to me afterwards, "Somebody must have left the door open at the jail."

Pete

THERE WAS a bony man in a plaid cape, rumpled evening clothes, black spats and one of those peaked Sherlock Holmes caps you see only in England and cartoons. He strolled in chewing the ivory knob of an ebony stick, a diet that couldn't nourish his pinched, old maidish face with the type of nose generally characterized as a snout, and eyes that were little triangles of blue water under hairy brows. We were asked to meet Sir Duffin Wilburforce, K.C.S.I.

He said, "Cheer-o," to me, and, "Charmed, my dear," to Pete. He screwed a monocle into his eye. The eyeglass flickered like a dim lamp in his face. A pale thread of a scar running from his eye down his jawbone was the electric wire to the lamp. He bowed over the stick. "I knew your uncle well, my dear. Gad! Doesn't he look natural?"

I'm sure the sailor who followed this Briton was announced by a name, but I was to remember him merely as "the En-sign," accent on first syllable. A square, copper-faced man wearing what seemed to have been an American naval officer's uniform. Gold frogs were frayed on the sleeve, but the buttons were missing, allowing the coat to flap open and give outsiders a peek at a naked stomach and a chest covered with hair and tattooing. He carried an oilskin reefer over an arm and wore one of those cod-liver-oil sou'westers aft on his head. His eyes were Alice-blue, and I didn't like them or the heavy revolver slung on his bullet-heavy belt.

"How they goin'?" he said in a voice that made nails of the words and grinders of his teeth. Leaning against a shelf of encyclopedias, he plucked a pipe from his pants and began to load it as if it were a gun, stuffing ammunition from a red tobacco can. I could have said, "Not so good," for I was meeting the man entitled Ti Pedro.

Ti Pedro said nothing at all. He didn't like me, either. Six feet of coffee-colored gristle speckled with green freckles, he stood with hands a-dangle; stared thoughtfully at Pete and me. He was naked to the middle save for tiny gold earrings and a hardboiled egg depended by a string from his throat. Dominican, Maître Tousellines told us, and at some time or other in a glamorous past, the tongue had been cut from his mouth. A mutilation which seemed to have deprived him of his speech.

"And this, if you please, is Ambrose."

WELL, I didn't please, but it didn't mean a thing to the tubercular-looking boy in the green jersey and slicker-bottom pants who sidled forward to stare at Pete. His hair and eyelashes were white, albino, loaning his eyes a sleepy, feathery look that was nasty. He carried a billiard cue in one hand and ran the back of the other across his mouth, fanning his eyelids at the girl. "Geez, it's been a long time since I seen a pretty twist." Then his eyes were here, there, everywhere, running like caged mice in his head. "Let's go—that stiff kind of gets me."

"They're getting better as they go along," Pete whispered. "Look at these."

These were an Aunt Jemima done with a ton of charcoal, leading a tame gorilla. Only it wasn't a gorilla, and I was to discover it wasn't tame. Instead it was a woolly headed Jamaican Negro with a face like a moose on the shoulders of a colossus.

Never able to support such shoulders, the legs bowed outward to form an "O," giving him a rolling gorilla walk to match the face. Maître Tousellines called it Toadstool, and we met its mother, the Widow Gladys. A billow of melting milk chocolate dressed up in chintz and a polkadot turban. A mouth like a slice of watermelon and teeth that were black seeds. Her five chins dripped in the heat while she studied us with eyes the color of tea. She had but one arm—the left being a dimple in a stub of shoulder—and she cuffed the ineffable Toadstool out of her way, and trampled forward to wish us a good evening.

"Cut it short," Ambrose whined out. "Get the Nazi in here and let's start the show."

Spurs clinkled down the library, bringing a shadow straight at us from Unter den Linden. Tousellines said, "This is Manfred." He came at us with an odor of rum, stalwart and Prussian from toes to faded tassels. The uniform, the mustache, bullet jaw, trained scowl were ghosts from Berlin, the sort of ghosts that used to frighten the Allied staff during the War and precisely the kind you'd never expect to be haunting the island of Haiti. Iron crosses on his chest, a black automatic on his hip, he was grim enough without that angry, liver-colored birthmark blotched across his cheek. And he was drunk as a toper. Standing very straight, he belched, *"Gesundheit!"* and saluted the coffin.

"Sit down," Maître Tousellines ordered querulously. "I am going to read the will."

There was a scramble for the chairs.

CHAPTER III

REST IN PEACE!

" *'I, ELIAS PROUDFOOT, being of sound mind and healthy body—'* "

Three pictures, that midnight, were to nail themselves in the gallery of my memory. The first was that row of so-called faces, ranged half-moon before the coffin—The Englishman's electric light monocle; the En-sign's pipe; Ambrose's fluttering eyes; Ti Pedro's tongueless mouth ajar; Toadstool's leer; the sweat-pearls on Widow Gladys's chins; Manfred's birthmark glowing like a stove burn—that batch lined up as if to start a game of Going to Jerusalem, and the little old lawyer, front and center, to referee the fun. When the lawyer faltered among "wherefores" and "hereuntos" to draw his own breath, nobody breathed, and the room was abysmal with the echo of pounded drums. And then the face of Uncle Eli with its blade-like nose poked above the cowling of the coffin, that strip of adhesive mending the punctured forehead, and the silhouette behind it on the wall.

" *'Do hereby set my signature to the following last will and testament drawn by me in accord with the laws of the Republic of Haiti—'* "

Cornelius was an ashen shadow hovering against the Complete Works of Bulwer-Lytton; and Dr. Sevestre stood behind me with legs apart, pitching that lead pea from hand to hand. Pete tightened her fingers on mine.

Maître Tousellines untangled red tape in the preamble, and arrived at the body of his document.

" *'It is therefore my command that if, when or at such time as I die: A—My body be autopsied and embalmed by Dr. Sevestre. B— Burial shall take place no sooner or later than three days after death. C—The funeral be of Voodoo ritual conducted by the hougan, Papa Leo, in manner of the Service Legba. D—That I shall be buried in my rosewood coffin in the assigned spot chosen by me on the morne, the grave to be exactly ten feet deep and the monument immediately mounted on the grave. E—That an iron stake exactly eleven feet long shall be driven down into the grave through the exact heart of the buried casket. Any omission or addition to the above renders this will null and void.'* "

The old lawyer's voice had ducked into his collar again; he stopped to fish it out. Beyond the window screens the drums were taking a quicker tempo; and an uneasy stir passed down the line of chairs.

"Well, the *verdammt* old fool!" The harsh outburst exploded from the German. "A stake in the grave, *hein?* He was afraid they would get him for a *zombie!*"

"Stow it, Nazi," the En-sign advised. "Can't you see the boss has a relative here?"

At the word "relative" the mourners leaned forward to stare at Pete. Sir Duffin picked the glass from his eye and winked his triangles solicitously. "Pay no attention to the Boche, my dear. The blighter is drunk."

"Who is drunk?"

"You are!"

"Pipe down, swabs, this is a funeral."

"Hush yo' mouf," the Widow Gladys injected, slapping Toadstool a maternal smack on the ear. The black boy had been staring at Pete.

Ambrose whinnied, "That stiff is givin' me goose pimples; can't you snap into it, Lemonade?"

MAÎTRE TOUSELLINES flashed the youth a sour glance; turned several pages of manuscript. "The clauses of the will shall be executed, *messieurs*. It will be necessary to drive the stake in the grave."

"He was afraid they would catch him for a *zombie*," the German repeated with a sullen wag of the head. The seven faces stared at the casket. Ti Pedro, the coffee-colored Dominican, fingered the egg on his wishbone, mumbling under his breath. Pete hugged my arm and tried to look as if she'd spent many an evening at similar funerals.

"But this is most absurd," the doctor spoke out behind me. "Attend, Tousellines, cannot you omit these details? For the sake of *ma'mselle?*"

The lawyer mopped his blue-black forehead with a lavender handkerchief. "It is the will and my instructions were to read the same." His eyes rolled down the arc of chairs. "Stop that noise, Ti Pedro. Have you forgotten that such talismans are against the law?"

"The hell with the law," the En-sign gestured his pipe. "What is this, anyhow? Did the Old Man leave us anything or not?"

"We now come to the devisees. To claim heritage they must hear the reading of the will and remain throughout the funeral ceremony. I ask you to give complete attention. It says: *'To each of the following named who shall remain at Morne Noir for the appointed period of time, I do devise and bequeath as follows—'* "

And then it was that the extraordinary cadaver in the rosewood coffin tossed its verbal bomb. One hears the term "mouthpiece" for a lawyer? I know where it came from. Lawyer Tousellines swivelled his eyeballs at Sir Duffin Wilburforce, and it was as if the little black man speaking was the dummy, but the ventriloquist lay in the rosewood casket, jerking the invisible strings.

" *'To my overseer, Sir Duffin Wilburforce, I leave my entire property, real and personal, valued at one hundred thousand dollars, provided the heir so named does not leave Morne Noir in any way, shape or manner for twenty-four hours after the driving of the stake*

*in my grave. Should the heir so named fail to carry out this stipula-
tion, the estate falls to—*

" *'Number Two: My plantation manager, Ti Pedro, provided he
does not leave Morne Noir in any way, shape or manner for twenty-
four hours after the driving of the stake in my grave, in default of
which the estate falls to—*

" *'Number Three: My master pilot, Ambrose Jones—' "*

Provided *he* did not leave Morne Noir in any way, shape or
manner for a similar period, in which case the estate went to
Number Four: one stable boy, named Toadstool. If Toadstool
defaulted the heritage fell to Number Five: his mother, the
Widow Gladys, housekeeper. The En-sign "business manager"
was listed Number Six. Captain Manfred von Gottz, "bodyguard," Number Seven. " *With the estate falling to each so named
in numerical succession in event of default by the preceding heir,
and lastly to my ward, Miss Patricia Dale. So reads my last will
and testament. Hereby subscribed and signed by me—Eli Elijah
Proudfoot.' "*

That was Uncle Eli's will! Maître Tousellines stowed it under
his coat tails with a nod, and for a minute that funeral parlor had
all the atmosphere of a spider's dream. Rage, disappointment,
jubilance, unbelief capered across the features of heirs numbered
One to Seven, flushed their faces all the colors of the rainbow.
Toadstool leapt to his feet and his mother struck him down.
Ambrose was counting on his fingers. "I'm sixth," came the
En-sign's sardonic drawl. Sir Duffin Wilburforce whipped to his
feet, monocle blazing. "Don't worry, you rotter! Or any of you.
It'll never get to you. I'm first, first, first, d'you hear? It's *mine!*"

OUTSIDE THE drums were bomming and booming. The
mourners shouted. A chair went over. There was powder in that
last will and testament, and I wanted most strenuously to get
Pete out of there, and by the look in her eyes she wanted to go.

But the spider's dream went into a spider's nightmare; and an
ancient Negro in an unscrupulous flannel nightshirt was standing in the library door.

"Papa Leo!" Maître Tousellines croaked.

The Haitian priest started forward, chanting. He wore a wreath of yellow daisies on his head, carried a dead white goat under his arm, a big red candle in his hand, and was followed by four black stevedores in nightshirts. These golems came down the library, lifted the rosewood casket to their shoulders without so much as a by-your-leave, and staggered, grunting like piano movers, for the door.

Ambrose cried, "Let's go!" and I felt the way I did when I smoked my first cigar. The mourners dashed out like rats on the heels of the Hamelin piper, and Pete and I were deserted among books and overturned chairs and blue shadows.

"Those brutes!" she tugged my sleeve. "All they want is his money. And he—it's pathetic the way he wanted them at his burial service. Cart, the least I can do is go; see him to his—"

We left the château and tagged the processional into the night. The drizzle had terminated. A cheesy moon lurked behind curdled clouds; the landscape was gray. At the bottom of the compound the drums were going like express trains, hurrying the black priest with the candle, the sweating pallbearers, the trailing crowd. That's the second picture I won't forget. That funeral cortège. Papa Leo in the lead; the trotting stevedores, casket swinging aloft; those seven outlandish mourners doing no mourning in the wake.

The parade cut crosslots through the wet, leafy black; taking that path where Pete had thought she was stepping on frogs. When he came to the station where the angel had stood, I saw the celestial had departed (taking fright, I had no doubt) leaving deep ruts in the mud. Farther on we overtook the angel, impelled uphill by a team of twenty black mules, a great to-do of equally black muleteers, much cracking of whips and jangling of harness and laying on of hands. Screeching and squealing on wooden rollers, the monument mounted the slope, a knot of glistening darkies shoving and cursing the thing on its way.

Then picture the noble brow of that hill above the bowl of

the valley, with a great tree standing lonely against the sky, the moonray silvering the skinless limbs, the Caribbean curving beyond. Two half naked blackamoors panting on long-handled spades, and a black rectangle like a shadow across the earth beneath the tree. I don't know what morbid impulse moved me, but I remember taking a nervous peek into that grave. A deep excavation with brown puddle water glistening on the bottom.

Papa Leo, the *hougan,* hung the dead goat on a limb of the dead tree; then stood over the grounded coffin, waving the dripping candle and singing *gulaba-gulaba-gulaba-gulaba* like a wattled turkey, while the four pallbearers bayed on their knees: *"Moon li mort! Moon li mort!"* which was Haitian for "the man is dead." Meantime the angel came barging up the heights, the drums throbbed like aching teeth, the presumptive heirs waited eager-eyed, candlelight fluttered on the wan, green face of the old man in his pink long-box. I wasn't sorry when the black priest hushed his liturgy, and the pallbearers set to work nailing a massive lid on that rosewood casket.

I WASN'T sorry to see the coffin lowered down the grave; to hear the hollow thump of earth-clods on its cover. But then we must stand there till the grave was filled, the mound levelled off, the earth packed hard; stand there and watch the business of the iron stake. Maître Tousellines, a shade lighter in color than before, fetched that solid crowbar from behind the tree. The gravediggers produced sledge hammers. Papa Leo held the monstrous spike in place.

Whang, bang, whang, bang! You've seen them drive tent-pegs in the circus? But this wasn't the circus. This was a new grave high on a night-swept bluff and an iron post sinking into the dirt. When but three feet of stake remained above ground, its point encountered a subterranean obstruction down below. Pete turned away, and I wish I had. The hammer blows fell harder; there was a sudden give—a sort of *whuff!*—and the stake drove level to the ground.

"Dormie pa'foom' M'sieu Proudfoot!" was Papa Leo's benedic-

tion. Maître Tousellines crossed himself, and echoed the blessing. "Let the dead sleep sweetly—"

Sir Duffin

We got away from the hill just as the mules were hauling the six-ton angel into his sentry station atop the grave. The mourners scattered on separate paths; I don't know how they reached the château. Picking our way through the dark, Pete and the old lawyer and I made the journey down the valley in dismal silence.

IT WAS two o'clock when I stood in that mouldy upper room with Pete, and grabbed into my Gladstone for a quart of Scotch. "Sleep sweetly," I had to comment. "Well, I must say your uncle fixed it so he'd be the only one after his funeral who could. Do you want yours straight or without ginger ale? I'm sitting up all night. To-morrow we clear out of here."

Pete frowned. "Maybe it hasn't occurred to you, Cart, but—"

"But what?"

"I—I spent all my money coming down here. There wasn't any return fare. And you heard uncle's will. No chance—not that I'd want any part of it—of my inheriting the estate, but it looks as if I might have to stay the twenty-four hours, anyway and—Cart, where's the painting? I must have left it with my things down in the hall. If anything happens to your canvas—"

She was gone before I could swallow, the door blowing shut behind her. I listened to her quick steps down the stairs; capped the bottle and tossed it aside; ran to the door. Dampness had warped the sills, and I had a moment's tussle with the knob.

Bam! Wham! In the night somewhere there were two jarring

reports. I whirled, sped across the room, kicked open the blinds, stepped out on the upper veranda. And that was the third picture I was to remember of that night. The lawn below eerie with moonlight. A man in white linen suit reeling drunkenly across the turf, crossing the gravel drive, wavering to pat the iron coach dog, then turning half-buckled to fall face-up on the grass. He drew up one knee, then lay still. It was Dr. Sevestre.

And a man I never saw before crashed out of the veranda below, raced headlong across the terrace. He was a brown man in a brown uniform, all buckles and Sam Browne belt. "I saw it," he bawled in English. "I saw it, in the name of the Law. This is murder, and no man may leave the premises!" He waved a bright sabre and his cheeks pouted on a whistle. Boots ran on the gravel. Presto! the lawn was crowded with uniformed men.

CHAPTER IV

NOBODY CAN LEAVE!

PETE HAD RUN up the stairs. When I ducked back into the room she was wide-eyed in the doorway, the rolled canvas under her arm, my case of paints in her hand. It was no moment for oil colors, either. Whistles were shrilling in the night; boots racing all over the château. Down the compound the drum family continued its bolero, while a dead man watered the lawn with his blood.

"Right here," I told her, "we say good-by to Haiti."

She dropped her bundles on the bed. "What's happened? I— it sounded like shots."

"Somebody just got Dr. Sevestre."

Handkerchief to lips, she stared at the opened shutters. "That's—that's awful. What are we going to do?"

"Pack up and clear out," I said, fiddling at my suitcase.

There was a step in the doorway behind Pete, and a big Negro in a canvas uniform, Rough Rider style, with broadbrimmed hat and leather gaiters, stepped into the frame. *"Ou là! Allons!"* He presented arms with a bayonet, grinning like a dental cream ad. "You and *ma'mselle* come."

"Who says so?" I objected.

"Haiti police. You come."

Pete clung to my arm, and we walked out on the gallery, descended the mahogany stairway down into the hall. A squad of black gendarmes were cackling at the front door, and I was ready to clout somebody. That Pete and I were in this devil's mess was more or less at my own insistence. A midnight funeral as grim as Uncle Eli's, followed directly by a homicide, was over-doing the thing.

So was the scene prepared for us in the library. The funeral parlor had become an impromptu morgue. Dr. Sevestre was stretched on a wooden fireplace bench, his face covered by his linen coat. Dark-skinned police were fetching the various members of Uncle Eli's funeral party from different quarters of that wretched house; no mourner, it appeared, had taken leave to depart. Toadstool and the Widow Gladys, routed from rooms somewhere in back. Ambrose out of the billiard room. The En-sign strolling in, pipe fuming in a pleasant smile. Manfred flushed from a door down the hall with a Bacardi bottle in his fist and his boots unsteady. Ti Pedro making dumb noises in his mouth and fumbling the egg under his neck. Sir Duffin Wilburforce arriving, indignant in a soiled undershirt with a bib tied under his chin, a shaving brush in his fist, one side of his jaw foamy with lather. Entering the library, they were ordered in line against the book shelves by a tall, cocoa-colored darky corporal with a hare lip—as evil a batch of fish as any drag-net could hope to catch.

As Pete and I stepped into the scene the brown officer with the cavalry sabre was shouting at Tousellines: "I want everybody, you comprehend! All of them!"

Maître Tousellines, yellowish at the temples, introduced us, in turn presenting the officer. "This is Lieutenant Nemo Narcisse, Inspector-Chief of the Garde d'Haiti in this district."

THE OFFICER glared at me and I glared at him. I don't know what he saw in me, but I saw a pompous little man compounded of French and African blood, his skin the color of an Alexander, a plump face with two quick black eyes, pomaded curls, a hand-kerchief up his cuff, his pouter-pigeon bosom wearing more medals than the Emperor of Japan. He made a very polite bow, showing very white teeth. I wondered if this were the police-man who had handed down the suicide report on Uncle Eli's demise with the reservation that he might have been killed by a *zombie;* and my heart sank for the third time. Politics in a police department are bad enough, and superstition could be worse. If the Law of Haiti believed in witchcraft, Justice might be a ghostly affair.

I started the one about American citizens.

He thrust a hand in his bosom, Napoleon style, and nodded perkily. *"Tiens,* I am the authority here. You and *ma'mselle* are in Haiti now, you understand, and both under suspicion of murder."

"Miss Dale and I had nothing to do with—"

"It is the *Code Pénal,"* the officer dimpled. "Unfortunately all suspects are guilty until proved innocent."

"But it's two o'clock in the morning. This lady is tired—"

He waved a hand to indicate that in Haiti there was always plenty of time. His super-important air heated the skin under my collar.

"I want to get in touch with the American consul—"

"In due course, *m'sieu,"* he nodded, "and meantime *ma'mselle* perhaps would like a chair." He pointed at the leather-and-buttons armchair in which Uncle Eli had been found with a bullet in his cerebrum.

"Thanks," Pete declined. "I'll stand."

"And now we're all on deck," the En-sign spoke out harshly, "why not cut the comedy and tell us what's it about. I see somebody pinched out the sawbones, but does it mean I gotta stay up all night? I ain't cryin', because I never liked Sevestre, myself."

"I will take that into account," the officer said softly, balancing himself on an arm of the leather chair and sending a slow glance up and down the line. "I will take into account that none of you liked Dr. Sevestre. His murder, I believe, is not the only crime in this nice little household of Morne Noir. I am convinced, *messieurs,* that *M'sieu* Proudfoot, himself, was the victim of an assassin's hand."

"What could that have to do with Mr. Cartershall or me?"

Pete interrupted with spirit. "We weren't in Haiti when—when *that* happened. If you will only let us telephone our consul—"

"Presently," the lieutenant bowed. "May I remind you, *ma'mselle*, the innocent—do they have cause for alarm? But no. I shall also expect their aid in this evil matter. I came here to-night because I am most certain your uncle was the victim of foul play. Was I so foolish as to believe *M'sieu* Proudfoot a suicide? *Non!* As for the *zombie* story—I spoke of that to put the real assassin off his guard. But then, we know the good doctor has just been slain, and I think he lies dead because he knew too much, eh? Do you see what I am getting at?"

Sir Duffin Wilburforce spluttered. "Who did him up, then?"

"That, *blanc*, is what I—Lieutenant Nemo Narcisse—am at your service to discover." He fixed his glance on the Englishman. "Perhaps you were not aware I was on the side veranda when those shots in front were fired? My men were stationed across the compound. I was also in the hall to-night while the will was being read in the library. What is more, while the funeral party was at the burial, I was searching your rooms, here. Perhaps I know more about you, my friends, than you would like to believe."

HIS SPEECH sent a little flurry down the line-up; and I was beginning to think the Haitian police weren't so foolish as their minstrel aspect might construe. The lieutenant went on in his liquid voice.

"*Eh, bien*, I am on the side veranda, and I see all of you return and enter the château. Ambrose came first, then the others, lastly *M'sieu* the American, and the girl. It was Dr. Sevestre who remained outside for a stroll on the lawn. He passed me where I was hidden on the side veranda, walking toward the terrace in front, and just as he moved beyond my sight I heard the two shots. I did not see them," the officer patted his oily curls with a dramatic gesture, "but I know they came from inside the house. *Voilà*, here is a child's problem! Some one of *you* fired those shots."

"Then that lets me out," Ambrose shrilled. "I was in the billiard room practicin' masse shots when I hear the guns, see? Why'd I want to croak the medico, anyhow?"

"Is it that he knew too much about the death of *M'sieu* Proudfoot, then?"

"I tell you I was in the bill—"

"But who was with you in the billiard room, *m'sieu?*"

"Nobody. I was takin' masse—say, what the hell are you—" The boy stepped out of line, his colorless eyelids fanning, his thin head sunk turtle-neck in his jersey collar, face inflamed. "What the hell are you tryin' to pin on me? I ain't got a rod and never carry one, see?"

Lieutenant Narcisse blinked sleepily. "How were you employed at Morne Noir? In what capacity did you serve *M'sieu* Proudfoot?"

"Pilot," the youth snivelled. "Run a launch over to La Gonave. Three days ago I hear the boss has croaked, and that Lemonade lawyer sends word I'm to be at the funeral, same as the rest of this crowd. That's why I'm here, and you ain't got nothing on me."

"And you," the officer turned suddenly on Sir Duffin. "You were overseer, here? Also, it seems, you are first in line to inherit the estate. Where were you when the doctor, to-night, was shot?"

"My dear fellow, where does it look as if I was?" The wry Englishman ran a hand across his jaw, scooped a palmful of soap-froth, slung it at the floor. "Naturally, I was in my boudoir, shaving. My ears, you know, being filled with lather at the time, I did not hear the shots. Therefore, I cannot imagine their origin." His triangular eyes watered with amusement and perplexity. "You notice, also, I am unarmed. At least, my only weapon at hand was a razor, and since the worthy healer's throat was not cut—"

"I notice," the officer interrupted the Briton's obnoxious levity, "that your room is near the front door."

"But of course I was in the throes of a shave, eh, what?"

"It would appear you choose an odd hour of night to shave."

"The funeral of my revered benefactor and employer had fatigued me, lieutenant, and I wished to be refreshed after sorrow."

"Permit me also to refresh your memory." Lieutenant Narcisse plucked a little book from a breast pocket. "The day of your employer's death I consulted the British agents at Port au Prince, wiring for information about you. I am advised you came to Haiti ten years ago from England; more explicitly, you came from the English prison, Dartmoor, where you had served a twenty-year sentence for murder."

THERE WAS a moment's silence in the library; then the Englishman blew up. The man's fury was extraordinary. Shaving soap bubbled with an apoplectic foam from his lips. "Well, what of it?" he screeched. "Suppose I was, you blasted fool! What would it prove?"

"Only that murder is no stranger to you, Sir Duffin. Only that you are already the criminal. Only that you might shave to provide for yourself a handy alibi. But you are not the only criminal before me, *non!* This Ti Pedro. This tongueless scoundrel from Santo Domingo—" Turning from the spluttering English caricature, the plump lieutenant poked his sabre at the Dominican. "You cannot speak, but you can hear. Then hear that I know you shot a Spanish captain, a few years past, in the Dominican army. Is not your room the room next the Englishman's? Answer me!"

The dumb one nodded.

"And you are *second* in line for this Morne Noir estate. Ha! You killed the doctor, too, *oui?* You sneaked down the hall, fired through the door, fled back to your room—"

Ti Pedro shook his head.

"Do you know the murderer, then?"

Ti Pedro blinked his eyes.

"Comedian!" the officer raged, "if you had the tongue in your mouth I would have you talking like a parrot. I am not finished with you yet." He made an angry flash with the sabre and wheeled suddenly at Toadstool. That bow-legged gorilla with the monkey shoulders split his moose face in a grin and began to chat in Creole at the officer. Instantly the Widow Gladys brought up a palm and calmly shut his mouth with a resounding clap. Her son's skull smacked the bookcase, bringing down several volumes, while the vast widow opened her milk chocolate lips and filled the library with a guffaw.

"Quiet!" Narcisse scowled fiercely. "You will answer in turn, speak English and one at a time. Every one among you will hear what the other has to report, *hein!* and if there are any lies I want to know of them." He prodded the sabre-point in Toadstool's black midriff. "Now, then, ape! You were with your mother in her room at the back of the hall?"

"Yessuh."

It was the first time I'd heard Toadstool's speech in English, for his mother had rigidly enforced the dictum about children being seen and not heard. Now his voice was thin and piping, pixie-queer in that black-blob body.

"Did you hear those shots?"

"Mebbe yes; mebbe no. Toadstool hear Rada drums."

"Son of a two-headed bat, did you or that black mother of yours come up the hall and shoot Dr. Sevestre?"

ANTICIPATING A slap, Toadstool ducked sideways; then said no. Widow Gladys giggled through a triumphant smile. "Toadstool and him mamma, we stay close our room, yes *suh!*"

"Listen to me, you fat crow. You and that rascally Caco boy of yours will be sorry if you try any tricks on Lieutenant Narcisse of the Garde d'Haiti. I am aware of how the British police in Jamaica had you exiled from their island for peddling drugs and *bocor* charms. Criminals, both of you!"

The Negress snickered.

"*Poissard!*" the officer scolded querulously. "How are you employed in Morne Noir, you and that ape of a son?"

"Toadstool he'm stable boy, fine boy, know horses. Widow

Gladys cook, wash, handle low plantation nigger, sometime midwife."

"Sell the field hands evil charms and drugs, that is more the truth. *Dieu!* I am surprised *M'sieu* Proudfoot should name you in his will."

"Him my good friend. Maybe sometime Ah owns Morne Noir."

"Maybe sometime you go to the guillotine and have your head examined. Witch, do you have any idea who it was killed Dr. Sevestre?"

In the shadows that smelled of books, the billow in the chintz swaddings slowly wheeled. The little tea-colored eyes were almost lost in folds of melting chocolate. "Ah thinks him, Nazzy, p'raps kill doctah man."

Manfred, who had been propped against the shelves like something preserved for a war museum in alcohol, roused with a shout. The Iron Crosses tap-danced on his gusty chest. "How dare you, you pig of ink! How dare you say Captain von Gottz slew that swine of a physician?"

"Ah hears, that's all. Quarrels with that doctah, yessuh. Two days ago. Doctah, he say Massa Proudfoot been murdered by certain kind of bullet. Nazzy, he tell'm doctah keep him mouf shut or maybe he learn some more about bullets."

"Shades of Friederich Wilhelm, but I will cut this female hippopotamus into barbecue!" The German's eyes sizzled. Rushing forward with a bawl, he brought his rum bottle crashing down on the polkadot turban. Glass exploded in a bright shower of amber fluid. But the Negress took the blow like a rock, threw up her arm and slapped that lavendar birthmark with everything she had. Everything she had was plenty, too.

It was a nice sort of caper for that library scene at three in the morning after a funeral. Hurled backwards by the blow, Manfred went tripping and crashing into the bench; outsprawled across the body of the murdered doctor. Dead man and German sprawled on the floor. Bedlam swept into the library. "Ki yi yi yi!" That was Ti Pedro laughing. A shout of mirth from the En-sign. Sir Duffin squealing applause. Gendarmes jumping with fixed bayonets and Lieutenant Narcisse yelling for order, and Manfred, on hands and knees, sober as ice and tiger-mad, and Dr. Sevestre watching with impersonal, sightless concentration.

Pete put her face in my shoulder, while I stood like a cigar store Indian, nerves going like a thousand mandolins. Then the German was back in line, the doctor back on his bench, and Narcisse assuring us the next one to move would be sabred.

RUMPLING THE feathers of his hair, the officer strutted the floor like an angered guinea hen. "How dare you outrage the dignity of an *enquête?* You German dog, jump out of line again and I will cut a bung-hole in the rum cask that you are, and let something more than Bacardi out of you!"

Manfred swayed, steadied, stood clenching and unclenching his fists, his jaw out-thrust like a quivering red cobblestone. "That female mastodon would try to frame me, *ja!* I would not be surprised if the black monster had shot the doctor, herself."

"While you, of course, are the soul of innocence. Blood of Saint Robert, but one would believe Haiti the stamping ground for the dregs of the white race, come here to pollute the brown. Why did Germany send you into exile for the mere matter of three wives, butchered one after the other in Berlin—"

"That is a lie!" Manfred snarled.

"The German agents at Port au Prince do not think so. So you had words with Dr. Sevestre?"

"The swine tried to tell me the bullet in Herr Proudfoot had come from my gun. Pah! I was on my way to Miragoane when I heard of the murder—and I wanted the physician to understand."

Lieutenant Narcisse glanced sideways at the body on the bench. "So you subscribe to the poetic notion that 'the dead understand all things.' A very pretty sophistry, captain, and one that may cost you your head. Observe." He picked his breast pocket. "This lead-nosed pea was taken from the dead doctor's grip. It is a dum-dum bullet, nine millimeter calibre. The doctor told me he removed it from the head of *M'sieu* Proudfoot, and that it had been put there by a Lüger automatic, such as the one you seem to be carrying."

Lieutenant Narcisse

"There is more than one gun in Morne Noir," Manfred snarled. "I was Herr Proudfoot's bodyguard, and I ought to know. All these swine are armed."

"They will not be when I am through with them, *oui!*"

"Are you trying to tell me the bullets in Sevestre are also from my gun?"

"I have not examined them as yet, but I am quite ready to believe it."

"I did not kill him," Manfred rasped, "because I was in that room down the hall, asleep. I did not even hear the shots."

"Can you produce a witness to your peaceful slumbers?"

"No."

"And you," Narcisse twisted his plump torso in the En-sign's direction. "You who are named sixth in the will and declared as *M'sieu* Proudfoot's business manager. Are you also the sleeping saint? But I have listened to rumors on the contrary. *Par example,* that you are a deserter from the American Navy."

The En-sign grinned, sucking the pipe and making little concave cones in his sunburnt cheeks. "You seem to of been doing a lot of snooping, Sherlock. I guess you're right. I got sick of working for Uncle Sam, so I went to work for Uncle Eli."

"I believe you already told me that on the day of *M'sieu* Proudfoot's murder you were in a fishing boat off the coast."

"I'm sorry, I was alone an' there weren't no witnesses."

"Where were you to-night when Dr. Sevestre was shot?"

The En-sign chuckled. "The gent's room, an' there weren't no witnesses, either."

CORNELIUS, NEXT to be questioned, stammered information that he had gone down the hall to prepare a couch for Maître Tousellines. He had heard the two shots, bleated Cornelius, and thought it better to observe developments from under the bed, the haven from which the gendarmes had dredged him forthwith. Narcisse focussed an eye on the little black lawyer.

"*Bien,* Tousellines, what have you to say? You did not retire, then, immediately after the funeral?"

The lawyer's sausage lip trembled. "On returning from the burial I escorted the other guests to their appointed bedchambers; then went to *M'sieu* Proudfoot's office under the stairs across the hall from the library. I was alone there, depositing certain documents, mainly the will, in my late client's safe. I had just opened the safe, *m'sieu* the lieutenant, when I heard footsteps rapid on the stairs. They appeared to stop in the hall—then I—I heard the two shots. I locked the safe at once and darted from the office. I am desolated to tell this, but Mademoiselle Dale was, at that moment, running across the upper gallery, and she went, I believe, into *m'sieu* the American's room."

The whole rotten line-up turned to glare at Pete when this bit of information was divulged. As for me, I could have wrung that raisin-headed avocat's neck for him, but Pete took it standing up. I never could have painted her eyes, the green flash in them right then!

"I had gone down to the hall after a package I'd left on the settee," she said evenly. "I was near the door when I heard the shots—they seemed to come from the library. But the library doors were closed and I couldn't be sure. I ran straight upstairs to Mr. Cartershall's room."

The Haitian officer bowed. "Thank you. And was *m'sieu* in his room when you arrived there?"

"He was."

"Certainly. And I am afraid I must ask you what it was you journeyed down the stairway to obtain. The package left in the hall?"

"A picture."

"Ah, but then, *ma'mselle,* you say no one quit the library?"

"Some one could have run out," Pete said, "but I couldn't have seen them from the upstairs gallery."

"*Ma'mselle,* was *M'sieu* Proudfoot your—eh—guardian?"

"He was at one time. I had received no word of him in a number of years."

"You did not like your uncle?" the officer smirked.

"I never said that," Pete countered. "He wasn't a close relative. After he came to Haiti I never heard from him until his lawyer came to me three days ago in New York."

"One thing more, if you please. Did it not strike you as strange that he should list you last as a possible heir to this estate?"

"Listen," Pete commanded. "I don't care about the estate. I came here because it was a last request and I wanted to see what Haiti was like. Now I'm seeing, I don't want any of it. I can't help the police. I don't know any of these people or—or anything. I want to leave as soon as—"

I said, "And that's that. Miss Dale and I aren't in this. Get us out of here."

THE OFFICER'S black eyes settled on me, filmed opaque. "You are the fiancé of *ma'mselle?*"

"Yes—No—I'm with her as a friend. If you don't give me a crack at that telephone so I can get the American con—"

"I am sorry to incommode you, *m'sieu,*" the pudgy man said with mock French politeness, "but for the information of the Law I first must inquire into your business."

"I'm an artist," I sneered.

My self revelation brought a grunt of disdain belching from the German at my elbow. The En-sign rolled an Alice blue eye at me and tittered, "One of those, blow me down!" Ambrose said, "Yoo-hoo!" and the Englishman dealt me an insulting ogle through his shiny monocle. Any one short of a professional garroter seemed to rate low in this Morne Noir ménage.

Narcisse did not seem impressed. "You paint the pictures?"

"Masterpieces," I corrected savagely. "So what?"

"Exactly that, my friend. So what. So what were you doing on the gallery outside your room while Dr. Sevestre lay dead on the lawn below?"

"I wasn't out there when he was shot," I bristled. I explained how I had heard the shooting and dashed through the shutters. From the glint in the Haitian's eye I knew he did not believe me, and I went on to add I didn't care a damn. I broke down further to admit that I didn't like the looks of any one or anything in Morne Noir, Haiti, and the sooner he allowed me to telephone for money and help to get Miss Dale and me away, the better.

"Maître Tousellines invited us down here. The authorities in Cap Haitien can check up for you. Now I want that telephone!"

The American consul would climb out from under his mosquito netting with a hangover and grumble in the phone, and I would holler for the U.S. Marines. Far in the distance bands would play "The Stars and Stripes Forever" and at dawn Old Glory would come bannering through the palms. That's according to Hollywood, but it wasn't according to Haiti. Not that night!

"I will call your American representatives, myself," Lieutenant Narcisse, Inspector-Chief of the Garde d'Haiti, told me with a bow. He strutted from the room. He was gone from the library about two minutes—a hiatus during which the darky gendarmes held the room at bay with bayonets, the air soured with breathing and the tension of those unstoppable Rada drums—and then he was back in the doorway, his dignity out of shape with rage.

"The telephone is dead! It is the only telephone between here and Le Cap, and some one in this house cut those wires!" He smashed his sabre into the scabbard on his belt with such vehemence that it started to rain outside. *Clang!* and then the deluge. Water slashed the library shutters; gushed with a cloud-burst roar. The room filled with the sound. An unhappy clock over the marble fireplace went *ding-ding-ding-ding*, and the old clock on the stairs, á la Longfellow, wheezed out a rusty "Four!"

Boots splayed, thumbs jammed in belt, medals dancing all over his bosom, Narcisse was speaking. "A murderer stands among you in this room. Those of you who think there is no law in Haiti will find to the contrary. I am certain *M'sieu* Proud-foot, whom you buried to-night, was assassinated. I know that of Dr. Sevestre. I know any one of you could have crept to the front of the house; fired those fatal shots. I am sorry, Mademoi-selle Dale, but I must examine your story at greater length. Nor am I satisfied with *m'sieu* the artist. As for the rest of you—by L'Ouverture's rotting bones!—I would as soon trust a jar of snakes."

His black eyes glittered at the line-up. He was thoroughly enjoying authority. "By the *Code Pénal* all are guilty until proved otherwise. It is a matter for the General of the Garde, and until I can summon him from Port au Prince the lot of you will remain under arrest in your rooms. Meantime my men will be pleased to relieve you of your weapons. Any one seen thereafter attempting to leave Morne Noir will be shot. No one can leave!"

"Don't worry, skipper." The En-sign stood forward and gestic-ulated his fuming pipe. "It's in the Old Man's will. They won't any of 'em *want* to leave Morne Noir. Not for twenty-four hours. Try an' get 'em out. They won't any of 'em want to leave in any way, shape or manner!"

But one of that little menagerie of heirs was going to leave before another hour was up. And the way, shape and manner of his going was no *bon voyage* departure, I can give my word on that!

CHAPTER V

ONE DOWN!

HOUSES, LIKE PEOPLE, are known by the company they keep; and that Morne Noir château was nasty, particularly in its upper hall. Once it had been a manor of considerable pretensions; French colonial, I suppose. There had been elegance and pride. But it had taken to wine and knavery and bad companions. Damp rot had crept through its foundations; it had learned to sneak. High living in the tropics had undermined its character and now, like a white man decadent, it had stooped to murder.

My nerves were just unhealthy enough to catch the mood of gangrened velvet portières and mouldering tapestry, dark panels and the sound of gurgling on tiles. Wainscoting had scabbed; woodwork assumed the stain of old iodine. Once mahogany, the doors to the bedchambers opening off the mezzanine had been varnished black. They looked as if they hadn't been opened for a long time, and there's something about closed doors. All the upstairs doors over the well of the hall were closed. Like evil thoughts masking festering schemes; and I'd feel easier knowing what lay behind them.

"Empty rooms," answered Maître Tousellines, trailing us upstairs. "Only the three front rooms were furnished."

Since Pete and I were to be lodged side by side in two of the fronts, I wanted to know who inhabited the third, the one next to mine on the right.

"That? That is *M'sieu* Proudfoot's bedchamber. Since his death it has remained closed." He paused with Pete at her door; begged permission to wish us both a goodnight. "I am most unhappy about this affair *miserable*," he quavered apologetically. "It was desolating that I should be forced to speak of *ma'mselle* running on the gallery."

"Never mind that," Pete said, "but how soon can you get us out of here?"

"I am sure it can be arranged as soon as—"

I said, "Now look here, Tousellines, you're responsible for Miss Dale's being here. You're a lawyer and you can start pulling strings and arranging passage for New York toot sweet."

He blinked unhappily. "Had I foreseen what was to occur to-night I should never have urged your arrival, *jamais de la vie!* Unfortunately, although *M'sieu* Proudfoot's legal adviser, I was not entirely familiar with his—this household. There were some matters in which I did not entertain his confidence. Matters— eh—somewhat the disturbing—"

I could see the little black man was worried. I leaned over the balcony rail, looking down into the hall. I turned back at him. "What are you trying to tell us?" I prodded, firing a cigarette to pretend confidence under stress. "Let's have it."

Whatever it was, the clack of military boots down below altered his intent. He swallowed solemnly. "I only wish to assure you, *m'sieu*, I will aid you in any way I can. You may have confidence, also, in Lieutenant Narcisse and his men. As a former interpreter and guide for your United States Marine Corps, when it was stationed here, the Inspector-Chief proved a man the most competent. He is starting a gendarme at once for Le Cap with a message for your consul. *Bon soir, m'sieu*—"

As we found out later, the gendarme never got to Le Cap with a message for any consul (because in Haiti you start off doing one thing and end up doing something else) but I heard the clatter of a horse Paul Revereing off through the night and rain, and felt better, knowing the rider had started, anyway. Maître Tousellines traveled down the stairs, and a black policeman tramped up half way to stand sentinel on the landing.

I DUCKED Pete into my room, switched on the bulb, and for the second time that night we were closeted alone. One thing I wanted, and I fetched it out of my Gladstone with a silent oath of relief. The old Lüger gun was pretty shabby, but there were shells in the magazine.

"There! They frisked all the others and dug up enough guns from their rooms to arm the peace conference at Versailles. Did you see the Tommy gun they found in Ambrose's duffel bag? Thank God they didn't discover this."

Pete watched me snap off the safety. "Cart, you don't think—"

"I'm through thinking," I told her, one eye on the closed door. "All I know is there's hell and high water, the dirtiest batch of week-end guests I've ever seen, and a doctor in the house. Take it."

"I don't need it," she shook her head. "The place is teeming with policemen. If I don't get some sleep pretty soon—" Her forehead puckered as if she might cry. I felt helpless and furious.

"You won't go alone to your room!"

"Of course I will. I've seen a funeral, a murder and an inquest, and I want a chance to let down my hair and smudge beauty cream under my eyes and cry a little, and that's something no artist's model does in front of her employer. I rather imagine those brutes downstairs will be snoring like cherubs the rest of the night, and Hallowe'en is over. Cart, do get some rest. You're losing weight." She smiled and patted my cheek. "Like a good boy."

I took her to her room; made a survey to see that the blinds were locked, the door would bolt on the inside, and there weren't any skeletons in the closet. After all, I was in the next room; and I planned to leave my door ajar and stand guard in the crack. Probably no soldier in the Allied Armies missed as many of the enemy as I did, but my mind was made up this time. Man or boy, the first individual who came up those stairs unannounced was going to get shot.

"Don't think I'll go to sleep," I complained sternly. (And then, to my undying shame, I slept like a Congressman.)

I left my door open five inches; pulled up a horsehair chair, and sat with a view down into the hall. I could hear Lieutenant Narcisse poking about, saying something about the scuttled telephone. A mysterious grinding, as if he were working the call-handle in a final attempt to wake up central. I'd glimpsed the phone on the wall at the foot of the stairs, one of those rural affairs with a wooden box under the mouthpiece and a little crank on the side. Apparently the local phone service had been put on the spot with the same neat dispatch which had finished Dr. Sevestre.

Lieutenant Narcisse abandoned his tinkering; went through a door somewhere. The sentry on the landing leaned on his rifle and yawned. Pete was right about the cherubic guest-list; the snoring from the rooms under the gallery sounded like a Pullman car made up at Buffalo. The house took on the drear complexion of any place late at night with the lights left on. Humid. A smell like wet shingles. A bannister creaking. Rain guttering and draining, guttering and draining. And faint through the walls that constant *tumpy-bum-bum*, as if from drums at the bottom of a well.

MY EYELASHES were sticks. I uncorked the Scotch; tried to locate the soft spot in the chair; wished the drumming would stop and the woodwork in the big square room behind me would quit squeaking. With the shutters closed the room was dopey, airless. Now and then a warped timber would crack, and the sound would lift me out of the chair by my hair.

I patched my unraveling nerves with another tug on the bottle; and then got to thinking about Uncle Eli's last rites. Easy to understand how an old man could get voodoo-minded living in a boneyard like Morne Noir. One could even believe the house had driven him to suicide; though why he had surrounded himself with such a batch of abnormals, invited them to his entombment and remembered them in his will I couldn't fancy.

Had one of those heirs-apparent murdered the old man; then taken his doctor for a ride? I didn't put it past any of those seven.

Sir Duffin Wilburforce with his master's degree in homicide from Dartmoor. There wasn't a grain of truth in those triangular little eyes; and he stood to inherit the estate. Ti Pedro with an equally sinister record, not quite as dumb as his maimed mouth made it appear. The tattooed En-sign? A navy deserter with a Jack-the-Ripper leer; and the others, somehow, were afraid of the merry-eyed man. Toadstool and his one-armed mother looked capable of anything from torch murders to cannibalism. As for Ambrose, I had made up my mind the minute I saw him never to let him get behind my back; while the pickled Manfred with his Prussian uniform and marred check was an exiled Blue-beard too sanguine for my stomach.

I tried to get my mind off those rogue-gallery faces, and every time I did I saw the funeral procession on that bald hill, the voodoo priest with the diadem of daisies on his brow waltzing up to hang a dead goat in the tree. Mules were dragging a stone angel up the slope, and black gravediggers hammered an iron stake into spaded earth. The room creaked, and another stitch came out of my nerves.

I SAMPLED the Haig and Haig. My spine wanted rubbing. It was four twenty-eight by my wrist dial. The gendarme on the landing yawned. I yawned. That wouldn't do. Better take a turn around the room. If I had something to read— There was a soli-tary book on the antique table by the bed. I took it back to the door-crack, sat down, knuckled a sandy eye. The book was old, vellum-bound, and left a brownish dust on my fingers. I blinked at the French title.

"*Histoire de Culte Vodu—par Hugo Catraville, 1848.*"

"History of the Cult Voodoo by Hugo Catraville, 1848." Just the title one would expect in such a house. In the mysteri-ous way books have, the volume opened by itself in my hand. Bookworms and stencilled little crescents on the page, but I could dimly fumble through the French, and it wasn't my idea of a bedtime story.

"Although, as we have noted, the religion of Haiti is nominally Catholic, Voodoo is practiced by the majority of natives, and Africa still casts its shadow across the Caribbean. Macandals, ouanga charms, talismans are commonly worn by the Haitian Negro; drums sound nightly in the hills. Contrary to popular belief, Voodoo is an established religion with a highly organized theology and priesthood. Priests are known as *papaloi*, priestesses as *mamaloi*, there is also a higher priest called the *hougan*.

"The Voodoo religion, in a manner somewhat similar to Christianity, is divided into two distinct branches or creeds, Service Petro and Service Legba, which in no circumstance must be confused with the Culte des Mortes, that dreadful Society of the Dead which claims to sorcerous power over corpses and is feared by Voodoo and Christian worshippers alike. The extraordinary machinations of this sinister cult have frightened not only natives of Haiti, but men of science who have studied the island's history. The sorcerers, known as *bocors*, hold secret meetings in the jungle, feast on human hearts, cast magic spells, and, it is claimed, have been known to raise the dead from their graves and enslave them in their power. These living corpses, called *zombies*, pass year after year in hopeless slavery, victims of their inhuman masters, lost souls robbed of either life or death.

"White men who have seen *zombies* tell with terror of their sluggish, obedient movements, their mute mouths, their glazed, sad eyes. Haitians live in constant fear of the Culte des Mortes. So it is we see in Haiti graves by the roadside, on the hill, in the open where no sorcerer may dig for the body. So it is we see relatives of the dead on guard for twenty-four hours in the cemetery. It is also believed that the beating of Rada drums, the suspension of a dead goat in a near-by tree or the driving of a stake through the body in the grave (a custom not unlike that employed by the peasants of Rumania, Russia and Transylvania to ward off werewolves) serves to frustrate the evil Death Cult.

"But the question of *zombies* is not to be taken lightly. No less an authority than General Galrileaun, who fought on the island under Napoleon, tells of a soldier who died of scourge, was buried with honors, only to be seen months later wandering darkly in the woods, his face—"

But that was in 1848.

Or was it?

I didn't know. I was asleep. I was asleep and dreaming. I was painting a picture of Pete on that hill under the withered tree. No matter how wildly I brushed, I could only paint a filthy red smear on the canvas, and Pete was calling to me, telling me to hurry. I wanted to cry out and tell her about a horrid gray shape that was rising like steam from the earth behind her, but it seemed I couldn't tell her until the painting was finished, and the oils were smearing red. All the time the gray figure was getting closer, a monstrous seven-headed thing wearing a stovepipe hat and its arms outstretched like a cross. It had seven faces, yet I knew it was Uncle Eli and I was getting smaller and smaller and farther and farther away, and the gray arms had closed around Pete and she was screaming and screaming. "Cart, Cart, Cart—"

Whoo! I bolted upright in the chair, icicles starting from my pores, those screams freezing cold in my ears.

"Cart! Help! In here—"

Good God! That wasn't a dream. Those were real screams and the voice was Pete's and it seemed to come from Uncle Eli's room.

THERE WASN'T any time to wonder where the gendarme on the landing had gone to. In my confusion I left my pistol in the chair and dashed out with the book; then had to make a flying leap back for the pistol. Pete's voice had stopped when I got to the door at the gallery's end, and I hit the knob with a yell. The door flew open with a gust that pitched me headlong into a scene I will remember until the day I'm dust! To this hour the smell of a room that has been too-long closed starts a melting sensation under my ribs. To this minute I can see that bedchamber with its curtained Napoleonic bed standing like a catafalque against one wall, its ghostly coterie of shrouded chairs sitting around in the blue dark like old ladies holding a veiled séance, the wakeful windowblinds chattering, the corners black as caves.

Pete was standing backed against the wall, ivory white in an ivory white lounging robe, her loose hair like a shawl about her shoulders, rigid with shock. In her hand there was a nickel-plated revolver about the size of a toy. She was pointing the gun at a gaunt walnut wardrobe that loomed like an upended coffin at room's end. The wardrobe door hung open, and a figure stood in the frame with a candle in his fist.

Darkness enveloped the lower part of the figure, but the flittering candleglow traveled upward to illume a face as gaseous, misty-featured and spectral as something just summoned from the Astral plane, forty degrees north of Death. The face was all mouth, and the mouth was one nose-bleed red wound.

The vision in that wardrobe would have made the Cabinet of Dr. Caligari an Easter gift-box by comparison. I saw it, and stood. A faint clamor in another quarter of the château seemed twelve thousand miles away. Pete was whispering, "Don't move or I'll—shoot!" and the mouth in the wardrobe door smeared with a smile like an incision for appendicitis.

"Do not remain in Morne Noir," it said in a belly-deep under-tone that hung the hot darkness with icicles. "Go straightaway. I am the ghost—the ghost of the wronged—the ghost who returned and killed your Uncle Eli—"

At that instant a soggy wind soughed from the wardrobe like an exhalation from an opened tomb. The candle went out and the face went with it. The hall door slammed on the draught, extinguishing the room with midnight. There was a piccolo screech, and a single shot that thundered in the black like a charge of dynamite. When that was gone, something whacked the floor. Then the hall door crashed open, releasing a dam of light, noise, faces and Lieutenant Nemo Narcisse.

I STOPPED my hysterical shadow-boxing and found the light switch beside the door. Pete lay on the carpet, fainted, and across the room a body was spilled out of the wardrobe, face to the floor, shoulders, crumpled, a broken candle smoking in one veiny fist. The body said, "Don't!" twice in a whisper muffled by the carpet; then stiffened like a tightened spring. I swung Pete to a stand, and she came around with her head on my shoulder and asked me if it was gone, while I glared stupidly at the faces strung across the doorway like so many wind-tossed Benda masks.

The En-sign's blue eyes twinkled at me; Toadstool and Ambrose and Ti Pedro were there; Maître Tousellines burlesquing in a nightcap and lilac pajamas, and the Widow Gladys cackling and colossal in a gruesome salmon-pink wrapper too short to hide vast, greasy black-and-brown bare feet. I was too sick to take any of this Barnum and Bailey, and glad when the gendarmes herded them aside with shouts and bayonets. I remember picking up Pete's nickel revolver, pocketing my own gun and dully watching Lieutenant Narcisse overturn the body of the ghost who claimed to have killed Uncle Eli. There was a big, red hole blown under the ghost's left shoulder-blade, and it wasn't a ghost in the glare of the electric lights.

It had been my imagination and something I hadn't eaten and the man's dramatic ability and something later determined as paint from my box of oil paints. An illusion dispelled by the lamps overhead, and the nimble black eye of Lieutenant Nemo Narcisse.

"Sir Duffin Wilburforce!"

The Englishman on the floor could not open his painted old maid's mouth to answer.

I YAWPED at the body on the carpet, wondering where my nightmare had left off and reality begun. The entire night was assuming the chameleon quality of a dream. In fact, one of those brittle little lizards was upside down on the ceiling over the dead man, watching the room with bright inquiry in its wee eyes and changing color with a sorcery all its own. I glared at this diminutive bogle, expecting to learn that the present scene was a mesmeric mirage emanating from its lizard mind.

Sixty seconds ago somebody's ghost had spoken from the otherwise empty wardrobe. A candle blows out, gunfire explodes, and an Englishman lies dumped on the floor by a bullet in his back—Sir Duffin Wilburforce, apparently, but not the Sir Duffin of the wake, the funeral, the three o'clock inquest. Not by a long shot or (for that matter) a short one! Narcisse, stooped in puzzlement over the Tory face, turned with amaze-lifted eyebrows.

"Red paint is smeared over his mouth. What devilment goes on here?" Hand on sabre-hilt, Narcisse paced and ranted with the fury of a stock company actor. "Another murder. Do not move, any of you! *Blanc!*" he spun on me. "Drop both of the guns—"

I tossed the nickel revolver and my automatic into a chair. Narcisse made a snatch for them. "How did you come by these weapons?"

"The Lüger belongs to me," I said, wishing sweat-beads wouldn't sprout on my upper lip, "and I don't know where the revolver—"

"It's mine," Pete said.

"Why did my men not take these from you in the library?"

"I left mine in my room," Pete said. "Nobody asked me."

"And mine was hidden in my suitcase," I said honestly, "and by God if I'd known what we were getting into I'd have brought a cannon!"

Narcisse narrowed his eyes to Chinese slits. "You have brought quite enough, my American friend. Will you be kind enough to tell us what you and *ma'mselle* are doing in this room with the dead Englishman?"

Pete stepped in front of me, shading confused eyes with a hand and pointing at the thing on the floor. "I was here first. I came in the room and saw—saw *him* standing in that wardrobe! I—I was too frightened to run or scream. I—I guess I did scream, though. Then Mr. Cartershall came."

Narcisse looked steadily at her, picking the handkerchief from his cuff and scrubbing his pink palms. "Why did you come to this room?"

Pete's head-shake was bewildered. "Honestly, I don't seem to remember—yes, I do! After I went to my room to-night I couldn't sleep. I got to thinking about all that had happened—to-night—and I was so tired—I just sat up for a while. I thought I'd give myself a manicure to see if it would make me sleepy, and while I was doing that I had a feeling—I heard something—"

"Something, *ma'mselle?*"

"I'm not sure what. This house, noises on the stairway, as if the whole horrible place was alive and tiptoeing. Anyway, I—I took my gun and walked out onto the balcony—"

I turned at her. "Why didn't you call me?" I demanded.

She gave me a wry smile. "You were snoring so, and I didn't want to wake you. I thought it was just nerves. Then I saw the policeman who had been on the halfway landing was gone—"

NARCISSE ROLLED black pupils at the hare-lipped gendarme. The hare-lipped gendarme took off his broadbrim and ploughed up his forehead with uneasy wrinkles. "Hones' to de Saint, I t'ink I hear noise same as white *ma'mselle,*" he husked in guttural English. "Little noise maybe rat in wall along stair. Maybe like somebody walk, too, creak, creak."

"In the wall?" Narcisse gritted.

"*Oui, m'sieu* lieutenant. Maybe rat, maybe *non!* I go down hall below look for you in library. You not there. I'm Louis in library when hear screams and shot."

"I was hunting the outside veranda for exploded shells," the officer said furiously. "*Nom de Marie!* but the next man to leave his post will find a most hard one in the guard room. Go on with your tale, *ma'mselle.*"

"But I was going back to my room," Pete went on in a colorless tone, "when I was sure I heard a door open in Uncle Eli's room, here. Not the hall door. A door inside. I opened the hall door and came in. The squeak I heard was that wardrobe door swinging open and—and candlelight came creeping out. I—I was petrified. The wardrobe opened up and—and that man was standing there with a candle. Then—Mr. Cartershall heard me—"

Narcisse examined me with a thin smile, wet-lipped.

"Ma'mselle made an outcry that woke you from sleep, eh?"

"Yes," I ground out. "I'd been sitting by my door, reading."

The lizard came skating down the wainscoting to hear better. The Barnum and Bailey onlookers jostled in the doorway, muttering.

"Alors, you rushed to this room and saw *ma'mselle* confronting the Englishman, painted as he is, in the wardrobe." The officer stuck out a thumb.

"That's a fact."

"Undoubtedly you know the reason for this Mardi Gras and why Sir Duffin should be standing in this cupboard with a candle?"

"For all I know he was waiting for a street car!" I snarled, sudden nausea reeling through my head. "I'm telling you, I ran in and saw it like Miss Dale tells it. Pete—Miss Dale—said don't move or she'd shoot, and that masquerading son of contamination said for us to go away from Morne Noir because he was the ghost of the wronged who had killed Uncle Eli—"

"M'sieu! Do you mean to tell me Sir Duffin said that?"

"Word for word," Pete cried.

"Then it went black as pitch," I shouted. "A lousy wind came out of the wardrobe, doused the candle and blew shut the hall door. I was too popeyed to move, or I'd have shot that skylarking English fiend, myself."

"Blow me down!" the En-sign spoke out from the doorway, rubbing his hands, his copper face creased with amusement. "This is gettin' good!"

Pete started to say something; but Lieutenant Nemo Narcisse interrupted her intent by turning his back on her, stepping gingerly over the corpse and into the wardrobe, where he let fly an explosion of staccato French oaths. Next minute his hands, pressing a panel at the back of the cabinet, had opened a door in the wall—a shadowy parallelogram about the size of the door to a broom-closet—and once more Uncle Eli's bedchamber was alive with that clammy, green wind.

THE HAITIAN went through with a stifled shout; the panel closed behind him; the wardrobe was empty as the feeling under my ribs. We could hear footsteps tapping behind the plaster wall; footsteps that died away, then came back rapidly like the fade and recurrence of volume in a radio. The panel reopened, exhaling stale breath and the perspiring person of the Garde lieutenant. Dusting cobwebs from his medals, he stepped with drama from the wardrobe and walked straight to Maître Tousellines.

"*M'sieu* the avocat, when you left the office under the stairs to-night, did you lock the door?"

Tousellines, licorice and lilac, bit his sausage lip. "The door to *M'sieu* Proudfoot's office? I—I did not think to lock it."

"That is how Sir Duffin gained access to the wardrobe in this room. A passage in the wall, descending to the office below. He stole from his appointed quarters without being seen by my gendarme on the landing; crept into the office and came up by way of the wall passage. But Louis heard him creeping up the inner steps. *Voilà!*"

Pete could hold quiet no longer. Fixed on mine, her eyes were shiny, almost gray with wonder. "Cart!" she cried. "Didn't *you* shoot him?"

I dizzied at her, "Me? But I thought you—"

"I couldn't shoot him," she whispered. "And if you didn't—"

Who did? Who shot Sir Duffin Wilburforce if Pete hadn't shot him and I hadn't? I stared at the body on the floor, my ears still ringing from that dynamite-clap in the dark. I listened to Lieutenant Narcisse telling me how neatly he had disarmed the rest of the household and locked their hardware in the office safe. I listened to Maître Tousellines babbling how he alone knew the combination and the safe in the office below was securely locked. I listened to the hare-lipped gendarme corporal, Louis, go down the stairs and come up the stairs with the information that the safe had not been opened.

"But some one," I heard myself croaking, "must have come up that passage behind the English freak and fired from his rear—"

The lieutenant promptly launched a cross-word puzzle. The room filled with the barks, bleats, whines and growls of the Inquisition and the sound of wind-thrown rain pounding the shutters. The lizard, reckless from curiosity, fell to the carpet, broke off its tail and fled under the houdini wardrobe. Drums beat a throbbing undertone to the game of question and answer, eyes went haggard and voices hoarse, but the answer, like the atmosphere in Uncle Eli's room, remained at zero.

Tousellines had been asleep in an alcove bedroom.

Manfred, Ambrose, Ti Pedro, Toadstool, the En-sign and the Widow Gladys, so help them God, had slept in their respective rooms, dreamed like babes until the moment of the gunshot. That was their story and they stuck to it. Furthermore, the lot of them were unarmed, were they not? Furthermore, a count of the guns stowed by the police in the office safe showed them all there. As Narcisse pointed out, *Voilà!*

"Ja!" Manfred concluded his confession of sanctitude, "but we agree on one thing, Herr Lieutenant. Somebody killed the British swine and it was done with a gun!"

"Miss Dale and I didn't shoot him!" I lashed back at the hint. I frowned at Narcisse and Narcisse frowned at me. "Look here," I hazarded, "if these—these sleeping beauties didn't kill Sir Duffin, and *we* didn't, how about somebody from the outside?"

"Quite impossible," the officer sneered. "Since midnight the château has been completely surrounded by a guard. A rat could not get by my sentinels. On my faith, it does not seem necessary. The rats are already in the house." His black eyes blurred with anger. "Attend, criminals! All of you! I am going to put a guard over every curst one of you; from now on it will be like the Siamese Twins, each one of you with a gendarme, *oui!* Two murders this night! Two under the eye of Lieutenant Nemo Narcisse, Inspector-Chief of the Garde d'Haiti! Do you think you can play with me like that? One of you shall pay!

"The one who shot down this Englishman, who killed Dr. Sevestre—when we find that one, on my word! I think we find the killer who put *M'sieu* Proudfoot, also, in his grave—"

Lighting his pipe, the En-sign gave a hoarse snicker. "You better stop your bluffin', Sherlock, an' find him damn quick," he said to Narcisse in a furry tone. "Take a hint from this limejuicer, here. My bet is he was shavin' an' swabbin' paint on his pilot-house to put on a spook act an' scare the rest of us outa here. Why? Because he stood first to rake in on the will, that's why, an' he wanted to chase off the competition. But the competition don't chase, an' Sir Duff gets kissed good-by with a bullet. Ti Pedro's in the hot spot, now. Myself," the sailor turned on heel and gave me a venomous, blue wink, "myself, I'm glad I ain't first in the will. I've a hunch it's like a football game I once played the Quantico Marines. One down an' six to go—"

The old clock on the stairs bonged six. Thunder tumbled wooden blocks around the sky, and the windows rattled under cloudbursting rain. Storm-sound echoed through the nooks and halls of Château Morne Noir; and a voice called up the stairway from below.

"Breakfast am served—"

CHAPTER VI

NEXT!

I SING THE restaurant business. It is here to stay. War and the moving pictures, death and politics and bullfights—we eat in spite of them. The ship sinks, but cookey brings hot coffee from the galley, though the stove be six feet under brine. Napoleon marches an army on its stomach, pampering the chefs. Henry the Eighth beheads a wife and goes out for lunch. Sudden death strikes an old château in dark Haiti; the library is a morgue; but the pantry carries on. The phrase is familiar: "His heart was in his mouth."

Louis of the hare-lip framed himself in the doorway. I found a cracked pitcher, lukewarm water with a little green frog in it for good measure, and I shaved. I cut myself four times. Then Louis wagged his finger, and I went down to breakfast. There was a grinning darky posted at Pete's door; a sound of water splashing in her room. I called to her as I went by, and she said she was all right.

But I'd encountered breakfasts more palatable. The Morne Noir dining room, that morning, was a combination Sing Sing, museum and Paradise Lost. A soggy, high-ceiled room at the back of the house, the plaster fractured on the walls, one side opening on a dripping courtyard where a marble Cupid with a cracked head stood in a broken fountain and didn't know enough to come in out of the rain. Weeds and tropical vines overran the courtyard wall. Daylight was absent, the court curtained with an oyster-colored mist through which the rain fell in lassos and spirals, wept and twinkled on the stones and pooled in puddles where mosquitoes bred. Most of the rain ventured into the dining room, glossing a varnished stuffed alligator over a ruined fireplace, clinging in drops on the ceiling. There were four green lizards and a brown lizard on the ceiling.

A meal in that room would be like feeding on the bottom of an aquarium, but what with Scotch dying in my stomach and my nerves already un-glued by the damp, I wanted coffee. Steaming Java might scatter the dreads of last night, and I'd wake up on Forty-Fifth Street, after all.

Nothing of the sort. The party was still going on, and the guests continued in their costumes. Lieutenant Narcisse had marshaled the Mardi Gras in the lower hall; the black guards of Haiti made a cordon with bayonets; we were marched to table. Narcisse pointed at chairs. Cornelius came web-footed from a pantry and swam around in the mist dishing out bitter coffee, bacon and grits. There was raisin bread. I cherish an antipathy for raisin bread that persists to this day.

I took to my chair amid a clattery of crockery and a battery of side glances; one long table and the boarding-house reach. Ambrose, who had been whispering to the lieutenant, sat down sullenly between Ti Pedro and the Widow Gladys. Narcisse and his gendarmes surrounded Toadstool at the other end, and I could hear them grilling the moose-faced Negro son in Creole, and it must have been warm for him judging by the way his dark skin bubbled. His mother, unable to slap the length of the board, sat smiling her slice-of-watermelon smile and eating other things with gusto and sound. Maître Tousellines, gray-faced under his stovepipe hat, rolled bread into little pills and popped them in his maw; and I remember Ti Pedro swigging coffee with a tremendous, freckled grin, swallowing like a hydrant, and beaming at his muted thoughts. I wondered at the Dominican's secret festivity until I remembered the will. And I wondered at it, then.

I WAS sitting between the En-sign and Manfred.

*Ambrose was
down to stay*

The En-sign's shoe moved under the table and stepped on mine. His copper face was low over his plate, and he regarded me from the squinted corner of an eye, talking softly while a strip of bacon dangled from the side of his mouth like a thin, limber brown tongue. The voice was so low it seemed to issue from the tongue of bacon. Lines tracked across his forehead, seriously.

"Lissen, bright boy, Manfred and me got something to say to you and pipe it low."

"Ja!" came the furtive whisper on the left. The German was gazing straight ahead, face a blank, coffee mug masking his

mouth. The birthmark brightened angrily as the hidden lips moved. "We would like a few private words."

"Before the girl gets here," said the bacon-tongue.

Manfred's blunt yellow head nodded furtively, and I had an acute feeling that a knife might catch me under the table from two directions, so I lit a cigarette and asked behind my hand, "What's wanted?"

Manfred whispered, "The En-sign and me, we know you shot the Englishman."

"And the doctor," the corner of the sailor's mouth said. "You was on the upper veranda when the doc was plugged, an' Sir Duff was a pipe. The girl couldn't of made such a hole with that twenty-two."

Manfred's shoulder was friendly against mine. "We don't blame you," he muttered into the coffee mug.

"Not a bit," the En-sign chewed, "and," rubbing the question off his lips with the back of a tattooed hand, "all we ask is, how far are you going?"

I said, with a mouthful of raisin bread, "You tell me."

"That was my idea," the corner of his mouth agreed. He leaned across me to stab a fork at the bacon plate, lips moving around in his face for me to hear. "We're onto the game, swab. You, her, the estate. All we want is our share, see?"

"Our share," echoed the German accent in the coffee mug.

"And we don't blame the skirt for bein' sore, left last like she was," the En-sign breathed, "but it wasn't fair to us, neither." His voice broke out loud, "Y'eah, mister, it rains all the time, now. It's what they call the *avalasse* season in Haiti." Softly: "It was a lousy will, an' me and Manfred got stung on it, too. The old man must of gone nuts. He was queer ever since that mutt Browinshields was muffed, and then all those crazy schemes he wanted to pull with the Cacos." The blue eye winked chummily.

"We play fair with you, my friend," came the German echo. "You tell the girl."

"What?" I inquired through a funnel of cigarette smoke.

THE EN-SIGN smeared butter on bread, flip-flopping the knife as if he meant to sharpen the blade. He folded the buttered slice; tucked it into a cheek. He chewed: "You're a wise swab. I don't know why you smacked the doc, but I suppose you got reasons. Narcisse ain't a dumb boob, though." His voice was barely audible through the masticating. "He may get you for the English job. An' you couldn't get away with the rest of 'em, see, not alone. Widow Gladys an' the Toad is tough stuff. Ambrose is worse. Ti Pedro's hell."

Manfred muttered into his coffee. "We take care of those."

"Easy," the En-sign mumbled, two tongues of bacon a-wag in his teeth. He looked at me with an expression on his forehead as if he were thinking about his mother. "You an' the girl friend won't do another thing," he purled *sotto voce*. "Your guns is frisked, anyhow. Leave 'em to me an' the Nazi. We got our ways, hear?"

I nodded at ashes drooping off the end of my cigarette.

He purred, "Then it's a three-way split an' the rest is up to us. Tell the babe it's no more'n our share an' that Manfred an' me bossed the deck before, run the whole job. Tell her why can't we keep goin' like it was, even if the New York office is out. Tell her we can still make dough, an' plenty of it. Just because prohibition's repealed—"

He blinked eloquently, leaned away from me and grinned at the table, reaching into a pocket for his pipe. I counted the four lizards on the ceiling; and on my left Manfred poured rum into his coffee mug and was sloshing the liquor around, staring at the miniature whirlpool with fascinated intensity. I tried to look as if I hadn't heard them, as if the roots of my scalp weren't throbbing. I grinned blandly at Ambrose down the table, and poured myself a fresh cup of coffee, leaning across the En-sign's unbuttoned chest for the pot.

"Prohibition?" I questioned sideways. "I don't get you."

The En-sign's Alice blue eyes twinkled cheer at nothingness in front of his nose.

He twisted to face me. "Got a match, mate?"

I held the small fire over his pipe. His mouth didn't move; the words seemed to come through the stem and out of the bowl in tiny puffs of smoke. "Cut the bluff, wise guy. You and her will play ball or else. Manfred and me are in or you two go out. I told you we had ways."

Manfred said something that sounded like, "And means."

"That's that," the En-sign said, leaning back in his chair as if his comment referred to his breakfast. Concealed from the dining room, he let his hand move like a predatory spider up my back. The fingers came creeping up my spine, closed like steel pliers on my neck-nape, dug in. For a blinding half second I could hear the vertebræ crack in that osteopathic and subtle pinch. I grinned at him politely, moved my elbow and poured a cup of hot coffee across his exposed stomach. He drove his chair backwards with a shout, jumped up, hand pressed to his scalded breadbasket. Everybody jumped up. Narcisse fled around the table with drawn sword, and Pete walked into the dining room, just then, looking as dewy in white with a starched sailor collar as if she'd just spent a night with friends at the Biltmore.

The nautical En-sign (with a starched sailor belt) straightened up to look at her, and the breakfast nook turned to stare.

"Sorry," I apologized to my table partner, "something stung me on the neck and I guess I jumped."

BUT I wasn't as cool as my speech when I crossed the room to sit beside Pete and pretend everything was under control. My little heart-to-heart chat with the navy man and his Prussian pal had spoiled my day. Manfred and the En-sign telegraphed little eye-messages up the table that came in black-rimmed envelopes, express, and I had a feeling the next time I was stung it would be for keeps.

"Thank Heaven," I pulled the Coué on myself, "the cops have all the guns in the place."

Only my thanks were unheard because there wasn't any Heaven. Not that morning. The sun had been drowned in a tropical flood and the sky over Haiti wept. The day wore weeds, and just when the morning should be brightest, the château was going to be darker than night, lighted only with gunfire where there shouldn't have been guns.

Narcisse, who didn't guess it, either, stooped at my chair. "As soon as *ma'mselle* has finished the breakfast will you both come to the office under the stairs?"

UNCLE ELI'S office under the stairs was a kennel-like lair, its door directly across the hall from the library. Once it had been the chapel, judging from the one stained glass window which cast a dim, shrine-like rainbow pattern on a tiled floor that hadn't been mopped in a hundred years. The ceiling at a slant, like a stairway turned upside down. The walls of panelled mahogany. The sort of roll-top desk President Chester A. Arthur might have used for the pigeon-holing of bills. Three or four junk-shop chairs. A square, black iron safe in the corner. A smell of cigars smoked in 1910.

Lieutenant Narcisse snapped on a dusty electric bulb; closed the door on the blackamoor gendarme posted outside; told us to please sit down. Pete sat down, trying to cheer me up with a smile. I faked one back at her, wondering which panel opened to the wall passage and the death-room upstairs. The Haitian officer swung a polished boot across the desk, squeaked back in his chair and looked at us with shiny black eyes. Some of the official bombast seemed to have been let out of his doublet. His curls were mussed, and his suspicious, mulatto features were sober.

He began suavely, "I do not wonder at your resentment, *m'sieu.* Americans are invariably resentful of foreign environment, forgetting that they are the foreigners. The situation—Haiti— a republic of color"—he spread his hands, studying the moons on his fingernails, "naturally complicates the matter for you. But why," he looked up quickly, "do you not admit to shooting the Englishman last night?"

"Because we didn't shoot him," I said.

He fished Pete's nickel revolver from the pocket of his tunic.

"*Ma'mselle,* here is your gun. A thousand pardons, but I am something of a ballistics expert in this country. Perhaps it will please you to know I was, at one time, with your police department in the Caribbean. *Alors,* your little gun is a twenty-two. Is it coincidence that the bullets I extracted from the body of Dr. Sevestre, before breakfast, are of the same calibre?"

"I didn't shoot him," Pete said without expression.

The Haitian moved his plump shoulders. "Did you know there were but five shells remaining in your pistol?"

"The man who sold me the gun told me to leave one chamber empty when I carried it."

THE LIEUTENANT nodded, returning the pistol to his tunic to yank my Lüger from his hip. "*M'sieu,* there are three bullets absent from the magazine of this, your gun, and bullets of nine millimeter calibre. That was a terrible hole blown in the back of Sir Duffin, eh?" He smiled at the Lüger. "A big hole and a big gun, *oui?*"

"Do you understand English as well as you speak it?" I angered.

"I was at one time guide and interpreter for your United States Marines, *m'sieu.*"

"Then understand Miss Dale or I didn't kill the doctor or that rotten Britisher. I'm no firearms expert, but all you've got to do is look at that muzzle to see the Lüger hasn't been fired since Nineteen-eighteen."

Scowling, the officer returned the weapon to his hip. A damp sweat polished his brown forehead. Rain came in buckets against the stained glass window, bringing the faint thumping of drums. Narcisse plucked at his lower lip. "Unfortunately I am not carrying equipment with which to examine these firearms. I can only believe the English *blanc* turned about in the wardrobe, was shot from behind, then spun and fell. The two of you were alone with him, then. What would you?" He made a Latin shrug. "I have questioned every one else in the place to no avail. Even that Caco scoundrel, the Toadstool, provides himself with an alibi.

Ti Pedro, who directly benefits by the Englishman's murder, could not possibly have done the shooting."

"That son of a Briton got what was coming to him," I suggested, "trying to play ghost and scare the life out of Miss Dale."

"You can tell the others I don't want any part of the legacy," Pete put in.

Narcisse squinted at a cocked thumb. "The doctor, before he died, testified that your Uncle Eli had been slain by a bullet of nine millimeter calibre, you comprehend."

"I suppose Mr. Cartershall fired that shot, too? We were four thousand miles away when Uncle Eli was found dead."

"This is a hell of a lot of nonsense," I raged. "All you've got to do is check with the American authorities and get us out of here. Yes, where the devil is that messenger you sent last night? What's more," I stormed, "if anything happens to Miss Dale while you're holding us in this rats' nest, I'll have the roof blown right off Haiti, put that in your book!"

Narcisse gave me an oblique stare. "What do you expect will happen to *ma'mselle?*"

"Nothing," I countered hastily, "and by the Lord, it better not! It's up to you and those minstrel cops of yours that nothing does!"

I shut up to light a cigarette. The Haitian's cheeks were olive-oiled in the stuffy heat. "I will do all I can to protect *ma'mselle. Enfin,*" he spoke at me, "but I would know what you and the German and the Yankee naval officer were talking about at breakfast a while ago, eh? What was it you whispered when you thought I was not watching, *m'sieu?*"

I glared behind my cigarette.

"And why did you spill the hot coffee so adroitly on your confrere?" he insisted.

"He made a remark I didn't like. Said I came here trying to marry an heiress," I lied, hustling the point. I wanted to tell the police about that little breakfast chat, but I couldn't have Pete worrying. Then I remembered a word of the En-sign's that had puzzled me.

"**LIEUTENANT NARCISSE**, what are Cacos?"

He regarded me sharply. "Why do you inquire, *m'sieu?*"

"You—a while back you referred to Toadstool as a Caco."

"It is a term for bandits, *m'sieu*. The type of guerilla rene-gade—you might say the gangster—who infests our mountains."

I traced the rainbow shrine pattern, faint on the tile, with a boot-toe; tried to put the next question offhand. "Do you know a man named Browninshields?"

The Haitian sat up with a jerk. "What do you know of him?"

Pete sat up, too, her worried eyes shading from blue to hazel. "Cart, what are you talking about?"

"I wanted to know if he knew a man named Browninshields."

"I did," Narcisse said carefully. "Where did you hear of him?"

"Read about him in the paper," I hazarded, not liking those black eyes. All at once they were augers boring at my head.

"Then you read," he was suggesting, "how Captain Brown-inshields of the American Coast Guard was shot dead on the dock at Cap Haitien last year when his boat put in for supplies." The officer heaved up from his chair. "A murder that created an international situation the most delicate. All we know of the assassin is that he employed a Lüger pistol, and the discharged shell had been purchased from a sporting goods store up in New York. You seem to have an excellent memory for names, *m'sieu*. Could it be you, yourself, were in Haiti last year?"

It was my face's turn to be olive-oiled. "I never heard of Browninshields before. I just happened to see the name in an old newspaper—at—at the port where we landed yesterday. I was never in Haiti before in my life and never want to be again. This whole thing's ridiculous," I shouted. "Murder all over the place and you pick on the two most innocent for your third degree while the rest of this underworld mob with admittedly criminal records—"

"Admittedly," he caught at the word. *"Ah, oui, alors,* admittedly. But how to vouch for your characters, *m'sieu.* Maître Tousellines, who brought you here, can speak no certain information on your past. For all I can determine, *m'sieu* the American may be all manner of a criminal. Now that we speak of it, that is precisely why I have summoned you to this private conference, *m'sieu.*" He sat down, watching my forehead. "The pink-eye, Ambrose, tells me you were with him in a Florida prison six years ago—"

My forehead must have been worth watching. "What!"

"Do you admit it, *m'sieu?*"

The officer blurred in front of my face. "Ambrose? Saw *me?*"

Narcisse shrugged. "He took me aside before breakfast and advised me to arrest you and send you away at once. He said you were a most notorious gangster—"

"Why, that double-damned, white-headed, lying—"

"He said you had, as he expressed it, done a stretch with him in the can, *m'sieu.* That you were the sort of expert who could open a safe or a bank vault with your fingers crossed. That you were known as a gunman for one *M'sieur* Capone."

"Oh, Cart—you—you a gunman in a Florida prison—oh—" It brought a burst of merriment out of Pete (hands pressed to cheeks she began to laugh) and a roar out of me.

"So I'm not only suspected of murder, but I'm a safe-cracker, a public enemy and a gunman. Don't tell me any more, it's too beautiful! Get Ambrose in here," I begged stormily. "Maybe he can remember something else. Maybe I'm Adolph Hitler! Maybe I'm—"

NARCISSE CALLED to the gendarme beyond the door. Pete wiped mist from the corners of gray eyes with a finger. Boots hobnailing up and down the hall produced Ambrose. He sidled through the door to stand before the Haitian officer, twitching and wheezing with asthma, fingers twiddling with a tweed cap, his albino eyelashes fanning.

He opened up with a whine. "What you want of me, chief?

You ain't got nothing on me. I was in the billiard room takin' masse—"

Narcisse nodded at me. "Did you ever see this man before?"

The mice eyes raced around the room, sped past me in a scuttle, darted at Pete, at the officer, then rested on the floor. "Yeh. I seen him."

"Where."

"At prison in Miami, Florida. Up in that skyscraper prison. He had th' cell next mine. He was doin' time for opening a safe at—"

"Ambrose," I said, thick-tongued, "you're nine kinds of a liar and you know it. You never saw me before in Florida or anywhere."

"Yeh?" His wheezing sounded as if his pinched chest were full of gum. His face distorted on the effort to breathe and lie at the same time, and he spun the cap wildly. "Don't gimme that stuff. They're tryin' to make me take the rap for killin' the sawbones an' Sir Duffin, an' I ain't going to take it, see? Not with no killer like *you* in the house. I got your number, see? Six years ago. Miami prison. Cell alongside mine. You use to talk through the bars an' tell me what a hot shot you was, how many guys you'd took for rides, an' how you could open safes like they was tin cans—"

I rubbed the ache the En-sign had put in the back of my neck and stared at the albino. He panted at Narcisse. "I'll tell you, this mug is a killer. He told me he was. Get him outa here, that's what you'll do if you're smart. Take him to Le Cap an' put him in the can! I know him!"

Narcisse spoke through white teeth, "Are you sure?"

"Yah," the boy puffed. "You think I could miss on that face?"

"And I can't miss on yours," I bawled. Then I missed. My upper-cut was out of practice. My fist made a foolish parabola past his pimpled chin, the blow throwing me off balance against the roll-top desk. Ambrose slapped me across the ear and caromed against the wall, wheezing shrill falsetto oaths. I lashed a punch that glanced off his shoulder, twirling him around. His cursing filled the close room with contamination. Pete's scream, "He's got a knife!" brought Narcisse tangling against me, and there was a second of free for all before I opened Ambrose's fist with a dropkick and sent a dirty little paring knife flying under the desk. I got his ears and banged his head against wainscoting while Narcisse sat on my back and spanked me with his sabre.

"See?" the youth shrieked. "He'll murder me—"

"Enough!" Narcisse roared. By that time the guard was through the door and we were all on our feet, Ambrose scream-ing I would murder him, and not a little truth in his accusation. Narcisse flailed the dusty air with his sabre.

"Enough! Enough! Stand so!" He bawled at the gendarme. "What room houses this pink-eyed spawn of an octopus and a shark?"

"Billiard room, *mon* lieutenant."

"Take him there and shut him in and do not so much as move an inch away from the door!"

AMBROSE CONTINUED to squeal that I'd kill him, while the guard booted him out into the hall. Narcisse slammed the door; swung back across the disheveled office, cursing. White at the temples, Pete sat in her chair. I could only stand and choke. Narcisse adjusted his medals; cleared a curl from his forehead, his plump face cinnamon.

"By the sacred name of ten thousand and two pipes, but yes! You comprehend, *m'sieu!* I know nothing about you, save that pink-eyed boy claims to have seen you as a murderer. I know nothing of *ma'mselle*. Foreigners, you come to Morne Noir late at night, armed, in the middle of a case the most mysterious. I find you together in the company of the murdered Englishman. There is no proof *m'sieu* did not assassinate the doctor. Then he speaks of an obscure crime that took place in Haiti last year. *M'sieu!* What proof have I that you and the girl are not working together in a plot to steal for yourselves the Proudfoot estate—"

"Good heavens!" Pete gasped.

"And that you are, indeed, a dangerous criminal!" the officer

crabbed at me. "There it is! I can only identify you and your character through the American authorities and my messenger has
not yet returned. If the road has been washed out by this curst
rainstorm it may occupy hours before the rider gets through.
Meantime—"

His voice was disconnected by a snaredrum flam of thunder
that broke like surf around the château, dinned across the roofs
and filled the house with a sound like breaking chains. The little
office shook with noise and there was a split second when the
church-window across the room glowed livid with outer lightning. *Wham!* Thunder followed like a blast. The electric bulb in
the ceiling dimmed and went out. Instantly the office was dark as
a cellar save for the ghost of a blue shine where the window had
been. Pete, Narcisse, everything around me vanished. A thousand off-stage wind machines sent a hurricane tearing through
the black outside. Inside voices were hollering. Doors began to
slam open. Somebody shouted, "Lights!" Boots ran.

I felt, rather than saw, Narcisse go by me; heard him kick
the office door open and dart out into the main hall. Midnight
and confusion filled that lower hallway, as if shades were stam-
peding in a cavern; in the blind black of the office I floundered
with out-thrown hands, trying to find Pete. Then I heard her
cry my name out in the hall; and played blind man's buff trying
to locate the voice. I remember thinking I'd cracked heads with
a bald man, and trying to choke the life out of the newel post at
the foot of the stairs.

"Pete!" I wailed. "Where are—"

"*Staaaaahp!*" A long-winded, quivering shriek knocked me
stockstill and stymied in a bath of ice. Coming from Nowhere
and Anywhere, the terror-driven cry pierced through the
dinning dark around me, knocked everything else silent as pitch.
For the sixty ticks of a minute it seemed as if the atmosphere
was dead.

Then, *bam*, a muffled explosion sounded somewhere in the
blackness, recessed, dull as the blow of a hammer on lead. Furore

broke loose. Shades ran by me in all directions, cursing, scuffling, and lifted above the clamor the sound of somebody rattling a doorknob like mad and Lieutenant Narcisse screeching, "Lights! Lights!"

ONE LANTERN—TWO lanterns came dashing out of darkness beyond the stairs; lights no bigger than match-flares in that high-ceiled, windy hall. The two gendarmes with the bull's-eye lamps raced up, waving them like frantic railway signals. The hall with its upper balcony, its extinguished chandeliers, its imperial stairway with me throttling the newel post came into view, all angles and crazy shadows. I don't know why nobody thought to open the front door. I don't suppose there was any daylight worth the admittance, anyway.

Pete, thank God, stood not far from me with white hands pressed to her cheeks. Directly across from the office, Lieutenant Narcisse could be seen trying to twist the doorknob from the door of a closed room that was sandwiched in between the library and the billiard room. A little crowd intermingled with the popeyed Haitian police crept toward the officer; gathered around like an accident crowd on a side street. The transom over the door was slanted open and pale tendrils of smoke were curling from the narrow aperture.

Gasping oaths, Narcisse released the doorknob and stood back. Drops as big as molasses glistened on his taffy-colored brow.

"Who is locked in this room?"

The hare-lipped corporal saluted. "I locked him in, *m'sieu* lieutenant. It is Dominican boy—Ti Pedro—"

"By the Seven Sacred Goats of Gonaives!" Narcisse squalled. "Give me the key to this door!"

The stricken guard fumbled in his tunic; found a big brass key. Narcisse jammed it into the lock; threw the door open with a crash. The bull's-eye lanterns jumped in; and the little "accident crowd" surged forward to look. Then it surged back at what it saw. With the hall in midnight behind them, the curious wanted to stay in the area of the light, but nobody wanted to stay in that opened room.

It was not an inviting chamber. The walls were puce-colored plaster, bare as a cell; there was one small window in back, thick-paned with dust and completely curtained by an enormous spider web. There was a heavy oak door in the side wall with rusty iron hinges and a rusty iron keyhole in which no key had turned for a hundred years, nor had the door been otherwise opened, nailed shut as it was by two spike-studded planks.

It was an even less inviting chamber when Maître Tousellines, huddled at my elbow, looked up and whimpered, *"Tonnerre!* it was in this storeroom where Uncle Eli kept the rosewood coffin—"* The coffin was not there, now. There were no other articles of furniture. There was nothing but a woven grass rug on the floor, and near that inner door which had not been opened, the hem of the grass rug was burning in little blue flames, fuming spirals of smoke that smelled like hay. The little flames quickened when the crowd fell back in the hall door; the glow of the burning carpet was weird blue and the light of the police lanterns no better. Firelight and lantern light touched a purplish tint to the body face down on the carpet.

It was Ti Pedro, and he was dead. Locked up by himself in that plaster room (no secret panels in plaster, by the way) with a window which hadn't been disturbed and a side door nailed fast, and the key to the hall door in a policeman's tunic, the Domini-can had been shot and definitely killed. That wasn't all.

I saw Lieutenant Nemo Narcisse go down on his plump knees beside the body, then stagger upright and stare at the blank plaster ceiling in open-mouthed dumfoundment. Where had that deadly bullet hailed from? Blood oozed from a hole drilled exactly in the middle of Ti Pedro's flocculent scalp. *He'd been shot in the top of his head!*

CHAPTER VII

FRAMED!

I DON'T KNOW how long the scene was posed—one of those badly done crimes in waxwork such as you might see for a dime if you go to Coney Island.

Except that the Coney sculpting would be better and the parodied crime more plausible.

Somewhere in darkness behind me the old clock on the stairs was ticking like a metronome; and I was a whole lot older when I yanked my eye from the smoky store room. One is as old as one's thoughts. In a brief eon of time I thought about Uncle Eli's will and funeral; about the doctor's sudden doom and Sir Duffin's rendezvous with death in a wardrobe; about my chat with my table partners in the breakfast nook and the business at hand.

I thought, "They're going to knock off every one else who made honorable mention in that will!"

I thought, "But the doctor wasn't in the waiting list, why was he killed?"

I thought, "Pete! And me! Caught in this black island sink. Drums and rain. Ti Pedro. They'll get to us after while. What's Tousellines gabbing about? Lord, what a face that Negress has. Why doesn't somebody do something to stop this? Do something!"

After all that thinking I was back where I'd started, and decrepit. Meantime I had an arm about Pete's shoulder, and the exodus from the storeroom had started. Lungs gathered breath about us, then broke in a hash of explosive blurts.

"Say! Say, by Gee!" that was the En-sign spitting hot-chewed nails. "Condemnation, if Ti Pedro ain't plugged right in the bean! Right on top the bean!"

"Foah de Massy sake!" from Widow Gladys. "Yo'all see dat, Toadstool?" *Crack!* "Y'all see dat, Toadstool boy?"

"By the soul of Saint Bouleverse!"

"Shot through the top of his doggone bean!"

"Ja!" came the German accent. "And the killer has set on fire the room to burn him!"

The En-sign rasped, "Yeah, and where'd the killer go to? How'd he duck outa this here room? Even the cops can see that winda ain't been up. That door to starboard ain't been open, neither, an' this hall door bein' locked—Keeripes!"—his tongue changed voice in shrilling bewilderment—"how'd the sniper get into this room?"

Toadstool's moose-like mask, the black-lacquered globe of Maître Tousellines's head, Manfred's plush birthmark, distorted faces leaning over my shoulder, peering, then rubbernecking back. The melting Haitian lieutenant and his troopers staring down at the punctured cranium of the murdered man. Green smoke roiling around the lanterns to confuse the eye. Hare-lip Louis stamping out the fired grass matting.

Then, the last smoldering strand trampled out, Narcisse drew his sabre and drove us into the hall. He closed the door of the storeroom; posed like an admiral waiting for a flashlight photograph. He glared at us, and we glared at him and the closed door behind him.

His eyes were crescent moons under thunderheads. He glared down the line, apparently wanting something he couldn't find.

"**OPEN THAT** front door!"

A gendarme scuttled to obey.

That house needed air. It didn't get it. The forlorn gray light of drowned day washed into the hall on a gust of mist; we stood like spectres at the last round-up, corralled by a fence of bayonets.

"You, you and you!" Narcisse spat like a cat at his squad. "Did I not order you to stand guard over these *blancs* and not move if the devil himself summoned you? Bones and blood, *oui!* Louis, you rabbit-mouthed black buffoon! You left your post when the lights went out and one of these little prisoners escaped and shot down Ti Pedro in the dark!"

Lanterns shrugged in chocolate hands. Butterplate eyes swerved uneasily under broad-brimmed hats. Corporal Louis spoke in that impossible, honking nasal achieved only by a split lip, a creole accent and darky fright—a tonal quality beyond description.

"*Moi*—heard light go out—then hear *m'sieu* lieutenant run f'om office, callin' foah lights, *oui!*" The corporal waved a khaki arm. "Gendarmes we leave our lanterns out back. We run fetch'm toot sweet."

"Bah! And while you were gone these—these—came out of their rooms and shot that Dominican in the dark!"

"*Gott im Himmel!*" Manfred spoke out. "Do you think we stay in our rooms all day to be shot like rats in the trap? Do you think we sit quiet when the storm blows out the electricity? *Nein!* I am no target. I, myself, run first thing into the hall."

"Bully for you, and I'm right behind you," the En-sign seconded his comrade. "I seen them glims was doused. Then I heard that guy scream. Right after there was that shot. Huh," he grunted at Narcisse, "I tell you, chief, we'll all get shot if you don't snap into it. We'll all get shot before twenty-four hours— like Ti Pedro in there—"

Narcisse swore, "But some one of you has a gun." He panto-mimed the maneuver. "Some one of you slipped out in the dark, broke into that room and jumped out again before I reached the door."

"And stopped to lock it after him?" The sailor's query was a vocal sneer.

Narcisse scowled. "You, Maître Tousellines. You delivered to me last night the key to that storeroom. Where is there another?"

The old black lawyer patted at his temples with his handkerchief. *"M'sieu* the lieutenant, there is not another. There is only that solitary key which I gave you."

"There must be another key!"

"There is but one," the lawyer stammered. *"M'sieu* Proudfoot was most cautious about the storeroom. It was there he cherished his rosewood coffin for safe keeping."

"How long did he cherish a coffin in there?" Pete wanted to know in a faint voice.

"Perhaps a year or so, *ma'mselle.*"

"What's that got to do with Ti Pedro gettin' sniped in the masthead?" the En-sign growled, waving a fist like a meat ball. "By Gee an' by God, Narcisse, are you gonna stand there askin' riddles instead of—"

Pete rebuffed the sailor with her level speech. "I only wondered how long the room had been closed."

"Ten thousand pardons," Narcisse bit through his teeth, "but I happen to be Inspector-Chief of the Garde d' Haiti, and I desire only to know how the room was opened when Louis had the single key in his pocket. I insist, Maître Tousellines, there is another key to this door!"

"There was but the one key, and that *M'sieu* Proudfoot carried on his watch chain. At his death I was to take it from him and open the room to produce the casket. Which I hastened to do. Then, *m'sieu* the lieutenant, last night I delivered the key to you. There is no other."

NARCISSE SWALLOWED lantern light. His fingernails clawed through his buttered curls. He looked up and down the shadow-crowded lobby of the hall, and clawed at the hooks of his tunic collar. "How, then, does the murderer make this entry and exit from that room? How does Ti Pedro catch the bullet in the top of the skull?" He snarled at himself, "I was at that doorknob in two jumps after the shot. And he is shot in the top of—"

"In the top of his nut," interrupted the ineffable sailor with a sort of laugh. "Say, Narcisse, why don't you look for an aviator?"

The Haitian officer scathed the En-sign with a stare. "An aviator?"

"Well, they're the kind of guys usually shoot a fella through the top of his head." His mouth went up. He gave a roar of laughter. Narcisse crashed the hilt of his sabre on the floor. The En-sign stood to attention, sober as the hypothetical judge. Guffawing at murder! I drew Pete three inches away from the man. He wasn't normal.

Manfred had something to say. He stepped at Narcisse with a grimace; made a Nazi salute; clicked a rightabout-face; stabbed a finger at the Widow Gladys.

"You waste your time, Herr Leutnant, until you fire one quick round of shots at this female witch. She was in the dark hall ahead of me, so. How do I know? Toadstool is with her, *ja*, and I hear the practised slap. So!"

Heads twisted at the Negress. She stood offside in a nest of bayonets like something in a zoo. At Manfred's pointed accusation, she made a half waddle forward, her arm uplifted for the assault; then she thought better of it, and grinned like a teak-wood Steinway.

"Lawd, how dat Nazzy man he do lie. Ah sho' nuff comes outen my room in de dahk, Toadstool he'm along by. But we bof' behind dis yer' German Nazzy, dat's so. He out in de dahk first. An' I don't hit Toadstool, did I, Toadstool?"

She hit Toadstool before the guards could stop her. Toadstool spun like a toy wound up by the blow; came around in an imbecilic crouch; and ended up by saying no, the Widow Gladys hadn't hit him and never did.

Manfred grunted, "Just the same, she is a witch. Does she not call herself the sorceress? Look at that boy of hers. A caco-demon, five parts *Fledermaus!*" The German draped his jaw on his chest, pulled his ears down to his shoulders, contracted his eyes on the Negress, and succeeded in impersonating Lucifer rising out of the fumes.

The widow giggled. "Lawd, lookit dat Nazzy man!"

"So!" Having pumped up the bellows in his militant chest, Manfred deflated with a shout. "Listen, Narcisse. Here is a room locked up like the military fortress in Salzburg! The window, it is not opened. The doors, they are sealed. A man sees something, cries out and is shot into the top of the brain. It is then set on fire, the rug! You call that human? *Nein!* I say it is the work of that *bocor* witch woman!"

"Where is your room?" Narcisse flicked his sabre at the widow.

She nodded her chins, indicating the back hall.

"Toadstool, he was with you?"

The Widow Gladys nodded. She elevated her hand over Toadstool's cringing head in the lazy way of someone swearing an oath. Toadstool made a quick affirmative head-bob. The widow lowered her palm.

"If she moves," Narcisse snarled at his guards, "stab her. *Bien!* You, Toadstool, come with me. Let us talk in your room where your mother cannot reach you. As for the rest of you, wait where you stand!"

TOADSTOOL SIDLED out of line and followed the officer down the hall, through the darkness of the dining room into further darkness somewhere in back. As for the rest of us, we waited where we stood, a row of guarded blanks confronted by a closed door. I didn't dare look at Pete. I could see her hands in front of her, clasped together on a bit of handkerchief. She was staring at the closed storeroom door as if it wasn't there. The black police with their bayonets and white eyes looked like dressed up Zulus from a So-This-Is-Africa movie; and the hall smelled dark green in the wiggling oil lights; and the whole scene was taking on that spurious cast that anything as real as death always takes. There were the library doors closed on the cadavers of a doctor and an errant Englishman. Here was this storeroom door shut on the body of a third victim. Fifty hours ago I'd been an artist in New York. Last night I sat through a wake in Haiti. Ten minutes ago I'd been sitting in an office under suspicion of murder. Now the lights had blown out and the murder was done. It wasn't convincing.

Wanting conviction, I found myself eying Maître Tousellines. He chose the moment to clap on his 1861 hat and extract and consult his grandfather watch. His judicial lower lip mumbled French at the time, as if he were fussing in a hurry to meet an appointment. He couldn't be a murderer. He looked like a page out of Mother Goose and I'd seen him with her umbrella. Then the corner of my eye picked up the En-sign's beefsteak face—

He'd been calling me with his eye. Now he caught my glance; signalled me with an oblique wink. Manfred was studying me, too. I was convinced.

The navy man jerked his head. I took a backward step, and the pair leaned toward me in a friendly way, both smiling on the side of the face that was toward me.

I heard the En-sign breathe. "Nice work, kid."

Manfred winked the eye on my side of his face. *"Jawohl."*

I gave them a vacant stare. Nobody home. The En-sign swerved a sideglance at the nearest gendarme, then scratched his upper lip with a finger and whispered under his hand. "You double-crossin' son of a pig, I ought to crack your head for burnin' my guts with that coffee this mornin', but you're actin' so clever—me an' Manfred gonna give you a las' chance—"

"A last chance," the German echoed softly.

Mice feet ran over my scalp. Pete was only a step away. If she overheard this—

I gestured pianissimo. The En-sign let his voice barely float. "Her an' you are gonna split with us, get that straight. We gets half or you don't get nothing but what we give you."

"What we give you," Manfred exhaled on a zephyr of beer.

"We know how you pulled this last job," the En-sign winked.

"We try to cover you by putting the blame on the black witch. We help you," the German confided.

"And if you don't give us a break I'm gonna spill the beans

and me an' Manfred will cook your goose," the En-sign menaced with his lips.

"Goose," Manfred waggled his head somberly. He was opening and shutting his big hands at his sides; his eyes were amber with malevolence; his smeared cheekbone had shaded lavender. I suppose my own cheekbones were shaded with frost. Looking at Manfred, then, I could believe those stories about Socialists beheaded by executioners in tuxedos. A swift glance at the En-sign' would ratify anything discreditable on the part of his compatriots.

"Go to hell," I consigned them with a secreted shiver; and I stepped up to Pete's arm, steering her closer to the nearest bayonet. I'd rather have stood with my back toward a team of Bengal tigers, and it took all my concentration to stay me from turning around.

Pete whispered up at me, "What did they want?" rigidly.

BEFORE I could lie to her, Narcisse and the Toadstool were focussed in the picture. The Haitian officer's features were out of place with rage, and he gave the blacker boy a shove that threw him against his mother, a haven from which he was promptly slapped.

"The boy can tell me nothing," Narcisse fulminated at us. "He and his infernal mother were shut in a room behind the pantry. It would have been impossible for them to race this far down the hall at the moment of darkness, to shoot Ti Pedro and fire that grass carpet and retreat before I, myself, pounded at the locked door."

Tousellines offered, "It was an execution the most swift."

"It must be the devil, himself." Narcisse rapped the floor with his sabre hilt. *"Mon Dieu!* I say it must. Observe, Tousellines. I leave *m'sieu* the American and *ma'mselle* in the office under the stairway. I rush into the darkness of the hall. I call for lanterns. There was a scream. Then a shot. In two jumps I am at this door and it is locked. *Voilà!* It is Ti Pedro."

"Waydda minute, skipper. Waydda minute." The En-sign butted in hoarsely. "Didn't I tell you to look for an aviator?"

"*Sacré!* Any more of this jesting and I will sabre you to a—"

"I'm only tryin' to prove Ti Pedro was shot from aloft some-how. Stow your temper for a minute an' listen." Shouldering off the wall, the En-sign swaggered up to the officer, mouth cracked in a grin that bunched his red cheeks up over his eyes. He put his hand on the face of the corporal and pushed the darky to one side. He let his triumphant grin go from face to face; then squared off in front of Narcisse.

"Sherlock," he chuckled, "did I hear you say you was in that office under the stairs with the artist an' the Judy, here?"

"You did, swine!"

"The lights blows out an' you rushes into the hall, leavin' them two behind?"

"*Oui*, and they were unarmed."

"Whaddle you give me," he pointed a thumb at the door behind Narcisse, "if I tell you how that Pedro swab was bumped off?"

"If you know something and do not tell the police, *m'sieu*, I will most certainly give you the guillotine!"

"Save it fer a snappier dome than mine," the mariner advised venomously. "The trouble with you is, yuh don't use yours."

"*Non?*"

"Nah!" He tapped a green-edged fingernail on a bronze medal pinned to the lieutenant's bosom. "You disarmed this bunch, didn't you? Then what? You locked th' gats in that safe in the office. Then what? You leave this artist mug and his dame back there with the safe? Then what? You run out into the hall and stand around in the dark—"

IT PENETRATED my numbed brain that this talk had some-thing to do with me. I took my hand from Pete's shoulder and pushed the En-sign's shoulder. "What the devil are you trying to tell these cops?"

He ignored me completely, except in what he said to Narcisse. "Don't you get it, chief? Didn't Ambrose tell you this guy's a safe-crackin' expert? It's plain enough for anybody. This artist fella opens that tin box, grabs himself a cannon, beats it into the hall—"

"That's a black lie!" Pete cried out. "I suppose—I suppose, Cart—if he did have a gun—could climb up through that little transom and out again—"

The En-sign put his tongue in his cheek like a cud of tobacco, and rubbed the swelling with the back of a hair-matted hand. He blinked one eye at the transom, then rolled it blue and wide at Pete. "That's an idea, kid! Say! Say! D'you get it, Narcisse? Sure! The wise artist shot Ti Pedro through the transom. Yeh! Say, maybe I missed my berth. Maybe I shouldda been a dick! He shot Ti Pedro through the transom an' that's why the Dominican gets a bullet in th' top of his nut!"

"So I think you hit the nail on the head," Manfred spat out.

Narcisse was now looking at me, eyes yellowed.

The En-sign went on harshly. "That's the answer to this job. That's how th' killer gets outa th' room. He wasn't *in* th' room to begin with. Yah! He shot through the transom, downwards into Pedro's noggin! Sure you did," he chuckled at me. "Sure, an' what an ace of a sniper you are! Why," he roared, "I'll bet you wasn't near th' door, here, neither. Where was you, bright boy, when th' lights come on? Where was you when they brung th' hurricane lamps?"

"He was standing across the hall at the foot of the stairs," Pete defended fiercely.

"I was standing by that newel post and you saw me there!" I choked at the sailor.

"I saw him, myself," Narcisse glared.

"You bet," the En-sign made cheerful assent, "cos' that's just where he was, this arty guy. And why was he there? Because he come outa th' office with th' gat he's took from the safe he's opened, an' he went hikin' up them stairs over there. Standin' on them stairs he can draw a bead smack down through this transom over here. A pipe for a gunman like him!"

I untied cords in my throat and gnashed out, "I'd have to be a pretty good gunman to take a shot like that in the dark, particularly when I didn't have any gun—"

"You musta had a gun, bright boy, an' maybe it wasn't dark." The man's salty face fissured in a thousand merry wrinkles; his coppery nose screwed up between happy cheeks. "I got that answer, too. It was lightning outside, wasn't it? Down in the hall we couldn't see it, becos' there's no windows in th' hall. But up them stairs over there, lookin' across through th' transom into Ti Pedro's room, here, you could see it. Lightning plays behind that winda in there an' brightens up th' room. You see Ti Pedro's head, an' you pop a bullet down through th' transom an' hit him atop his nob!"

STEPPING OUT of shadow, Pete stood forward with fists clenched at her sides. "And since you've taken over the case," she accosted the En-sign scornfully, "perhaps you'll explain why a gun fired in total darkness on those stairs wouldn't be seen by us down in the hall?"

"Maybe Bright Boy muzzled the flame with a nose-blower or something. You tell us how he did it."

"And how was it," Pete cried, "the sound of the shot, when heard by the police lieutenant and the rest of us, seemed to come from Ti Pedro's room?"

The En-sign hitched a sweat-stained belt on his tattooed (and blistered) stomach muscles. "You said 'seemed to come,' didn't you, girlie? That's a give-away. It was thundering outside. Them voodoo drums is still goin'. The whole dam' house is fulla noise as a ship in a storm. How do you know where a sound comes from? You can't never tell in the dark. Manfred," he twisted about to blink at the German, "where'd it seem to you th' shot was?"

"On the stairs, Herr En-sign."

"Narcisse," I bawled, "they're trying to frame me, and if you believe—"

I must have made a move at the officer, for Corporal Louis put a bayonet-point into the knot of my necktie and held me suddenly at attention. Tears were drops of quicksilver sliding down Pete's marble cheeks. I saw Narcisse snatch a lantern from one of his men; go sputtering across the hall to the stairway. The bull's-eye sent a yellow path mounting the steps ahead of him, and he was half way to the landing when he stopped, grabbed up something with a shout, came leaping down the steps and at us. Curses of astonishment rose in the windy gloom, my own curse leading the chorus in key and profanity. Narcisse carried a gun in his hand.

"It was dropped—or thrown—on those stairs. You were right, *m'sieu* the En-sign. Here is the pistol!"

CHAPTER VIII

THE FACE ON THE FLOOR

WELL, IT WASN'T anything else but. Not an automatic or a baby .22, but an old fashioned duelling pistol with a barrel as long as a piece of lead pipe and a long, curved, chased-silver handle, single-ball, vintage of colonial days.

Everybody looked at the pistol.

Lifting the muzzle to a splayed nostril, the officer sniffed audibly. "So! It has just been fired!"

Everybody looked at me.

I looked at everybody. Amazed satisfaction leered from the En-sign's mottled countenance; I saw his glance slue sideways at his infamous German partner; saw Manfred's eyebrows go up.

The Haitian lieutenant's teeth glittered as he barked, "Have any of you seen this weapon before?"

"I have."

Everybody looked at Pete. Pale, she was pointing a white finger at the gun in the officer's fist. "I saw that gun when I was a little girl. Uncle Eli's house in Florida. He kept it with a lot of others in a trophy case—he—that was Uncle Eli's gun!"

"But I—I have seen it, also," came the unexpected admission from Maître Tousellines. "It is one of a collection of which *M'sieu* Proudfoot was most choice. Always it was locked in the office safe."

Narcisse glowered, "I did not see it when I locked up the other weapons in die safe."

"It was in a little strong box," the lawyer gurgled.

93

"Who could open the strong box? Who has that key?" Narcisse shouted at his black compatriot. "Who?"

"Not I!" the old Negro wagged. *"Non,* I have not the strong box key. Nor do I know where it is. I could not open the box."

"Ah, but *ma'mselle* knew of this loaded pistol and its where-abouts," the officer's eyes flashed black lightning at Pete. "And her American friend could open the safe and the strong box, eh? I begin to believe *m'sieu* the En-sign speaks more truth than poetry when he accuses the so-called artist of this murder."

"I told you I had it figgered," the En-sign gloated.

As for me, I could only stand there in that ghost-gray hall, my brain in complete coma, everything going flibbergibbet around me, and listen to those rats railroad me to beat the New York Central. Away off in the gloom, drums were trains in the rain; the hall of Morne Noir was a dim cavern of Inquisitionists; dead men stiffened behind doors; I could only stare with my tongue out at the weapon in Narcisse's hand. If it hadn't been for Pete they might have got me, right then. My head had stopped.

BUT PETE'S warm-haired head hadn't stopped. In the space of five minutes the lights could go, the mute from Santo Domingo could be trapped and shot, murder in every shadow, storm and Witch's Sabbath—and when it comes to nerve I'll put my wager on the frailest woman, any time. She laughed. Her eyes narrowed green at those devils around her, and she laughed a cold laugh that shocked the color out of the darkest of those visages.

"Don't be a fool!" she spoke to the officer in the way women can speak to men. "The En-sign's story is all right, except it isn't true. Assuming Mr. Cartershall could open the safe in that dirty office—and Heaven knows he can't open a Gladstone bag with-out pinching his fingers—why should he go to the trouble of breaking into a strong box to get that ancient pistol when the safe was full of all kinds of guns?"

"Because the other guns, *ma'mselle,* were not loaded."

"Very nice," she said, tight-lipped (in my defense, and me

standing beside her like a gawk), "but who set fire to the grass rug behind this door?"

Gulps from the audience.

"A shot from that stairway might go through the transom of this door," Pete scathed, "but it wouldn't hit a man directly through the top of his head. More likely it would hit him above the ear. Besides, just before we heard the shot we heard a scream. Somebody screamed 'Stop!'"

"True!" Narcisse bowed.

"And Ti Pedro never gave that scream," Pete's voice broke on a sob. "The voice screamed, 'Stop!' and that Dominican in there didn't—didn't have any tongue to—to scream out a word like that." She whirled on the En-sign, on Manfred. "There goes your murderous little plot to frame Mr. Cartershall. Who set fire to that grass rug? Who gave that scream?"

Under the girl's verbal attack German and sailor retreated against the bayonets. Head high, chin up, foot stamping, Pete turned on the gray police lieutenant. "You leave us alone! It was dark and the hall was full of—of other murderers! Listen, you! The inside door, nailed shut in there. What room is connected with that fastened door?"

The Haitian lieutenant scowled. "The billiard room—"

"Tell me! Tell me, you! Who was in the billiard room?"

The door to the billiard room, down the hall, stood shut. Narcisse glared at the door. "Ambrose was in there, and—"

"Who would benefit most by Ti Pedro's murder?" Pete lashed out. "Who was named third in the will?"

"Ambrose!" The hall echoed to the yell.

"And where," Pete finished, "is Ambrose?" She turned about, hugged my arm, put her face in my shoulder and began to cry. God knows what I did. In the cathedral-like gloom of that shade-infested hall, we stood like two lost souls while hullaba-loo broke like the Tower of Babel at quitting time around us.

Ambrose! Ambrose! Where was that pink-eyed, tubercular Munchausen? He wasn't behind the chintz-and-chocolate bulk of the Widow Gladys, or behind the shining black shoulders of the Toadstool, or the lawyers' redingote, or the portières or anything else in the hall. Like a blow on the brain it came to me I hadn't seen him in the "accident crowd" gathered to spy at Ti Pedro's death-rendezvous; hadn't seen him since lanterns re-lighted the dark. Only Pete had owned enough mind to mark him absent.

"Ambrose! Good God! Third in the will—"

Some one else had remembered that numerical progression, too. Some one else had Ambrose's number!

NARCISSE WENT by. I saw him snatch a lantern from a gendarme's paw; make a rush at the billiard room door. The rest of us mobbed after him. He opened the door with a kick; then stood. The rest of us bunched and bayed on the threshold. Light sped into the room before us and explored a shadowy pool table, its mahogany legs and sagging pouches, its flat green cloth worn bald here and there and scarred with old cigarette burns, its little cluster of colored balls huddled together at one end of the field as if in fear.

Thunder boomed above the plaster ceiling, shaking the circular green shades of the dark overhead lamps. Rain tattooed on the shuttered side windows; and the weak lantern-light strayed beyond the table and grew weaker. So did the watchers in the doorway.

"Ambrose!"

The youth on the floor beside the table was spread-eagled. Arms and legs stretched X to mark the spot. Our combined lungs chorusing his name could not get a rise out of that lad; he was down to stay. Pinned like a bug by a hatpin. Impaled by a wooden lance that was speared through his skinny chest to nail him flat on the carpet.

Only (and you might say, this was the point!) it wasn't a lance. Ambrose had been speared by a billiard cue—a billiard cue that had been sharpened like a pencil, its polished shaft sticking straight up at the ceiling, allowing Ambrose to study the handle with white-lidded, horrified eyes, and his mouth wide open to yell. But that yell had been smothered by a gag; and let me live to a millenium, I'll never see the like of that gag again. I thought at first he had choked on a crimson crabapple. Jaws fastened apart by that unswallowable sphere in his mouth, he looked for all the world like a magician stuck in the middle of a trick.

What a trick that was! The deadly cueist had made his score. The shot had been called and played. Jammed in Ambrose's mouth was a billiard ball. We could see the little white circle with the number. Number Three!

PICTURE THAT decayed billiard room ominous in shadows and enfeebled light; that white-haired boy on the floor with a sharpened cue sticking up out of his wishbone and that billiard ball popping from his mouth; the thunderstruck huddle hoodooed in the door to the hall, and that other door nailed shut on the other room and the other dead man.

Nobody laughed. Nobody could move. Then Narcisse pulled himself together with an effort that made the fat sizzle on his forehead, backed out of the billiard room, slapped shut the door with a crash. The crash brought pandemonium. It started with a sob and mounted to the hollering of Jerusalem's Wall. Tousellines moaned a prayer to his patron saint, and those about him took up the cry of calamity. Toadstool and his lovely mother were backing away from me, pointing black fingers, jibbering. I stepped on a policeman's foot, and the Haitian screeched as if he'd been tagged by the Grim Reaper.

Nobody wanted to stay in that billiard room. Nobody wanted to go back into the dark hall. There was a moment of hubbub, bravado, consternation and fright (such a coterie of gargoyle faces as Cocteau might have sketched during an opium fit) through which I shoved like a dummy with its straw out, and fought to shield Pete from mass panic. We were thrown back in a bargain-basement rush to the other side of the hall where there were certainly no bargains. Anything to get away from the doors on the library side. The library doors that were closed on doctor and Briton. The storeroom door, shut on the dead Ti Pedro. The billiard room portal, masking what had happened to Ambrose.

Best door in the house was the front door, open to the veranda and clouds of sooty rain; but two Haitian Guards stood with crossed bayonets in the frame, and the crowd could only back against the stairway.

My face was guttering at the temples. I clutched Pete's shoulders and spoke down to her hair. "Stick with it, Pete."

"I—I'm all right."

"They can't get away with any more. They can't!"

She said something I couldn't hear. Every one in the hall down to the last gendarme was saying something. Now was the time for all good men to come to the aid of the party. It sounded as if the guests wanted to go. Twenty-four hours was a little too long, and whoever was trying to scare us away had outdone himself on this latest prank.

But we were going to play Questions and Answers again. A monstrous, blue-black .45 automatic glinted in Lieutenant Narcisse's fist. He appeared to be unwell. Pomade was melting in his curls and lubricating knots on his forehead; sweat formed in a row of glittering jewels on his upper lip. Nostrils opening and shutting, he stared dumbly at us, then at the billiard room door, uncertain, as if doubting what lay behind it.

"FIVE MINUTES," he doubted. "Five minutes of darkness and two men are slain. Ambrose came to the office, talked, marched across the hall to that curst game room; a cat's jump later he is killed." He began to breathe hard. "You, Corporal Louis. You shut him in there!"

"*Oui!*" The gendarme shuffled his feet.

"There is no lock on that billiard room door?"

"*Non, m'sieu* lieutenant."

"That Ambrose, he was all right when you shut him in?"

"Pink-eye boy all right, foah de Gawd!" the hare-lip honked. "Ah kicks him in room. Close de doah, Ah do. Just so Ah see pink-eye boy catch up cue an' staht to play. Louis waits front de doah an' heah de balls click-click. Den lights go pouf! Louis go fetch de lanterns."

"By Petian's soul! And the killer slides into that room and sticks him like a boar. *Oui*, it was Ambrose who gave that scream. He saw the assassin coming at him." The automatic jiggled in the officer's grip. He scraped water from his upper lip with a grassy tongue; made a sudden twist at Manfred. "Captain Manfred von Gottz, your room is opposite that billiard room. And by your own confession you rushed into the hall the moment the lights departed."

"Hein!" The German's jawbones were bulging, yellow; the blemish on his cheek like red velvet. *"Aber,* I did not spear that white-headed mongrel. Where would I have on me the billiard cue? Or the knife with which it was pointed?"

Narcisse said thickly, "German dog, if the assassin had on his person a knife, why does he bother to fashion himself a lance?"

"Because the lance strikes deeper than the blade, *ja!*"

"M'sieu the Captain von Gottz speaks from experience," the Haitian officer reminded. "Is it not you were once captain of Prussian Uhlans, eh? Perhaps you know too much about this lance—"

"Dunderhead! Have I any knife to sharpen such a spear? Herr Proudfoot would not allow those who worked for him to carry knives."

"Ambrose had a knife." It was my own voice getting into the mêlée where it didn't belong. "He tried to stab me with it back there in the office and I damn well kicked it out of his hand." I laughed coarsely. I was acquiring some of the Morne Noir mannerisms, suddenly determined to play these criminals at their own vicious game and throw some mud on my own hook.

"Listen to me, lieutenant," I demanded. "You wanted to know what this sailor and this German swine were whispering at breakfast; by God, I'll tell you! That navy deserter and his Boche friend told me they had ways to finish the others. They said they were going to get Ti Pedro and Ambrose. They—"

The En-sign had been leaning on the balustrade, stuffing tobacco in his pipe, eyes riveted on the billiard room across the hall. My outburst dropped him in a crouch, his face turned savage as a Molly Maguire. "Who put a nickel in you?"

"You did," I said with a calmness that astonished its owner. "You and your Nazi boy friend. I'll put a stop to this Greek chorus of yours. If you think you can frame and threaten Miss Dale and me—"

"Why did you not speak of this at once?" Narcisse sputtered.

"I was going to," I snapped. "But I thought they were pulling a bluff and I didn't want to scare Miss Dale. When Ti Pedro was shot I—I didn't have a chance to speak. Now I'm telling you. I wanted to tell you when you asked me in the office—"

I STOPPED to grab breath, and before I could get started again, the En-sign's mouth was chewing:

"Don't be a fool, Narcisse. This guy is ribbing you with a pack of lies. Look, Narcisse. By Gee an' by Gawd, if he kicked a knife outa Ambrose's hand in the office, like he says, then that would give Bright Boy a blade to sharpen a cue with, wouldn't it?" He straightened up from the crouch, his mouth a hyphen between the red parenthesis of his cheeks. He poked the pipe stem at me. "I betcha you speared that little harpoon in Ambrose, yourself!"

I shed a little of my self-collectedness. "You and Manfred said you were going to murder those two!"

"You wouldn't send an innocent guy to hell for somethin' *you* done, would you, Bright Boy?"

Calmness departed. "You lousy rat, are you trying to frame me again?"

Of course he was trying to frame me again, the same way Manfred was consistently trying to frame the Widow Gladys. Not that I couldn't believe the Negress and her son capable of murder in any degree, but I doubted the one-armed woman's ability to wield a spear in so drastic a manner. Whereas Toadstool might have done so with a smile, I considered neither him nor his mother endowed with the imagination that must have been behind that billiard room scene. These deductions I made in my best Gaborieau manner (oil colors being my medium) and was furiously convinced that Manfred and the En-sign were close as crossed fingers behind this noon-hour massacre. Not being a Paris fiction detective, and Pete being present, I could only call the En-sign a rodent and ask, thick-tongued, if he was trying again to frame me. Trying? That was a laugh.

"Nah! I'm just tryin' to help th' police, an' save my life before you get down the list to me." The mariner was once more amused. Cheeks fiery as carbuncles, throat chuckling, he leaned against the stair-rail, coolly adjusted the pipe in his teeth and held a match before eyes as blue and guileless as those of a cathedral-window saint.

"Sherlock," he advised Narcisse, "I see this here pair of murders plain as I'm seein' you. The girl, now. *She's* the sniper what shot Ti Pedro. Look. Her arty boy friend opens the safe, quick as light gives the dame the loaded pistol. She beats it up the stairs an' pots the Dominican. Meanwhile, *he* takes th' knife he's grabbed off Ambrose, ducks acrost to the billiard room, yanks a cue off the wall and with one swipe cuts himself a spear. Ambrose sees him an' lets out a squawk. He whales the spear into Amby, beats it back acrost to the stairs just as his girl friend shoots Ti Pedro, an'—"

"Wait!" Narcisse held up a hand at the En-sign; spun at me. "Where is this knife you grabbed from Ambrose in the office?"

"I didn't grab it. I kicked it. For God's sake, lieutenant, can't I tell you something?"

"I have no doubt you could tell me a great deal."

"It wasn't only at breakfast those two threatened Miss Dale and me. They were giving me the high sign while you were questioning Toadstool a few minutes ago."

"That is a lie!" Manfred shouted.

The En-sign cried plaintively, "Narcisse, this arty mug is a triple liar. He was threatening Manfred an' *me* at breakfast! Tellin' us to clear out of Morne Noir or him and the Jane would smack us down."

"You're a liar," I shouted.

"*Herr Gott!* it is the pot calling the kettle black," Manfred shook a fist at me.

DESPERATION WRIED my tongue; tied up my vocabulary. Everybody was shouting now. Liar! Liar! Diogenes would have run out of lamp oil in that menage of mendacity. I shall always remember the En-sign as one of the few talented people who could yell a falsehood and perjure himself like an advertising man—that is to say, misrepresent with a smile and look you straight in the eye.

He was looking me straight in the eye. "By cripes, Bright Boy, you got a nerve," he was bellowing. "Trying to plant these butcherings on us, and all the time you know it's you and your babe."

I burbled at the sailor, "I'll kill you for this!" and tried to hit him, but Pete held my arm.

"Sure you'll kill me," the En-sign was crying in a wounded tone. "You'll kill us all if the cops don't put you and your girl out the way. Four murders just since the funeral. By Christmas!" he flung at Narcisse, "didn't Ambrose tell you this bird was a safe-buster an' a Capone gunman! Didn't Ambrose say he seen this yegg in the trap six years ago at Miami!"

"Ambrose lied!" I cawed.

"Why would Ambrose lie about you, Bright Boy?"

"Because he wanted the police to get me out of here. You and he and the rest of your murderous gang. Trying to frame Miss Dale and—"

"Ambrose had the goods on you! You ain't no artist! You're a homicidal maniac, by Gawd! Ambrose reckanized you; an' you put him on the spot so's he wouldn't blab. You an' the dame will put us all on the spot—to get the Old Man's estate—if this dumb Haitian cop don't nail you. Pinch 'em both," he shouted at Narcisse. "Pinch 'em both before they kill us all! Same as they killed Amby an' Ti Pedro—"

"He didn't kill Ti Pedro and Ambrose!" Eyes blazing, Pete spoke a flow of low, fierce words. "You navy deserter—you inhuman thug! You're trying to confuse the police! Don't listen to him, Lieutenant Narcisse! You listen to me! I think I can tell you how Ti Pedro was killed—"

Narcisse lifted an elbow; shoved Pete out of the way.

"Can you prove, *m'sieu,* that you are this artist you claim to be?"

I couldn't budge my tongue.

"Fool!" Pete cried at the officer. "If he's a gunman would he be carrying a box of paints and—the *canvas!* The painting! Why," Pete's eyes were wide blue, "he's even got a portrait with him! My portrait! Upstairs in the room! Show him, Cart!" she sobbed. "Show this fool!"

Narcisse gritted at me, "You have this work of art with you?"

Dumb, I nodded.

Shadows and struggling faces, the gray hall with its doors closed on the murdered and its front door open to black rain and drum-thumped mist reeled in front of my eyes. *Bong!* The old clock on the stairs started filling the gloom with the tolling of twelve. Noon? I had never seen a noon so merged with midnight. The big gun in the police lieutenant's fist was levelled at my jugular vein.

"I give you ten minutes," he was dicing the whispered words through his teeth. "If you are an artist I will believe Ambrose lied. If you are an artist I will be convinced you are not gunman and murderer. You have canvas and paint-box, *oui?* Perhaps that is but part of the disguise. But the talent, that is something you cannot pretend. *M'sieu* the artist, I desire to watch you paint!"

"Paint?" I gurgled. "In this madhouse?"

"*M'sieu,* I give you ten minutes to prove you are an artist."

CHAPTER IX

CACOS!

FIBS, FALSEHOODS AND fairy tales. Ambrose saying he'd seen me in Miami jail. The fired pistol picked up on the stairs above the newel post where I'd stood when Ti Pedro was shot. The knife I could have snatched in the office to sharpen the cue in the albino.

Looking back on that mephitic morning, I often wonder how many of the innocent go down in the quicksands of Circumstantial Evidence. A better jury might have been prejudiced. My face was against me. I couldn't explain the burning grass mat in the locked storeroom or the bullet hole in the top of Ti Pedro's head, and if Pete knew the answer (and strangely enough, she did) they gave her no chance to speak. As for Ambrose, I had hinted at a desire to kill him, the gesture was certainly well motivated, and he was certainly killed. Therefore, I had ten minutes to paint.

Ten minutes in which to prove myself an artist. From all that hallucinatory fiasco of demonism, death and storm, I recall those particular instructions as the maddest. Breakfast after murder, that is more or less traditional. Portrait painting is something else. To leap from a sweat-bath in the Chamber of Horrors, into the frivolity of smock and palette! Ten minutes in which to paint and prove I was an artist. A thousand years ago (or day before yesterday) an Academy at least had given me ten days. Wasn't it Holbein who spent a week on a broomstick? Ten minutes—

"Allons, donc!"

Tropical Haiti couldn't wait. I looked down shatterpated at

the blunt snout of Narcisse's service automatic. Narcisse's service automatic was pushing on my belt buckle. The Haitian's eyes were onyx beads on hatpins. He bowled me over. "Paint, *m'sieu!*"

In that dormitory of criminals summoned together by an old man's crackpot will? In that jungle-hemmed manse where death struck when your back was turned and drums pounded in rain and freaks chittered? That was no studio. That house had an atmosphere about as sweet as the twilight in an octopus cave. I continued to stand with my mouth open a little.

The taffy-dripping police lieutenant held a gun in my middle, and there was no time for temperament.

"You and *ma'mselle.* March!"

Sweet Land of Liberty, if he didn't mean it! He swung on his gendarmes, spluttering Creole. Corporal Louis honked an order. The black police fixed bayonets and conducted Manfred, the En-sign, Widow Gladys and Toadstool toward the back of the hall.

Then, *tramp, tramp, tramp,* Hare-lip Louis on one side, two awed gendarmes on the other, Tousellines bringing up the rear and Lieutenant Nemo Narcisse in the lead, Pete and I were marched up the stairs to the mezzanine, along the balcony to the front room. The room assigned as mine, between Pete's and the late Uncle Eli's.

Darkness was not remedied by candelabra lighted on the bedside table. Candles can't pinch hit for the required "north light" of an artist's quarter. The fluttering yellow gleams were solemn as a church. For further fantasy there was the sound of rain whooping across the outside balcony, the undertone of funeral drums, the senseless expressions of the minstrel police force. All the foolish and sinister tenebrosity of a college fraternity initiation.

"Good Lord!" I managed an aside to Pete. "They really mean it."

Her chin puckered; whether for laughter or tears, I couldn't tell. She whispered, "Mount the canvas, anyway. I'll slip to my room for the costume—then they'll see—"

SHE WAS gone for a moment, during which I got in a few of my more stellar oaths for Narcisse's benefit. "There's the painting," I concluded with heat, growing madder by the second and doing my cause no good. "I haven't an easel or frame to mount it on."

Suspicion bunched his frizzy brows. "I did not believe you would have, *m'sieu*." He shrugged. "Anybody could carry such a picture."

"Confound it, I'm trying to finish it for a showing. An art exhibit! I brought it here to work on."

"And you neglected to bring this easel that is necessary?"

"I thought I could buy one here if we stayed for—I mean, I intended—it would be imperative for me to work because—"

"And I give you an opportunity to work, *m'sieu*."

"Damn it, man," I implored. "While we dance around in this blankety blank comedy the real murderer is loose down there in the hall. Would a gunman be lugging this picture and—take that gun off my stomach!"

He did not take the gun off my stomach. "I repeat, how do I know you do not carry the paints to mask your true identity?"

I whirled on Tousellines. "What a hell of a lawyer you are! You saw me in New York! You saw my studio! Why don't you tell this cop you visited my studio to call for Miss Dale?"

The old black man screwed up his face in dismay. "Please, *m'sieu*. I have seen artists' studios in the cinema only. I wish to aid you, but in all honesty I did not carefully view your habitat"—the lower lip drooped unhappily—"to speak truthfully it—I do not recall it as looking like—like an artist's quarter—"

Narcisse nodded craftily. "There is but one way to prove. If the man is an artist the talent will convince. It you are the artist you will paint."

I could have rung like a smashed alarm clock, but Pete slipped

"Paint!" Lieut.
Narcisse whispered

into the room in her organdie frock and saved me that extremity. Together we spread out the canvas. Puttering like a born idiot, I looked around for a place to mount the thing and finally decided (sanity to the four winds!) the door of the clothes closet would do. Ten minutes had collapsed to five! I fumbled through my paint case and found tacks. Pete took off a shoe and limped across the carpet to help me. We pounded tacks with a high heeled shoe while the Law of Haiti and its moon-lipped pettifogger looked on like pickaninnies absorbed in the raising of a showboat poster, and dead men spoiled downstairs.

The pounding covered Pete's whispered, "For Heaven's sake, Cart, get this over with before I lose my mind. Just play around with the brushes and they'll see—"

THEN SHE took her pose in a nearby chair, trying to smile the same smile. Not smiling at all, I mixed a mess of paints on the palette, trying to look like an artist. In rattled befuddlement, I dropped an expensive tube of Winsor Newton, dandelion yellow; and when I stooped to recover the tube I gave it a boot that sent it slithering across the floor to hide in a cranny somewhere near the door. No time to pick things up. My nerves were popping like roman candles, and I had to give at least the appearance of Leonardo da Vinci.

"Paint," Narcisse was demanding. "Paint, *m'sieu!*"

Shadows stood up over my head and looked down from the ceiling; the black art committee gathered at my back; the sweating officer muzzled his automatic in my spine, ordering production; and lunacy lay just around the corner. I daubed bits of color, flecking the brush, standing back and cocking my head at each stroke in the approved pantomime.

"Paint!" Narcisse whispered.

I made a couple of impressive strokes at the face. I could feel the critical eye of the judges sizzing like electric batteries over my shoulder. A man couldn't have read a newspaper under such scrutiny.

"And are you painting, *m'sieu?*"

I swung around in rage. "What in damnation do you think I'm doing?"

"Then Ambrose did not lie!"

"What?" I howled.

"An artist would paint the likeness! Do you call this art?"

"But—"

"And you put blue on the throat and a streak of white paint for the nose—"

Then I saw! I don't suppose that Haitian police officer had ever seen or heard of modernistic technique. Like the one about the genius poet at the lynching who was told he must write a poem or die. The unhappy poet composed a masterpiece in blank verse and was lynched because it failed to rhyme. To that Haitian art committee, a blue shadow and a highlight on the nose didn't "rhyme." And when you stand on top of an oil painting and the lighting is bad—

"Your game is up, *m'sieu!* Fraud! You and *ma'mselle* go to the General of the Garde in irons, *bien sur!*" He was mincing backwards, mouth askew with anger, gun pointed. "I arrest you both for—"

"Nothing of the sort," Pete cried in fury. "You don't under—"

I COULDN'T stand that pointed gun any more. Dodging sideways, I struck out hard and slapped the massed palette square at the lieutenant's face, grabbing the gun barrel and deflecting a fast shot through the window blinds. The gun-shot crashed like a French seventy-five, the bullet tearing cloth from my armpit and crackling through the bamboo shutters. Paint splattered fifty ways. Pete's scream came faint through the cannon-smash; the air was filled with brushes, oils, oaths, smoke; I saw her wrestling in the clutch of the hare-lipped corporal; and a thin gendarme jumped on my back like a black cat, pinning my arms.

We did an adagio twirl, that black cop and I, while Narcisse stood raging, his mad face clown-spotted, polkadots and polychrome from chin to hairline, red, blue, white, yellow, modernistic for fair, the palette stuck to his hair like a custard pie. He wiped a smear of carnelian from his upper lip, and came to me.

"I would shoot you where you stand, *m'sieu,* if you were not already condemned for four murders, on your way to the gallows. Assassin—"

He mopped his harlequin features; squalled at his men. Pete was dragged toward the door. The black behind me prodded a bayonet at my shoulder blades; sent me staggering across the room. The portrait tacked on the closet door ("Southern Hospitality, by E.E. Cartershall, '34") watched proceedings with calm amusement, summery and graceful with posed picture hat, as if Pete, herself, was standing there in the gloaming; the candles on the table flittered like frantic moths; shadows went every which way; and down in the lower hall something else was happening.

I was aware of a policeman's whistle shrilling in the gloom, and someone was drubbing the front door. Sentry boots stumped down the hall, and then the front door slammed open with cackles and yells. Narcisse scrubbed scenery from his face with a sleeve, and snapped an order for quiet among the comedians behind him. Upstairs we stood in tableau. Glad tidings!

The messenger was back from Cap Haitien! Maybe the consul was with him, diplomats, the Marines. We were saved!

Not yet! Not by any manner of means. I saw a muddy figure come slowly up the staircase, leaving a track of puddles. On the landing he saluted at Narcisse, and the lieutenant stalked across the balcony in something like dignity to meet the man at the stairhead with sharp words. The dispatch bearer talked with his arms, semaphoring like an Indian. To my sudden alarm, I saw this darky messenger was shockingly wounded, a livid cheek-gash spilling crimson down his jaws as he talked. Narcisse clapped a hand to his forehead. He leaned backwards. He leaned forwards. He said, *"Mon Dieu!"* The wounded envoy handed his superior an envelope; the officer snatched it, tore it open, staggered backwards as if he'd been hit.

"What is it?" Pete's whisper was distracted.

I yelled, "Did he get the American consul?"

NARCISSE WALKED stiff-legged at us, smeared like a witch doctor from collar to hair line, black eyes savage as a cat's in a cave. "Into that room, both of you! Every scoundrel in this house will remain here until my return. Tousellines, you will come with me to the office where I will give you a rifle and orders. I am leaving you in entire charge!"

"Tousellines? In charge of Morne Noir?"

Narcisse turned at me, his mouth spitting fire like a Gatling gun.

"Do you think this means I am through with this affair, *m'sieu.* Do not think this gives you leave to escape! I deputize *M'sieu* the Count of Limonade to shoot any or all of this house who do not remain in their rooms—"

The little black lawyer stood aghast. There was a stoppage in my windpipe. Pete cried, "What does it mean—"

And Narcisse ground through his teeth, "It means I am ordered away with my men immediately, *ma'mselle.* All available police must go, no matter the consequence. Word has just come of a Caco uprising. At three of this morning Cap Haitien was attacked by bandits, the Banque Nacionale blown up, the terror loose through the hills! It is said," his voice squeaked tenor on the blurted cry, "it is said the Cacos are led by a *zombie*, do you comprehend? Headquarters sends for every man and my command! But I warn you both—"

He twitched his glittery glance at me, backing from the door-way with aimed pistol. "I warn you both! It will be far more dangerous for whites to leave this house than to remain hidden inside. I would not attempt to flee Morne Noir, *m'sieu*. And Tousellines has orders to shoot if you so much as step from this room. If you value yourself or the girl, stay where you are!"

WE STOOD hand in hand and stared at the slammed door. I heard the squeal of the key; the boots trampling down the stairs; uproar in the hall. Maître Tousellines' high-pitched falsetto; more slamming doors; boots fading on the veranda; shouts; rain-smothered calls.

Pete, expressionless with dismay, wandered to a chair and sighed down. I jumped for a window to peer through shutters at a landscape like a waterfall. Beyond the veranda rail the compound blurred off into fog thick as night. Leftward the bald hill swooped distant above a wedge of rain-thrashed jungle, a vague and misty escarpment with soggy clouds tumbling along its summit. I could just make out the silk cotton tree, like a tiny hand of bones reaching up through tatters of vapor, and the speck-white guardian angel sentinel over its grave.

Down the blotted compound the sullen *tum–bub–bum* of the indefatigable drum family continued its lament, the sound loudening and fading like the pulse of a sickened heart. Like the pulse of my own heart, when I saw that dim knot of mounted gendarmes go wheeling down the gravel drive past the iron coach dog, bunch together with Narcisse in the fore, and gallop off in the water-clouds. Like horsemen from Sleepy Hollow, they misted away at the foot of the compound; there was only the terrace and a wall of rain, and what was left of the Law had gone.

I turned from the window, pale as a fool, I suppose, and looked at Pete. Pete sat in her organdie frock, small, white, looking at me. A Caco uprising. Cap Haitien sacked and a bank blown up. Black guerillas prowling the storm, and led by *zombie!* Pete and I—marooned in a château with its downstairs stiff with murder, its rooms alive with brigandry and a darky lawyer named Limonade left in charge. It had been poor enough sport with those Haitien police, but they'd meant well. Now the lid was off and I was sitting on it.

"Tousellines! Alone down there in that hall—"

I couldn't stopper a shaky oath. I had to plug it with Scotch from the Gladstone. Pete sat watching her portrait tacked on the closet door, two large tears strolling down her cheeks. She shook her head at the bottle.

"I'm not crying. I was only thinking—*I* got you in this—"

I stood over her angrily. "This expedition was my idea. And I'm going to see you out of it." I swallowed for courage, paced the room a few times, tried the locked door, then sat on the edge of the bed and glared. Candles. Pete's picture on the door of the clothes closet. Rain and drums. Pete. I feigned amusement, making a vinegarish mouth-pucker. "Great Christmas, what a mess. Somebody tells a ghost story and the local constables leave to see it."

"Cart, it's a nightmare."

"None of it's happening," I said hopefully.

"I can't believe any of it," she told me in a low voice. "That's what frightens me more than anything."

"What?"

"The feeling that it's all an illusion. And behind it all an awful menace, this depressing rain and those drums and—not so much the danger, but the sort of dream where you want to run and can't because you don't know what to run from."

I swallowed some more courage.

"**IT'S QUEER,**" Pete whispered, her white hands tight on the arms of the chair. "I can't seem to weep over those—those dead men. It's like reading about the Chinese. Two million China-men die in a flood, and we turn the page and laugh at the comic strips. This is so dreadful, I—I think I'm going to laugh. It isn't just murder. I think it's more terrible than any of us know."

I said passionately, "One of that bunch is trying to knock off all the others to get the estate, that's certain."

"It seems like that from the will."

"That will may have been cooked up," I tongue-wagged. "And one of this gang—"

Wet woodwork creaked across the room, jumping me off the bed with uplifted bottle. It was only a warping floorboard. I sat down.

"I think one of this gang killed your Uncle Eli," I floundered, "and monkeyed up the will to clean up the whole household. Bring them all together and pick them off one at a time. I think this *zombie* scare is a trick to get the police out of here."

"But why was Dr. Sevestre—"

I shook my head. "I don't know. Unless he was going to testify about the bullet he removed from Uncle Eli's head. You know what the Negress told, about Manfred and the doctor fighting and—"

"I don't think Manfred killed him," Pete said.

"That Bluebeard would crucify his mother."

"He was soaked in rum last night. A marksman fired those shots at the doctor. A steady hand."

"Whoever's behind this hell, I'll tell you one thing," I pointed the Scotch bottle. "This bunch has been running rum."

Pete sat up straight. "But since prohibition—"

"That's just it. Repeal came along and busted the smuggling business and this mob went broke. Say they've been working under cover from Haiti, operating in secret from this château, pretending employment with Uncle Eli."

"Rum runners," she gasped. "I never thought of it."

I said brightly, "Repeal washed them up, and sometime last year they killed that American Coast Guard captain—"

"Browninshields!"

"Right," I panted. "The En-sign gave that much away at breakfast. They murdered this coast-guardsman and maybe your Uncle Eli knew about it, saw it done, something like that. So they put him on the spot, and frame his will in an attempt to snatch the estate."

She watched me, eyes widening.

"I think we've got it," I muttered. "The gang put up the job on your uncle, but one of them's double crossing the rest. And they maneuvered you down here to pin the guilt on you. Because, with your name last in the will it would look—"

She shuddered, her temples white, strained. "It might be the reason."

"I hope to God it is," I said vehemently. "Don't you see? They aren't going to touch you, then, but they'll leave you as a set-up to get the blame. Me, too, now that I'm in it. They'll try to frame us, just as they have been trying; and leave us to take the rap. And no court on earth can prove us guilty."

PETE'S EYES were dark with candleshine. "Cart, *who?*"

"Well," I husked, "they've narrowed it to four, and if it goes any farther, by the simple process of elimination—"

She counted in a tense voice, "Toadstool. His mother. The sailor. The German."

I growled, "They've gone down the line, one, two, three."

Pete looked at me. "Cart, listen. Who is it in mystery plays, in stories,"—she tried to smile—"who is it in stories always turns out the guilty one? I mean, isn't it always the one you don't suspect, the one who seems least guilty, who looks impossible?"

I followed the thought around in my head.

"Cart, who looks the least guilty to you? Who in this awful château—which one of this household couldn't be the murderer with any apparent rhyme or reason?" She was staring at the door to the balcony, her eyes mined deep, strange in her shadowed face.

I thought, "The only trouble is they all look the most guilty, even I. And if I was writing a mystery play I'd know the idiots who attend them would be looking for the villain among the least suspect, so I'd make the killer look guiltiest and nobody would guess him."

This mental acrostic made me a little ill. Good Lord! Pete's face had gone white as chalk. Here I sat like a bumpkin trying to comfort my nerves with Scotch and conversation, the police were goose-chasing after phantoms ten miles away, and almost anything was getting ready to happen.

"Look here, Pete, we're not going to stay locked in here waiting for the next move. I'm going to do something. That lawyer wouldn't dare take a shot at me. If he thinks I'm going to sit meekly up here with that den of tigers prowling downstairs—"

"Cart!" She caught my sleeve. "What are you going to do?"

"I'm going down into that hall and take that little African by the nose and make him open that office safe, that's what. We're going to hold all the guns in this game from now on."

No optimism could make me believe Tousellines was going to keep Numbers Four, Five, Six and Seven caged politely in their rooms until the police decided to return. I'd better haul the other side of my lap off that feather bed and down into the office after the artillery before the others of the house party discovered the same idea.

It was a good idea, at that, but it was born too late. I'd no more than tightened a notch in my belt and moved for the door, when a furious burst of gunfire started Fourth of July in the hall beyond and knocked the stuffing out of my thoughts.

CHAPTER X

DEATH IN THE AFTERNOON!

I WAITED, STUPEFIED, for the shooting to quit. I couldn't count the shots. There were too many of them; for half a minute they came so fast the noise streamed together in one continuous din, like a team of riveting hammers running an armament race.

Pete stood up out of her chair appalled. The château boomed and banged with the loud enthusiasm of Black Tom erupting on Sunday. It was a midnight attack. Somebody was going over the top. Bunker Hill never rivaled that outblast. Then it stopped. Dead. I could almost hear my wrist-watch ticking.

I shoved Pete roughly into her chair—"Don't move!"— smashed the quart bottle on the doorknob, and rammed a shoulder at the wood. The lock gave like cheese. The door bulged, stuck, then opened farther than I'd have dared and spilled me out on the balcony. My arms hugged the balcony rail to keep me from sprawling; then fastened me there in a crouch, and I couldn't get away. Anybody on the hunt could have sniped me for a stunned tapir, but the gunmen in the lower hall (to my fortune) weren't looking at me.

Under the balcony Maître Tousellines, no longer on guard, wasn't looking at anybody. I thought he was dead. His eyes were squeezed shut and his forehead was battleship gray. A little red soap bubble glistened on his big underlip. He lay on the floor under the gagged telephone near the stairs, his globed head pillowed against the wall, knees splayed, arms limp and palms open, beggar-fashion, at his sides. There was just enough light from the candles flickering in sconces down the hall to see him by.

The stairway was brighter, bathed by the mellow colonial light. Toadstool, at the foot of the stairs, didn't see me. The apish little Negro was mounting the stairs, bending every faculty to the task. Something was the matter with Heir Number Four. His great, doormat shoulders were at last too much for him; he was grunting like a piano mover, legs bowed, grotesque, wabbling as if under the oppression of Atlas. His feet struggled and his parenthesis knees were rickety while his vast shoulders glittered with thousands of inky sweat-beads.

On the bottom step, it seemed an hour before he achieved the next one up. Left hand glued to the banister, he had to haul himself upward with all his might and main. Looking down on his preposterous shoulders, I couldn't see his moose-face; but his head was lifted in an upward fixity as if he was Elisha, or whoever it was, mounting the golden ladder and spending his life's blood to get there. In his right hand, the butt fast in his armpit, he clutched a shiny repeating rifle.

THE WIDOW Gladys, facing my way, didn't see me, either.

She stood on the stairway landing, interested in the doings of her son. His slow-motion struggle to ascend amused her, and she was looking down on him, regarding him with a hugely maternal smile, slowly nodding her chins, like Mamma urging Baby to his first adventurous climb. The swaddled bulk of the Negress was shaking with a suppressed inner mirth, a silent Mammy giggle that shook her like a great chocolate pudding and jiggled her larded cheeks. One might have supposed she had skipped upstairs ahead of her infant, turned and beckoned; and another minute and she would peal a laugh. But a crimson current was flowing down her side, welling from a red gutter that was scooped on her dimpled, armless, left shoulder. And her vast right arm was akimbo, wrist resting on the shelf of her hip, and in that big hand a chunky black revolver.

It was a charade—mother and son playing a game. The house

and its hall were silent, the walls listening. I'd imagined hearing those shots; it was only the clock ticking. That smell of burnt powder, those smoke-wisps lingering over the stairs were figments of neurotic fancy. In the candle-lit quiet, Toadstool gained another step. Save for her subterranean merriment and the seismic heaving of her mountainous bosom, Aunt Jemima never moved. But there was strain in the air and the gloom would snap.

It did.

I heard Toadstool's voice. "Morne Noir b'long Toadstool all mine."

The Widow Gladys whispered, "No!"

"All mine," Toadstool panted.

The Widow Gladys smiled, "No. Toadstool, no!"

Toadstool's right hand slid along the barrel of the repeater and fastened into the trigger. Holding left-handed to the banister rail, he pointed the repeating rifle as a lame man might point a crutch. *Flash! Flash! Flash!* Silence burst into a succession of shocking explosions as the black boy worked the repeater, and I could almost hear those bullets hitting, like blows on a soft pillow. At each successive blow, the Widow Gladys gave a violent shrug and fired, squeezing the revolver on her hip. Noise flamed from the revolver, *slam-bang!* above the tinnier report of the .32 rifle, and at each slam-bang Toadstool would scream.

Battle smoke rolled blue on the stairway. I wanted to shriek and stop it, but I couldn't. They were riddled in a trice. They kept on shooting. They swayed and tottered and continued upright and firing like a pair of black Rasputins, too tough to die. I don't know whether death or the sheer weight of the lead in them finally brought them down. They dropped at the same time— the Widow slopping down like a bag of laundry on the landing; Toadstool toppling forward and sliding down the steps, his chin going *tubbedy-bub-bub-bump* until his bare feet touched the floor and held him stiff. His mother's revolver capered down the steps to look at its handiwork. The noise disappeared down the back corridor. The smoke cleared. Pose!

"Cart!" Pete screamed from the room. "Are you all right?"

"Stay right where you are!" I broke from sick inertia and fled around the balcony to the stair-head. "Don't come out, Pete! That black woman and her son—just killed each other—"

GASPING IN powder smoke, I banged down the landing, cleared the Widow and got to the bottom two at a time. I picked up the black revolver and tucked it into my pocket; then stooped to wrench the rifle from Toadstool's grip. His dead fingers hung on and I had to tug. I was sweaty and seasick, but felt a lot better with those weapons in my possession. Typical of my scatter-brained condition that I never thought to wonder if they'd been emptied.

Then a snore rippled out behind me, and I spun with a shout frightened to my mouth. Maître Tousellines. I'd forgotten the little black man under the telephone. He wasn't dead. His snore woke him up. He gave a mulish snort, wrinkled his ace of spades nose as if to dislodge a fly, rubbed his chin drowsily, opened popping white eyes and sat up in the scene of carnage with a jump of alarm.

"Morte de Dieu!" He took in the bodies on the stairway with a howl; saw me standing over him with the rifle; rolled along the wall with a bleat of fear. I had him covered.

"Get up!"

He hauled himself upright, rumpled and moaning, hand to jaw. I kept one eye out for trouble at the back of the hall, one eye on the lawyer. "How'd those two get out here? What happened?"

"M'sieu—I—Narcisse gave me that rifle you have and told me to stand guard by the newel post where I—where I could watch all the rooms. That woman and Toadstool—*Dieu!*—they were shut in—the closet beyond the billiard room."

"You had this repeating rifle?"

Eyelids batting homerun glances of terror at the stairway,

he swayed on his feet and gulped like a flamingo. "Lieutenant Narcisse armed me with the rifle."

"And you gave it to Toadstool, there?"

"*Jamais de la vie!* The ruffian took it from me, *m'sieu.*" He clapped his jaw as if to nurse an aching molar; stood trembling. "Sacred stove! but I looked up, you comprehend, and saw that fiend and his sorceress of a mother walking up the hall from their room. They had pried off the lock. I told them to halt or I would shoot. And then I saw the Widow was pointing a gun at me, a black pistol."

I patted the weapon in my pocket. "Where'd she find this gun? Did you give it to her?"

He groaned. "Does *m'sieu* think I am mad? But no! She walked out of her room and the pistol, it was in her hand." Tousellines ogled the chintz laundry bundle on the gloomy landing.

The chintz was changing to red flannel, and I couldn't watch. Toadstool was worse. I nudged the lawyer with the repeating rifle. "Where did she get the pistol?"

Tousellines gulped, "The woman was a wizard. She said it had flown through a window in her room. The shutters were open and the gun had flown through like a bird and dropped into her hand."

"That's a hell of a story," I quarreled, savage in growing anxiety. "What happened was, you opened up that safe in the office and passed around some of these guns."

HE FAIRLY jigged with fear. "Oath of the Saints, *non!* The woman she was grinning and pointing the gun at me as they marched down the hall. They made me hold up the hands, and the Caco boy snatched from me the rifle. *Dieu!* and the police not a half hour gone." He scrubbed perspiration on his bald head with a green wrist. "They warned me if I so much as opened my mouth to call they would blow off my head. *M'sieu!* That widow started up the stairway saying Morne Noir now belonged to her and she would take care of you and *ma'mselle.*"

I sent a glance of horror at the red laundry bundle.

Tousellines worked his face. "I believe she would have killed you, but for that Toadstool! *Sacré!* He stood beside me with my rifle and called softly to his mother to stop her on the landing. He told her to attend! He said Morne Noir did not belong to her, but was for him. Then he lifted the gun barrel and struck me across the jaw. I—I do not know how this happened—"

I didn't know how it had happened, either. A revolver flying through a window to arm that black witch and her son! Then his feud, this mess on the stairway. I could understand them shooting out an inheritance between them, but I wanted to know where the Negress found her pistol and how many more errant guns were flying around Morne Noir. No amount of shouting and scornful skepticism could make Tousellines alter his little story.

"I tell you, she was possessed of the devil. *Tiens!* Every gun in the house was locked up. Then she produces a pistol with which to punish her son. But she was not his real mother; there are those who claim she summoned him from the regions of darkness." Drops stood and grew on the old colored man's forehead. "Perhaps that is how she gains herself the weapon."

I could almost believe it, but not quite. "Now *I've* got the weapons," I declared loudly, "and I want them all. You're going to open that safe in the office for me, Tousellines, and from now on I'll do the shooting, you hear?"

"You are not going to kill me?"

"I'll kill the first damned one," I shouted to the world, "who makes a move at Miss Dale or me. I'm taking charge in this château, right now!" I leveled the rifle at the lawyer, and he turned the color of liverwurst. "I want everyone out here in the open where I can watch. Where's the German? What's become of Manfred?"

As long as I shouted and stamped I could bluff that scene on the stairs.

Tousellines pointed a shaking blue finger down the hall. "The

German is in the room beyond the office, *m'sieu.* The door across from the billiard room."

"Where's the En-sign?"

"In the room next to that, *m'sieu.*"

I SHOVED Tousellines away from the wall, stepped over Toadstool's ankles, scouting the shadows for something to shoot at. The house was a tomb. The doors across the hall were the portals to grave vaults. The doors on the staircase side—Manfred's and the En-sign's—were quiet as sin. I'd announced my dictatorship to a pair of dead Negroes and a third who looked half dead from fright. A chill of apprehension trickled down my spine. When I cleared my throat the sound came loud as cogs rattling in a piece of brass pipe.

"Get the German out here." I shoved Tousellines. "Call him into the hall."

Tousellines hesitated, then rustled to the door he'd indicated as Manfred's, and delivered a quavering summons. As well have tried to call Ambrose out of the billiard room, Ti Pedro out of the storeroom, the doctor and Sir Duffin from their respective biers in the library. Manfred's door was adamant.

I lifted the repeater, walked stiffly up the dim hall, waved Tousellines aside, and crashed the sulking door with a kick. I walked in behind the rifle, and Tousellines walked in behind me. Then we turned right around and walked out. Vacant room. No Manfred. Nothing of notice save a side window that had been smashed open, the blind ripped away, a lame shutter hanging on a torn hinge. Rain stormed over the sill, and the veranda, dimly visible outside, was adrift in swimming weather.

"Out the window, and I'll bet he broke that glass when the guns were going."

Tousellines protested at my coattails. "But *m'sieu* the lieutenant did not think they would dare. Consider the Cacos!"

I didn't wait to consider the Cacos. Nor did I do any polite teasing at the En-sign's door, but walked at it with leveled rifle, and drove it open first crack, certain of what I would discover in the burly mariner's room. I was not to be disillusioned. Another side window and wrecked shutter with a blowing gray curtain of rain and a glimpse of foundering veranda and pouring day. Vacant room. No En-sign.

Tousellines' awed voice reached my hearing in a stammerous aside, "Turn me into one pepper mill, but they are gone!" and I stood in the middle of that lightless chamber with my throat ticking, my ears out like bird dog's, running what used to be popularly called the whole gamut of emotions. Since the doctor's death, events had come almighty fast and thick, what with the murders of Sir Duffin, Ti Pedro and Ambrose, the subsequent retirement of the police, the war of attrition on the staircase and my final ultimatum to the world. I was just growing used to the fact that Toadstool and the Widow Gladys were no more; (I was going to look again to make sure). That the En-sign and Manfred should have capitulated, withdrawn through windows—folded up like Arabs, disappeared, and gone home!

I lowered the rifle, and stared. It was like that first minute of silence that swept over France in November, when you wondered if everyone was dead, and then you began to glow with security and happiness, forgetting the lad who was killed by the last shot. I put the rifle butt on the floor and began a smile at Tousellines.

I said, "By God, they *are* gone!"

AND THEN it was just too true to be good. My relief at their being out of the house ebbed to anxiety as to where they were. I'd cheered too soon; there was once a False Armistice. Wired with nerves, I backed into the hall.

The old darky lawyer set his eyeballs travelling. "If the Cacos catch them they are going to be sorry. The mountain bandits are most cruel with the whites. In the days of the Marine occupation when a Caco captured a white man—"

A lot I was concerned with the safety of that couple! I took the old black man by the scruff of the redingote. "Tousellines! We've got to get out of this château!"

"You?"

"Miss Dale and I. You've got to help us get out of here!"

"The Cacos, *m'sieu!*"

Cacos weren't the only terrors riding that rainstorm out there. I visualized Manfred, drunk, skulking, venomous with his bullet-blunt head and stove-burned cheek. The En-sign with his Alice-blue eyes and rattlesnake mouth, his tattooed and blistered stomach and sadistic hands.

"We've got to chance it, Tousellines. You know the road. Any road. You've got to take us out of this. Where are these Cacos!"

He described a sweep of the arm. "I wish I could know, *m'sieu.* They are thick as snakes in the forest. It is most dangerous to try."

"Do you call this house a haven?" I snarled. "We're going. Horses! There must be some around."

He gulped, "A stable at the foot of the compound."

"You'll fetch the guns out of the safe," I directed quietly, "and we'll ride. You must know some place we can hide. I'll leave that up to you. You'll go, or—"

He worked his sore jawbone, shrinking under my eye. "Anything to assist, you comprehend. I must warn you the roads will be almost impassable. *M'sieu,* I am a lawyer, not a—a guide. But I will try." He hesitated, then went on breathlessly. "I think Melotville would be our most opportune attempt. But, *m'sieu—*"

I shoved him into a run. "Hurry it, then."

"If *ma'mselle* departs she forfeits her right to the estate."

I saw the bodies on the staircase and snapped, "We're clearing out. Get the guns," and pushed Tousellines toward the office door, and started a run up the stairs. I didn't stop for star gazing on the way. Pete would have an automatic, and I'd have the rifle; if we kept our fingers crossed we'd escape this hecatomb. The grass on the other side of the fence couldn't help but prove greener.

"Pete!" I called to her as I broad-jumped the huddle on the landing. The door to the front room where I'd left her was closed. Thunder bounded around in the rain outside, and my hail was smothered. I sprinted along the balcony, and shouted her name again as I yanked the door-knob. The draught of the door flurried the candles on the table, animating the wall-shadows. Pete was there, standing in the door of the clothes press across the room, smiling at me, calm, ready to go with picture hat in hand.

For a tenth of a second I thought she was. Only for an eyewink that portrait, shadowed in with dusky candle-glow, was natural as life. Then I went stockstill on the threshold with a cry.

Pete was not in the room!

CHAPTER XI

ONE MORE

"PETE!" I CALLED her name and I broke through window-shutters, to the outside gallery. Water swooshed through green strings of vine, wetting the veranda like a ship's deck, twinkling where the drops burst on the leaves and wood. Pete was not there.

I drove my face through the vinous screen into the gray downpour, hunting the landscape below with frantic eyes. A brown river seeped across the terrace where Dr. Sevestre had been shot; shrubs and bushes blew flat in their beds; the compound, hemmed in by walls of pouring mist, lay like a weedy lake. Nobody in sight.

Drenched as a turtle, I jumped back into the room, cursing myself sick. My God, I hadn't left her alone five minutes. I knew. She'd gone to her room for a nap. I raced out onto the balcony, shouted her name, slammed through her door. "Come on, Pete, we're leaving—we—" Empty. Her suitcase on the bed and something pink-fluffing on the back of a chair. I backed out choking, pawing at my hair with a frightened hand; made a dash for Uncle Eli's chamber.

Uncle Eli's chamber was dark and vacant, the door of the wardrobe half ajar and the carpet darkly stained in evidence of Sir Duffins early morning end. "She's frightened," I advised myself drearily. "Those devils on the staircase scared her, and she's hiding."

I choked because I knew that wasn't true. I chased down

both sides of the upper balcony, slamming into one room after another, shouting into the fusty emptiness of long-shut chambers where the sound of my voice started hollowed echoings and the opening of the door brought down clouds of atticky dust.

"Pete! Miss Dale! She's not up here!"

I toiled down the staircase four steps at a time, jumping the body on the landing, slipping on a wet step and hitting the bottom beside Toadstool with a screech that brought Tousellines out of the shadow on the hop. I cleared the dead darky to catch the live one by the throat.

"Don't stand staring! Miss Dale's not upstairs! She's not up there—anywhere! Did you see her? Where could she have gone?"

"Ma'mselle was not in the room?"

"She's gone, I tell you. Hunt! Help me, you fool! We've got to find her! They—they may be killing her—"

He could only stand panting with his tongue lapping his bulged lower lip, black face zero with fright.

Too crackbrained to see anything if there'd been anything to see, I poked my face into the office under the stairs and bawled her name. Then I crossed to the library and slid the doors and glared at bookshelves and empty blue shadows and the doctor and the Englishman side by side in silent contamination. After that I banged into the storeroom where Ti Pedro lay in a smell of burnt grass with a hole in the top of his head. After that, slowing on sickened legs, I visited the billiard room where Ambrose had been squelched with cue in heart and the Number Three ball in his teeth. I was ill when I toured the dining room to see monster black flies buzz in clouds off the breakfast board; and Tousellines hunted the two rooms at the back, the kitchen, the pantry; and Pete wasn't there.

I DREW the black pistol from my pocket. I shifted the rifle to my right hand. Cold beads streaked down my face.

"Tousellines, she was up in that front room and she's gone."

"I am desolated, *m'sieu.*"

I husked, "We've been through every room?"

"Every room in the château, *m'sieu.*"

A queer suffocation clogged my chest. "I don't see how Pete could be out of the house. While we were down here in the hall and—do you think the Cacos—"

"We would have heard them coming," he moaned. "They would attack first the huts at the foot of the compound."

"Go down to those huts," I said very quietly, prodding him with the rifle, "and see if Miss Dale is there or has been seen. If you should see her—or Manfred or the En-sign—yell. Send back two horses. I'll go around the outside of the house. Get started."

I pushed him out the front door; turned and ran through the dining room into the court where the marble Cupid with the fractured head was idiotic in a shower bath. I was soaked to the skin in a second. Puddles boiled over my shoelaces; buckets came around corners and took me in the face. Beating bare-headed through plunging, swirling cascades, steamy and tasting salt, I clanged through an iron gate and started along the rear wall of the château. Steep hill swooped down behind the house, the upper heights buried under the weather. Freshets came leap-ing and purling down the muddy slope, pouring a river around the château. A dyke had broken in the sky. Swashed in mud and warm water, the raffish old house seemed adrift on the hill, as if its dark wings were moving along in the rain and I was standing.

Pete couldn't be out in this flooding afternoon. I couldn't find her if she was. Tracks would be obliterated. My God, if that devil of a sailor, that German wolf had trapped her—Blowing like a narwhal, I reeled through mats of blown vine, clumps of bougainvillea and hydrangea; thrashed through huddles of spouting palmetto, keeping close to the wall and trying to see five feet ahead. My boots sank to the ankles in quaggy garden-ing. My face wept. That was a day for dolphins, not for murder and a girl disappeared from an old dark house.

"Pete!" Her name choked in my throat. Murder, then! I'd play it at its own game. Shoot first and ask afterwards. If those jackal inheritors, Six and Seven, had laid a hand on the girl—

A waterspout gushed me around a dim corner of stone; I stopped; crouched; held breath; huddled under the flowing eaves of the side veranda. With the vine screen behind me running like a green millrace, it was like hiding under Niagara. Someone was moving through a thick clump of plantain not ten feet ahead of me; someone hunched low, creeping through the glistening wedge of tropical leaves with animal stealth, a shadow under the splashing storm.

I tightened, knotted in my blind of shrubs, trying to sight the rifle. The shadow stirred in the plantain patch, parting the great fronds with a shining stick, lifting its head through the green in a turtle-like scrutiny. The drenched head was turned away from me, but I knew that red, creased neck. The En-sign! He didn't see me, but was steadily regarding a stand of coconut palms some fifty feet distant from the house across a guttering yard of weeds.

THEN I saw something else! Something that looked like a stalking crocodile inching along belly to mud behind the palm grove. Manfred! The big German, flat in the rain, was nosing through the brush across the yard, for all the world a man-headed saurian, sliding over the mire with his eyes glittering at the house, the field-green Boche uniform melted with the landscape; and as I watched he reared his blunt head and scanned the brush where I hid. He clutched a curved banana knife, a long scimitar-sized machete, in his grinning teeth; his features were blurred, but his strawberry cheek was livid as a wound and his eyes pierced the rain-swirl like dots of acid. He did not see me, nor did he see the shadow in the plantain clump.

The En-sign, hunched in the plantain, could not see Manfred, either. I could see them both, and I froze on bent legs; watched drowning, lungs chugging to burst. In the pour from the leaden sky, the doused daylight, the picture was dim, flickery as an ancient cinema film. Then the En-sign spied Manfred's advance and congealed in a squat. I saw what was up and wanted to howl. That murderous sailor was stalking Manfred, and the German killer was angling *him!* The elimination contest was carrying on. Manfred grinned with his butcher knife; and in the En-sign's fist was a long, tapering lance, its tip sharpened like the point of a pencil. The sailor had taken a cue (no pun, either) from Ambrose's killer. Manfred was going to get it.

What a sweet little game of hide and seek that was! I was watching a finesse of murder, cross-purpose and secret attack that would have made the underground cheatings of Europe look playful by comparison. The En-sign studied the shadow in the palms with the taut-spring intensity of a tiger luring its lunch. Oblivious to the ambush-hidden peril, Manfred squirmed and scouted toward the veranda like a hunting python. Carnivore and snake.

I was hypnotized. I watched in bated fascination. I saw the cue slowly lift in the En-sign's fist; saw him shift and balance for the throw, spear aimed at his prey. I waited for the rocket to go. It waited. It hesitated. Then the lance was lowered; I blinked water from my eyelids and glared. Manfred was nowhere to be seen!

Sensing sudden jeopardy, the crocodile had vanished in the rain; as if the waterfall had absorbed the German, blotted him from sight. Flesh walked on my neck, for I'd seen those green uniforms vanish atop a trench in much the same way, and I knew he could not be far. I searched the palms, the brush under them for glimpse of an ear, an eye, a moving weed, a knife-glint. The rain came battering across the weedy yard, blinding, gray-white. A baffled exclamation drifted from the plantain where the En-sign crouched. I could see his spear poking the leaves, his head screwing around, eyes hunting the lost target in a beady, lizard-quick gaze. Another second and he'd see me crouched against the vines. I could have shot him on the spot, but Manfred's disappearance had addled me, and I didn't want that banana knife buried in my spine. I had to find Pete—

HE SAW me! The En-sign's China-blue eyes gazed straight

into mine. He was not two yards away, and his pupils blazed like heated needles blowpiped through the mist. He whipped to his feet, waist deep in the plantain, arm cocked back for the throw. I shouted and squeezed the trigger in my wet clutch and the hammer only clicked. The repeater was empty!

And that billiard cue spear would have come flying through my heart if the man's arm hadn't been smashed by lightning out of the rain. *Rat-ta-tat-tam!* The fusillade poured from the veranda vines right at his shoulder. Fire lashed through the green wall, shattering the cocked elbow, spotting his throat, his jaw, the side of his head with red holes. The En-sign, who had wanted his share of Morne Noir, got it!

I saw the spear loop out of his fingers, fly sideways, fall in the weeds like a defective squib. I saw crimson liquid scatter in the rain; saw the sailor go down as if the mud had opened under him. There was a crashing among the palms across the yard—a wild face uplifted—Manfred burst out of hiding like a flushed dinosaur. He gave one look at the green-screened veranda; the blade dropped from his teeth; the shots crashed—*bam! ram!* and the German shrieked and fled down the juicy field. *"Gott im Himmel! Ach, Gott im Himmel!"* The python chased out of Eden never had such eyes. He was baying like a hound.

I think I squalled Pete's name. The German never heard me. Stark, staring like a madman, he rushed across the side yard, hurled himself off down the compound and out of sight. A final shot spurted from the masked veranda. *Bam!* The bullet pruned blossoms from wet branches touching my cheek, and for forty seconds I was too staggered to move. I couldn't see through the rain-flogged vines, but the marksman on the veranda behind them was running. Footfalls fled away, going fast. No heavy tread, like a man's; but a quick, light-footed scurry, fading toward the veranda in front.

I dropped the useless rifle, gripped the black pistol, started out of the shrubs only stopping for a sideglance at the En-sign's smashed face reddening the green, and broke through vines to the porch. The long deck of the veranda was deserted. I raced to the front of the house. Nobody. But the door stood wide, and I made the hall just in time to hear a rat-like scuffling in the office under the stairs; and I made the office only in time to see a panel glide shut in the wall behind the roll-top desk.

The desk had been shoved to the center of the den; I couldn't believe that strip of wall had moved. I attacked it blindly, filling the dim cavity under the stairs with dust and bedlam. Strips of mahogany splintered under my punching gun-butt, slivers sheared away, then the whole panel caved inward like so much kindling; and I was staring, dunce-headed, down a corridor black as a mine shaft and dank as the entry to an Egyptian crypt.

Out of the pitchy passage came the breath of a hundred and ten staled years and the scurrying echo of quick-slippered feet. Whoever it was, he had finished the En-sign and only missed me by a milicron. And where was Pete! With her name on my lips and a curse for the tunnel, I swung the gun and jumped through.

CHAPTER XII

PROCESS OF ELIMINATION

DR. SEVESTRE TO the En-sign in sixteen hours; perhaps that would win the non-stop massacre marathon in any man's country (Chicago handicap), and the little process of elimination couldn't go on. But Haiti, that afternoon, was no man's country, and Death wasn't taking a Holiday in Morne Noir. I look back into the tunnel with confusion. With the murder of Dr. Sevestre, I hadn't been able to see the forest for the trees; in that tunnel, with the trees all chopped down (to muddle a metaphor) I couldn't see anything. And I'll never know how near I came to dying in that rat hole. Who was ahead of me there? I couldn't see.

We ran. Sometimes I fell down flights of loose flagstones; sprawled headlong in hillocks of soft dust. Most of the way the black hole seemed on an upward slant; darkness drank up the last hope of light at the first turn, and there were dozens of turns after that, each ten shades darker. I tallied the bends on my face, stubbing my jaw against corners of invisible masonry and scalping myself on low-lofted rafters, full tilt at hairpin curves.

The rabbit gone mad and pursuing the ferret. I could sound that mole-like scurry in the lead; and I trailed it headlong up a passage as tortuous as the buried track of an abandoned roller coaster. Every foot of the way was narrow as the channel for a gas pipe, stifled with dust from the flying feet up ahead. My elbows skinned raw on the close-pressed walls, and I coughed and staggered on running legs, burrowing in subterranean night where every turn might throw me down a mile or greet me with gunfire. I went on. The underground chase seemed to last for miles and years.

The airless tunnel writhed for breath, upward and downward, on and around like a vein of ink on its way to the black heart of Haiti. I'd like to find out about the sappers who engineered that historic feat; an earthworm couldn't have planned it. They must have been probing for China.

Thud-thud-thud my boots drummed the floor, running into exhaustion and out of exhaustion, dogged and on like Volga boatmen too tired to stop. Dirt caked my clothes. The pistol was a ton. But Pete—Pete was gone, and the fugitive up ahead had tried to kill me, and I could hear his feet in the asphyxiating black, *thud-thud-thud* when they were out of step with mine, always a turn beyond reach. I wanted to cry out and order them to halt, and could not get my teeth out of my lower lip. But I struck my head against a hanging bulge of earth and brought a terrifying shower of slag clattering down from the ceiling.

My shout of alarm was suffocated almost as it got away, and the runner ahead must have heard, for a laugh came twisting back through the sponge-thick, channel blackness and turned my heart to a goose egg. Lord, what a cackle that was! "Yee-hee-hee-hee!" The sort of outburst Satan would give with a fresh soul on the tines of his pitchfork. The brand of inhuman mirth that rattles the doorknobs of monkey houses and insane asylums.

Let the mine collapse. My temples iced at the shocking sound. I'd once heard a madwoman laugh like that as she stood on the train tracks of a New York subway. Ten minutes, twenty minutes later in the smother of that under-earth passage my ears were curdled with the diabolical echo and my legs didn't want to go. All in all, I don't believe I ran through that earthworm corridor more than half an hour; that evil outburst dragged it half a century, and, had it been repeated, I'd have turned and fled like a mouse.

WE CAME to a stretch where the bends straightened out and

The light blinked on, and Cart saw a strange sight

the tunnel took a direct line to wherever it was going. Now the walls on either side were wood, my heels hammering a floor of timber. In the sceneless black in front of me the scurry lengthened to a frantic stride. *Pat-pat-pat*, the author of that deviled merriment was drawing away from me. Thud-thud-thud, I ground my teeth, pumped aching legs, hung on.

It was queer how we locked step in a sort of rhythm, faster and faster, running together, so that the pounding of heels joined together in the dark was as if one man sprinted in the passage. For a hundred yards it was straightaway and echoed like a single pair of heels—suddenly I slowed with the muscles jerking on my neck nape. It had sounded like one man running; now it *was* one man! The thudding of my own slowing boots. The boots that had been in front of me had stopped.

Only, somehow, it was different from that. As if (I went stock-still and aghast)—as if my slowing feet had carried me over the place where those other heels had halted. As if, in the absolute night of that invisible tunnel, I had run clean through the unseen fugitive.

The unseen had stopped, turned to mist in the blackness, and, before I could check my race, I had passed through the vacuum where the thing had been, and now it was behind me.

Every hair on my scalp was lifted. I dead-stopped. Was that my own breath, or was some one there in the dark beside me, breathing? I took four steps forward; reached out my right hand and struck solid wall with the pistol barrel; threw out my left hand and caught a head of hair. Instantly the silence shivered into screams. I shouted; yanked. Nails clawed my mouth; raked my jaw. Fists drubbed my cheek bones. I got an arm around a body lithe as a catamount. Cloth tore as we waltzed, wrestled, fought blindly along a wall, rolled on a wooden floor.

I knew, then, I'd run out of the tunnel into a room, and I struck about with the revolver desperately, hitting nothing. Then metal clanged on metal with a little shower of sparks. My fingers grabbed wildly and caught the barrel of a rifle. I twisted and yanked, my mouth smothered in hair. Teeth sank in my forearm; I squalled; the rifle discharged with the jolt of Armageddon; blackness gulped the gunfire; I rolled in thunder and powder smoke while claws raked my forehead and a tiny, stifled voice was screaming, "Cart—help me-e-e-e—Cart—"

I lunged to my feet, yelling, "Here I am—My God!"

"Cart—darling—"

Light streaked white out of blackness and hit me in the face. That shaft of brilliance could have been the last bolt from heaven. The room, flashed suddenly into view, went topsy-turvy before my eyes. I shall always remember every detail of that chamber at tunnel's end. That square compartment, perhaps eight by eight, floor, walls and ceiling of heavy planks, bare as any monk's retreat. The narrow door of the tunnel's entry draped with mauve powder fumes. The glare and smell. Once it may have been a secret arsenal or a hideaway against marauding Caribbean pirates; it housed nothing of the sort now. The floor was covered by a carpet of loose dirt, not unlike a barroom floor (and most of which was adhering to my face), and the sole article of furniture was a shabby pine table of the kitchen variety standing near the tunnel's throat. On the table top (odd the homely touch invariable to some fabulous scene) sat a half loaf of raisin bread.

And, flashlight in one hand, rifle tight in the other, her eyes bright purple under the tangled thicket of her hair, Pete was posed against the table.

I STOOD for a long time looking at that underground room, at the tunnel's door, at Pete. Then I uttered her name twice as if I'd never heard it before, was trying to learn it; couldn't believe the sound of it.

She propped the rifle against the table, freed her fingers from the barrel and stood there pushing back her clotted hair from her forehead with the back of her hand. Her organdie frock was torn down the seam under her left arm, her elbows were smeared, and there was a big splotch of earth on her cheek. She hadn't been hurt.

"Cart—It *is* you," she said in a small voice.

I don't suppose I looked like myself or anybody. I was as black as a Polak from a bituminous pit. I gaped at Pete with my mouth like a mounted pickerel's, hands hanging.

"Oh, Cart—" The electric lamp wavered in her hand; she drew in her lower lip, fighting tears. I stumbled to her, pawing and stammering.

"Pete, in God's name! How! And I—I didn't know. That shot might have killed you—"

"I almost killed you," she wailed faintly. "Look at your arm."

"I might have broken your head with the pistol. Lord, I almost shot you! Pete, why didn't you stay in that room?" I was scared and domineering. "If I'd killed you down here I—"

"But I heard you coming in that awful tunnel, and I was going to shoot," she said in a flat voice. "I didn't dare snap the flashlight, and when you touched my hair I—I was so frightened I—" She rubbed at her splotched cheek, eyes bewildered. "I was too scared to do anything but fight and I—I'm not used to rifles and it fired off by itself."

I looked at the gun, startled. "Where'd you find it?" I pulled the light from her fingers and set it on the table and drew Pete under my arm, looking over her shoulder at the rifle and trying to get it through my comprehension.

She gasped. "Honestly, Cart, my head's spinning so I can hardly think. Is—your arm all right—where I bit you?"

It was hurting like the devil, and I was glad of it, after the roughing I'd given her. "You can't hurt an artist's feelings." I babbled nervous jocularity. "Not after what happened at the judging to-day. Do you know you called me darling?"

"D-did I?"

"Yes. That goes both ways."

"If that gunshot had struck you—"

"Pete, *where?* Where are these guns coming from? This one?"

She drew a shuddery breath and reached for it. "You know when there was shooting in the hall and you ran out of the room and told me not to move—all those shots—"

QUEER. IT hadn't happened two hours ago, yet it seemed in memory I must grope back as many years. "Toadstool and his mother. They were shooting it out on the stairway. Riddled each other right in front of me. My God! Old Tousellines lay knocked out on the floor—"

"I saw it," Pete said throatily. "You called out after the shooting stopped, and I heard you go down the stairs. I had to see what was happening. I crept out on the balcony, and there they were—that awful pair—dead. I heard you questioning the lawyer about the guns—"

"Damned odd about that," I snarled. "He tried to tell me the Widow was a witch, the pistol she had—this one—had flown through the window into her hand, or some cock and bull thing like that."

"I heard you talking," Pete nodded, "and I was going to go back into the room, when—I don't why, Cart, but I—you know the feeling some one is looking at you? I felt that way. Just as if eyes were watching me at my back. Eyes in the door of—of Uncle Eli's room again."

"Did you see them?"

"No! And I suppose it was nothing. Nerves. But I went to the door and looked in. Nobody there, of course. Then you know the wardrobe where the Englishman was killed. The wardrobe with a door inside that leads into a passage through the wall down to the office. The whole dreadful house must be honeycombed. Anyway—I walked into Uncle Eli's room and then went into the wardrobe—"

I shook her arm. "Pete, you didn't!"

"I wanted to see," she insisted. "And it was empty, so I went down. You were down in the hall, and I thought I'd step out of the office and be there with you."

"The whole place shrieking with murderers, and you walked down through that wall passage alone!"

"But it's just a flight of steps and it opens through a little panel right next to that old iron safe. So I—I stepped out into the office and was going to run straight out into the hall. Then I saw that old desk had been shoved away from the wall, and there was a panel on *that* side, half open, and another passage. That's where I found this gun. It was leaning against the desk and the flashlight was right beside it. I was going to open the door and call to you, but I heard you somewhere away in back of the house thumping a door and calling for Manfred—"

"I told Tousellines I was taking charge," I clipped through shut teeth that were dry and made my mouth thirsty. "Thought I'd round up the gang where I could watch 'em. Knew the En-sign and the Dutchman wouldn't sit in their rooms like late schoolboys, not after that artillery battle. Don't you get it, now? They're all killing each other to inherit this château. Wilburforce—Ti Pedro—Ambrose—Toadstool and the Negress—gunning each other down and the last survivor wins."

HAND TO the hollow of her throat, Pete swayed against the table, steadied herself, eyes closed. "It's been horrible—"

"Then when I found the sailor and the German had busted out of their rooms and weren't to be seen—"

"Cart!" Her eyes opened in round alarm. "They may kill you—"

"Never mind me." I could be bold now that everything was over. "They gave me a chill when I couldn't find them. When I dashed up to the front room and couldn't find you I blew up. Didn't you hear me shouting?"

She shook her head. "I thought you'd gone out back—"

"Maybe you think I didn't. I went through every confounded room—you weren't in the office when I looked in, and I was too jittery to notice anything else—and then I set out to tear up Haiti by the outdoors. When I saw the navy cur in the bushes by the side veranda with a billiard cue in his fist—I'd have shot him myself if I hadn't spied Manfred. He was after the En-sign, too, and the sailor was out to get *him!*"

Pete's eyes widened. "Both out there? In the rain—"

I gasped, "Didn't you see the German?"

"Didn't *I* see him?"

"Why, he was over behind those palms," I described. "With a big knife in his mouth."

"But I couldn't have seen him there," Pete said, "because—"

"Because you thought I was Manfred," I explained for her, "and you took a shot at me where I crouched. Don't worry, it wasn't too close. Manfred went down the compound like a terrified elephant. I don't think he'll be coming back, from the look on his face. You've put them both out of it, Pete," I said, taking her hands in mine, "and this whole terrible business is over. I really ought to kiss you for saving my life—"

She stood before the electric torch that staged us both in its glaring bath, and Alice at the end of her Wonderland tunnel couldn't have owned such eyes. "Cart, what do you mean about me saving your life?"

"Why, the En-sign had me spotted. The rifle in my hands was unloaded. He stood up to throw that javelin, and he'd 've speared me like a codfish—"

"Don't!"

"But you killed him," I cried. "You shot from the veranda just in the nick—"

"I didn't kill the En-sign," Pete said rigidly.

"Wh-a-a-at?" It came up out from under my ribs.

"I'm trying to tell you, Cart. I didn't shoot the En-sign. I wasn't on the side veranda."

HOLLOWNESS MELTED my insides. I could hear my words in that airless crypt like echoes started in a catacomb. "You didn't—find that rifle in the office and go out on the veranda and shoot the En-sign through the vines? You didn't run back into the house and down the tunnel, with me after you—thinking it was some—"

"No, I didn't. When I heard you at Manfred's door, calling to him, I—I thought I'd explore the passage by myself. I took the gun and turned on the flashlight and followed it—the tunnel—to this room. It must be over a mile long. I kept thinking the tunnel would end."

"Let me get this straight," I blared. "You ran down here all by yourself?"

"I wasn't running," she insisted. "I walked all the way. Then I came to this dead-end room and was on the point of turning back, when I heard you coming along the tunnel. I didn't know who it was. There's no way out of here, and I was terrified, afraid I was trapped. So I switched off the light and just waited. The sound of a man running came nearer and nearer, then stopped in the dark right in front of me—grabbed my hair—it was *you.*"

"But I was chasing somebody," I chattered. "Somebody right in front of me. Somebody who gave me the laugh, and then we were running in step so it seemed like one man in the dark. Suddenly I had a feeling I'd gone by the thing." Nerves came unstitched in my throat, and the bright dugout swam. "But he couldn't have turned to slip around me in that passage! I was blocking it behind him! Pete, where the devil? Where could he go?"

My tongue stalled on the question, and there it was. A little room like a rabbit's den deep underground at the end of a tunnel. One door—the door I'd barged through. No windows; no shadows where one could hide. Blank, timbered walls and floor. A kitchen table and a half loaf of raisin bread. Pete standing there.

But somebody had shot from the veranda, clipped the En-sign and potted at me. Some one had sped into the house and down the office rat-hole with me heeling after. Those quick-slippered feet and that ghoulish laugh! My brain gagged and stuck. A one-way tunnel ending in an earth-bowled mine chamber, and some one racing ahead of me. There was no other place for that "some one" to go, and, as far as I could see, that "some one" wasn't there.

THERE ARRIVES a time during mayhem, murder, war or any similarly related and cruel antic invented to rag the human emotions when the horror wears into the absurd, the little safety valve on Endurance blows off like a peanut whistle, iced nerves put on a coat of callous. So our sentimental war pilots grin cheerily at the young men falling under them in flames, our undertakers whistle "When You Wore a Tulip" at their work, and our city medical examiners light cigars at suicides. Maybe that's why Lazarus laughed.

Murders? Up till one night ago I'd been a portrait painter. Aside from a few unidentifiable objects polluting a barb wire fence in France, the only murders I'd seen were hanging framed on the walls of American art galleries. Then a murdered man's so-called funeral, and twenty-four hours at Saturnalia. A physician shot down on a terrace. Sir Duffin Wilburforce killed in a wardrobe where he couldn't have been waiting for a street car. The mute Dominican with a bullet through the top of his head in a locked storeroom. Ambrose javelined in the pool parlor. A widow and her boy cheerfully assassinating each other on the stairs.

Murder by that time was almost monotony, and I'd hardly whitened a hair at the En-sign's worthy execution.

But a killer who could vanish in a subterranean tunnel was

something else again, and a callous peeled off me to expose every jumping nerve. I bristled on the scalp. I rolled a gaze of cold fear around that under-earth chamber. I remembered that mocking ghoul-laugh and those quick feet leading me through the black, and it was no sport standing in that mine-deep crypt alone with a girl.

What wizardish thing could I have pursued there? Manfred? Could he have reëntered the château, ducked for the passage?

But Manfred hadn't fired that blast from the veranda vines. And light-slippered, scurrying feet—the only man left alive in that house—

I grabbed Pete by the arm; shouted the name. *"Tousellines!"*

"The lawyer?" Her whisper was low with unbelief.

"It's *got* to be! Who else? I left him going out the front. He's behind all this. There's nobody left but—"

"But where is he? If you followed him down the tunnel—"

THE FLASHLAMP on the table illuminated every inch of the room; there wasn't a shadow's shadow of the man. Guessing that blue-jowled little Negro barrister was one thing, and finding him out was another. No tracks on the dirt-smeared floor; our fight had obliterated any hope of footprints. Besides, where could footprints go in a dugout eight by eight? We covered every inch of flooring, scratching and pawing like excited hens. We pounded on the floor for a hollow spot. Pete thumped with the rifle butt, while I hammered with the black pistol. We went over every sliver of the boarded walls, beating at planking with solid earth behind, raising the din of a thousand carpenters and finding no flaw. I went so far as to yank the drawer from the kitchen table. Nobody in there. I looked under the loaf of raisin bread. I banged the floor again. But no resonant echo answered our pounding; the only hollow sound in the room was the bumping of my heart loose in my ribs, less solid than those earth-backed walls and floor.

"Then he got by me somehow in the tunnel. Maybe there's a side passage where he could've ducked." I wanted to get out of that stifling hole. I grabbed the flashlight and sent the white stream into the tunnel's gullet. "Come on!"

There was no side passage in the tunnel. Narrow walls scraped my elbows, solid planking underfoot, a hand's clearance overhead until we reached the turns where the one-way passage was a channel cut through dirt. The white ray groped ahead of us, picking out the turns, the places where masonry had collapsed, the slag-mound where I'd bumped my head and the unseen had voiced that laugh. Where the bright electric illumination should have dispelled apprehension, it only served to blacken the mystery. Pete hurried me on, hugging the shotgun; and I was sopping with perspiration that wasn't inspired by anything like heat.

Once Pete looked back at me. "Cart, are you sure somebody—"

"I tell you, I saw the panel closing. I heard feet running. I was right behind and there was a laugh and I—"

"But there's no way he—"

"Let's get out of this," I muttered. I was in a temper. Unseen gunmen can't disappear like so much smoke, even in black tunnels under Haiti. I couldn't have imagined those shots at the En-sign or dreamed that hyena laugh. I'd chased somebody into that dead-end room, somebody who wasn't there. Tousellines! It had to be the lawyer.

Somehow he'd turned in the dark, maybe run through my legs, got around me—

"Watch the steps," Pete warned. "They go down here—"

A little farther, now, and we'd be in the death house. The drowned afternoon would be consumed. Bodies stiffening, moldering in the rooms lining the hall, decorating the mahogany staircase. The En-sign lying under plantain leaves out in the rain. Storm-water sweeping the jungled mountain with night. Now I could catch the beat of Haitian drums, the sound penetrating underground like taps from a sunken submarine. We climbed a flight of trippy flagstones.

"Here's the house—"The flashlight revealed splintered panel-ing; streamed on into the ghostly office. I helped Pete through the wall and stepped over kindling wood after her.

We stood in the office listening to rain and drums.

I whipped light at the office door. It was closed. It opened.

The hall was yellow with the glow of candles, and three men stood in the door. Spirits of '76! Lieutenant Narcisse, Inspector-Chief of the Garde d'Haiti, with a bandage turbaning his head and a carbine in his fists. The hare-lipped corporal, Louis. And Maître Pierre Valentin Bonjean Tousellines, LL.B., Comte de Limonade.

"Thunder of God!" the Haitian officer screamed at us. "We have spent the last hour, Tousellines and I, looking for you!"

"TOUSELLINES AND you—I spent the last hour—" I fumbled a hand to find the edge of the desk; leaned there gulping, looking from Narcisse to Pete, my popeyed gaze finally coming to rest on the purple-black countenance of the little darky lawyer.

"We looked everywhere," Narcisse ground out. "I came to the château after you, and discovered Tousellines in the huts down the compound seeking the girl. He said *ma'mselle* had disap-peared. Then he said he heard shots beyond the terrace and feared you had been captured or killed—"

"Bon sang de sort!" The lawyer's words shook the wattles under his chin. "I heard these shots and I rushed back to the château, only to find the En-sign—that one!—lying dead by the side veranda. Then I fled down the compound to call Cornelius, who had heard nothing and was all afternoon with the field hands at the *bamboche*, the drum dance. Then the police arrived—"

"We have just come to the house to search the rooms for you," Narcisse gurgled, wringing water from his cuffs. "Nor is Manfred anywhere to be found. Where, then, *m'sieu*, have you been?"

I stepped aside to show them the splintery aperture in the office wall behind me.

"Down that rat-hole after a ghost," I said insanely, "but it seems to have turned into a loaf of raisin bread—"

Eyes blue, wide, luminous, Pete turned at me. "Stop it, Cart! Raisin bread—"

"I'm not at all mad," I affirmed grimly. "You know that's all we could find down there. On that kitchen table—"

"But why didn't you—I didn't notice it," she cried. "Don't you see? Good heavens! Raisin—"

"M'amselle! M'sieu!" The Haitian lieutenant came at us, frantically throwing out his hands. *"Mon Dieu!* this is no moment for the jest." He spun at me, throwing words in a shrill inflection that soared higher and higher and pierced my head like the shrieks of a poll parrot.

"The Caco bandits are everywhere! Haiti—it is afire with revolution. Even now they may be marching on Morne Noir. My police cannot hold. The army is coming from Port au Prince, but cannot be here in time! The bandits, they come through the jungle like wolves. Wolves—"

His mouth was going like the loud speaker of a radio tuned off-key, interference by the bad weather, strident with static; an excited war correspondent spouting news flashes from the front. In a minute he would shout, "Oh-Kay, Chicago!" and the Bull Watch Company would give the correct time. Nothing of the sort. News flashes still coming—

"The Cacos must be stopped before they kill us all! It is uprising—led by a *zombie!* The guards have captured a Caco who tells us they were led last night by the *zombie of Eli Proudfoot"*—he fairly screamed the name—"the *zombie* of Eli Proudfoot, who rode the night wind with dead eyes of flame, rode to summon the bandits. The police in Cap Haitien—at the bank—they saw it, too."

Pete put a hand to her throat. "Uncle Eli?"

Tousellines cried at her, "We do not believe such things—"

Narcisse shouted, *"Non! Non!* It is rumor to incite the natives, but we must stop this story; we must smother this report or the whole country will rise. We must prove at once your murdered uncle is dead. We go to resurrect the body on the hill. I bring this corporal of gendarmes to stand guard in the château with *ma'mselle.* All others must come. I have summoned the Christian field hands. *M'sieu,* you will come as my prisoner. All hands must help in the digging, and we depart at once!"

CHAPTER XIII

ZOMBIE!

"CACOS COMING!"—"BANDITS LED by the *zombie* of Eli Proudfoot, who rode the night wind with dead eyes of flame!"—"We go to resurrect the body on the hill and prove it dead!"—"All hands must help in the digging!" Skipping and jumbling, the shouted headlines herded themselves jigsaw through my head, danced around in the madhouse chamber of my brain. I was given no time to collect the pieces for calculation.

I remember stumbling out of the office with Pete; staring around the hall. The corpses had been removed from the staircase. The library doors were wide, a lantern posted on the threshold, and a row of stiff feet and sheeted bodies faintly visible beyond the tide of light—some with shoes, some without—suggesting a bad accident.

Down the hall the front door was open; a crowd of tarry faces struggled and surged beyond the veranda, where resin torches glowed. The graveyard detail.

I heard the old clock on the stairs. It couldn't be right. Nine o'clock. The afternoon had been killed, too. Narcisse was answering some question I had stammered, blattering in my ear.

"Oui! Oui! When I left with my men this afternoon we rode straight for Cap Haitien. The road is washed out ten miles down and the horses were forced to a detour. It was then we were met by gunfire, attacked by the Cacos. Two gendarmes killed. Police from Le Cap arrived in time to save us, and we slew the guerillas,

all but the one who told us of the *zombie*—the *zombie* of *M'sieu* Proudfoot that had led them last night—"

"Did you see the *zombie?*" Pete cried in a shocked voice.

Narcisse panted, "It is just superstition. But the Cap Haitien police—they think they saw it. Last night, for one cannot see *zombies* in the daytime, that is the legend. The captured Caco declared it promised to return and lead them again to-night."

I swore. "Blankety blank rot!"

"True," the officer panted, "but the mountain blacks are of the most fanatic. This story spreads like the disease. We stop them only by producing the dead from the grave, proving it a corpse. We must have him out by the time they get here. It is our one chance—"

"The Cacos have gone mad," Tousellines echoed.

There weren't enough corpses in Morne Noir. We must dig up another. I didn't want to leave Pete behind in the château, under guard or the contrary, but she shook her head bravely and said she didn't want to come. No, thank you! Not to that "digging." I saw her upstairs to her room, and I think I told the hare-lipped Louis I'd kill him with my bare hands if anything happened to *ma'mselle* while we were gone. The corporal saluted. If he thought anything of my threat, if he thought anything, he didn't show it.

THEN SOME one thrust a spade in my hand, and I couldn't think either. We departed at once; and in that dark harlequinade confected of torchlights and shovels, voodoo drums, mule-hoofs, gun-shine and moonshine and mud and the barking of dogs, a Rodin's Thinker couldn't have thought. And if Dominicans could be sniped off bull's-eye through the top of the head, dueling pistols appear out of nowhere, guns fly through shutters into a widow's hand, and tunneling fugitives laugh and turn into loaves of bread, why shouldn't I go brainlessly running through night with an inquisitive grave-shovel?

The rain had quit in despair. A melon-rind moon sailed high and anæmic in a yeasty smudge of clouds. Bent on its noisome enterprise, the parade slogged off in moonlight and mire. Down the compound I could look back and see light barring yellow the shutters in Pete's room, the yellow dusk of the opened hall. Water lay in flat, gleaming sheets down the terrace, the whole compound was awash, the jungle hedging around made the disturbance of a million leaking faucets. Feet squashed on the march like the Russians going across their death-swamp to Tannenberg. It was gloomy as Russia and might have been, save the air was warm, turgid, tropical and smelled green.

"Avant!" Narcisse yelled.

I won't forget that foraging party. Black mules jingling in the lead. Narcisse with his bandaged cranium, ghostly as an Arab atop his horse. Four gendarmes exploring the shrubbery along the way with nervous carbines. The batch of "Christian field hands" dog-trotting in line, their stevedore faces reddened by the resin flares, shovels swinging, big mouths chanting to the drum-rune from the huts, and the sound anything but Christian. I walked next to last; and Tousellines brought up the rear, handkerchief to forehead, eyes all over his face, twitching along like a startled turkey.

Last night's funeral had been no stroll down lovers' lane. This party of resurrectionists, out to undo the funeral, loaned it downright gayety by contrast.

I looked back at the château, shadowy on the slope.

I could only snarl, "Listen to me, Tousellines. If anything happens to Miss Dale while we're gone, I'll kill everybody!"

My tone must have carried conviction this time, for he shrank back four steps, crossing himself vigorously.

We couldn't leave the compound, though, before the night dealt us another shocker. The swimming pool. Spurring on ahead, the police lieutenant clattered abreast of the concrete *bassin.* I saw him rein in with a vicious jerk that reared his mount on hind legs; saw him swing from saddle, draw saber from scabbard, and go stiff-legged to the edge of the pool. Then he staggered back with a *"Alt!"* and the parade stopped short, jarring down its length like a string of freight cars.

Shovels hit the ground and mouths flew open. It was Manfred. He was in the pool, but it wasn't any moonlight swim. Not in that weedy natatorium. He was to be seen, if one cared to look, floating along the bottom, his birthmarked German face magnified by the water over it, eyes peeping suspiciously under heavy lids.

"Waaaaah!" the field hands bawled.

"Drowned!" Narcisse spat.

"The château," announced Tousellines thickly, "belongs to *ma'mselle.*"

"Move on!" the lieutenant squalled.

WE MOVED on. Those darky grave diggers weren't the only ones who wanted to bolt. I could have steeplechased. The parade curled through a ferny thicket, followed the black mules into a forest of drooling trees, marched into cotton-thick night. My flesh crawled. Tousellines aside, that Prussian Bluebeard had made the last possibility. Drowned in a swimming pool—then who had lured me into that dead-end tunnel?

Parade-master Narcisse reined in at the pathside; waited for me to come up with him; then leaned down from his saddle and desired to know how I had drowned so neatly big Manfred. We didn't go into it because we had something more immediate to go into. Up ahead the mules were skidding, floundering on the miry hill. The slope was guttering fudge; men and teams going down in the paste. Narcisse rowelled his horse, raging forward to hurry the mules. With a muffled cracking of whips and calling of Creole oaths, the animals were started again up the insecure rise.

High at the crest I could distinguish the aged silk cotton tree and the heavenly sentinel mounting guard on the grave. Watching that angel grow against the windy, scudding sky, my eyes swam and my stomach knotted. Manfred. The En-sign. Widow Gladys. Toadstool. Ambrose. Ti Pedro. The Englishman. Seven bloodhounds killed, and the doctor for good measure. Twenty-four hours of murder, matricide, infanticide, drowning; a château turned to a slaughter house; an island country hemorrhaging. An old man's will had read like a death list and his funeral initiated pogrom. I hadn't done it. And Pete—

Suddenly I had to find out what was under Uncle Eli's *pierre tumulaire*. I had to know what lay under that gravestone. The parade reached hilltop and gathered under the tree. Tackle screeked, whips smacked, the moonlight echoed to a circus-lot clamor as black men and mules struggled to dislodge the giant stone angel from his outpost. The watcher silently resisted the depredation; then slithered away so abruptly a dozen mules went down. But the stone colossus was hauled to one side and out of the way; and when I saw the iron stake in the earth I laughed and remembered and cursed myself for a fool and spat on my hands.

No time to lose. Cacos were coming, and we wanted Uncle Eli. Had a little bird told me who was going to *be* in that rosewood casket, I'd have laughed no laugh, nor set to work with such a will. But the only little birds on that hilltop necropolis were the graveyard birds, only a little darker than myself, getting to work with their spades.

SHOVELS WHACKED in, and sods thudded. A chain was hitched to the stake, the mules strove, the iron post uprooted with a sepulchral groan. The spades worked. The trench dropped foot-deep, ankle-deep, knee-deep. An earthy smell mingled with the musk of sweat and the pungent torch-smoke. The night watched us and we watched the night.

The flares held aloft in a red, smoky ring. The tarred faces melting under them. Jungle shadows creeping uphill to look. Wind whispering off the night-veiled Caribbean. The horned moon nesting in the dank upper brandies of the silk cotton. Four gendarmes patrolling the lower dark. The granite angel playing onlooker (I'd watched Radio City excavations with that same expression of inanimate stupidity). Narcisse, major domo in his muslin turban, sword in one hand, carbine in the other, pacing, cursing, bossing the job. *"Allons!* Faster!" The nodding backs of the shovelers. Whistling lips. Shiny foreheads. Sweat-steam on licorice muscles. A gobble-like chant to time their swinging spades with an echo out of Africa. I would like to paint that picture.

Fume-red and fog-green, blue-dark and a patch the color of an old man's bald spot in the sky, a-swim in dusk and black. But you can't paint the smell of an island night after rain, and no brush could put down that gravedigging torch song. And sensation goes beyond color, unless one thinks of pale green. I don't mean blisters on the palm and an ache in the spine. I mean a cavity inside and cold skin. Exhuming the dead in that lofty cemetery surrounded by a murder mystery and the night holding its breath for a bandit attack—the original John Ghoul of London would have looked over his shoulder.

"Dig!" Narcisse instructed. "By Damballa's Oath! Dig!"

We dug. The sod had been packed hard. We worked in gangs of four. It's easier to fill a grave than empty it. I dug like a gopher for twenty minutes, then spelled off with Cornelius, who had brought his skinniness from somewhere.

When we spelled off, I leaned against the angel, sweating, picked a cigarette from my opened vest, tried to drag some sedative from the tobacco, and watched the château below in the bowl of the valley. The roofs were sinister and moon-silvered, the house a crouching shadow on the slope. The swimming pool lay like a pane of blue glass dropped on the flat field of the compound; the outhouses below were points of light and the drum family continuing its mutter.

I was glad Pete hadn't come, but I didn't like her down there. Our path to the graveyard had made a roundabout, circling route down the valley and up again to detour a wedge of swamp; I couldn't get a bearing on the house to discover where her window-light should be. Times I was certain I heard something down there; then the singsong from the open grave obsessed my ears and I couldn't be sure.

But nothing could happen to her with that gendarme on guard. Every one else in the place was dead.

NARCISSE'S BLACK eyes were on me as mine were on the

château. Standing by his picketed horse, he trailed me with a glance when I moved, shifting the gun like a magnet needle. I yanked what was left of a handkerchief out of my hip to scrub my sore hands and took a peek at Tousellines. He was standing with his Abe Lincoln hat clapped to his bosom, upright at the foot of the grave. The hole was hip-deep.

"Your turn, *m'sieu* the artist—"

Narcisse's teeth were scissors, shearing the word "artist" out of tin. I picked up my shovel and dug. The grave sank to my ribs. Shoulder-deep. Five feet down through solid clay, each scoop weighing half a ton. My back stooped, now, with no volition on my part. I was a robot, rusty, but working. Six feet. I remember a sudden stoppage of vibration in the air; remember looking up out of the trench into Touselline's face and hearing him tell me it was midnight and the twenty-four hours of funeral drumming had come to an end. Seven feet. I was thinking that, the grave being exactly ten, we should come to something presently.

Then the spade jarred in my hand, *bump;* the shovels around me were scraping earth from a rosewood lid; I climbed out of it. I didn't approve of standing on coffin lids; at least not on that one with that stake-hole splintered through its heart. Nor did I hanker to stand on the lip of that violated grave and watch the lid pried off with shovels.

There was no time for raising the casket, and Narcisse ordered it opened on the grave-bottom. The levering shovels jimmied and creaked; nails tore loose with a crying sound.

"Nom de Dieu! Sluggards!" Narcisse bawled down. "Remove that cursed cover and lift him up here!"

Creeeeek! The sound of the lid ripping off was the sound of everybody's ripping nerves. It was too much for the Christian field hands down below. The lid came up, and they came up with it. Narcisse swung forward with his bull's-eye lamp and sped a white ray into the grave. Torch-flares and goose-livered faces crowded forward; leaned around me and looked down. Somebody gurgled like a throat drinking iodine; another said, "Aaaah!"

like a connoisseur with an opened jewel box in his hand; and Tousellines, beside me, squeezed my elbow numb with a gray-knuckled fist.

But the corpse-quiet body in the coffin said nothing, absurdly little in that rosewood longbox, like a doll wrapped up for delivery with its prim-toed boots sticking from the end of the wrappings, pointed up at us. A doll wrapped up! I didn't remember that black cloth cape that shrouded the body from head to foot like the windings of a mummy. Where the fold of the cape was cracked open over the face, like the peep-hole of a Moslem woman's veil, one wax-lidded, shuttered, sleeping eye showed through. I could see where the hands were clasped in repose under the shroud

Of course it was Uncle Eli in that grave-cloth. But I didn't remember any such mantle!

Then my eyeballs chilled in my head; my stare was freezing on that black-wound body. It wasn't what looked like a dark stain over the breast. I was goggling in panic at a shoe—the prim-pointed toe of one upturned boot—

My mouth flew open to yell. A whiplash cracked twice in the night behind me. I spun, screaming nothing. Tousellines pitched against me, clawing at a hanging arm. A voice screeched, "Cacos!" The dark downhill began to explode.

I DIDN'T have a chance to reach the pistol in my coat. You can't dig graves wearing the coat of your only and best suit, no matter the reduced condition of the garment. I'd shucked the jacket and hung it on the angel. Before I could broadjump the grave, bullets were coming like a blizzard from all points of the compass, woodpecking the tree, ricocheting off the angel's face.

Singing like an artillery shell, a hurled club blew over my head, and I dodged for the tree. Shadows were running on the slope below. Darkness sparked and crackled like a corn-pan on fire. The whack of police carbines as the Garde d'Haiti opened up. The slam, bang, thud and whang of all manner of gunnery downhill. The croon of flying lead, the whine of thrown knives, a startling chorus of caterwauls, shrieks, grunts, howls, mingled with the screams of the fleeing Christian gravediggers and the shrill shouts of Lieutenant Narcisse, and sent a rumpus of echoes running down the valley.

Already a khaki gendarme was down, mysteriously unable to rise, kicking as if he were trying to pedal a bicycle. Cornelius was rolling in the mud, struck somehow in the throes of a fit.

Stovepipe hat jammed over his eyebrows, Maître Tousellines crouched behind the mound of fresh sods, nursing his broken arm. Narcisse was sprawled flat on the clods, firing loudly at the dark. Little showers of dirt kept squirting up around his bandaged dome. The three remaining gendarmes lay belly to mud in a line beyond the tree; I couldn't see them, but I could see the fire of their guns; jumping one-two-three in the gloom like motorcycle exhausts. The gravediggers had departed in the direction of the Caribbean, and I never saw them again.

Thrown to the ground, the torches blazed like election night bonfires on the hilltop; the enemy was protected by night; and we were surrounded like an island. I wanted my pistol badly, finding myself armed with nothing more than a shovel. Under cover of the earthworks, I inched along with my eye on the angel where my coat was being torn to ragtag. It was tough traveling on that shot-swept hillcrest. I cursed myself bitterly for having abandoned Pete to the mercies of the château down below. By lifting my head and daring extinction, I could see the roofs in the valley. The valley was quiet, shadowy, moonlit. No lights showed in the house. I consoled myself with the thought that our preoccupation with the cemetery had decoyed the enemy assault to the hilltop. Small consolation when I remembered the cadaver in the grave at my back. It iced the water on my temples.

I dared a dash for my coat; ran headlong into a knot of Negroes who soared out of shadow and were at me like panthers. Negroes everywhere. I didn't get the pistol. I was thrown back against the monument. Face averted from the opening in the ground, I had to fight like a barbarian to save my life. Time stood at zero while I slapped black topknots with the shovel.

Cart was fighting for his life now

It was like hitting gongs. The shovel rang. Blue bodies twirled and danced around me. I saw heads and hit them. Things hit me. I don't know why bullets didn't. Explosions were bursting on all sides. A stone caught me hard in the eye. My nose bled. Smoke, flame-balls, knife-shine, tooth-shine, black arms boiled around me where I stood under my guardian angel and stirred the tempest with a shovel.

I STIRRED that little battle into a witch's cauldron. Through that roaring surf of bodies and noise I caught crazy-quilt glimpses of Caribbean, jungle, valley, the moon-lit roofs of the château, and every time I thought of Pete I howled like a Choctaw and hit another head. Narcisse went pirouetting by me like a tackled football end. Tousellines sat on the ground with the top sheared from his hat and his arm in his lap. I guess the gendarmes were somewhere. It would not do to think of the man in the grave under the tree and those prim-pointed boot-toes. Fighting was better. Don't slug till you see the whites of their eyes.

Of course this heroic bit of biography wasn't as bold as it sounds and lasted half as long as the telling. The shovel rang *damn! damn! damn!* on half a dozen heads like black coconuts;

and there must have been a hundred of those Cacos. Fifty for Narcisse. Fifty for the angel and me. I stood there with my nose-bleed and shinered eye, walloping out with the scoop, and I couldn't miss.

Somehow Narcisse had climbed the pedestal of the monument and was hanging there like a Bolshevik on Union Square, waving a bloody fist and hollering over the heads of the mob, *"Gran moon li mort! Cacos—ici—Voilà! Moon lit mort!"*

Tousellines shrieked at me, "Let them come, *m'sieu!* He tells them the old man is dead—demands them to look in the grave and see—"

Whatever the officer was trying to tell them, his howls only served to inflame the riot, drawing a volley that sent him leaping from his rostrum. *"Non! Non!"* was the roaring response. *"Papa Proudfoot gran' zombie—"* Narcisse was thrown crabwise through a smoke-billow. Lights banged all over the hilltop. If those Haitian natives were marksmen I'd have been shot to sponge, but they made up in ferocity what they lacked in science. *"Papa Proudfoot! Papa Proudfoot!—Zombie! Zombie!"* Anything Narcisse could say wouldn't drown that battle cry.

Loudest of all it screeched from a twisted mouth that swam at me through the din. A big black man, naked to the belt, with a rifle club-fashion in his hands. Sinews egged out on him like lumps of wet coal; his face was all out of shape; his mouth—I remembered that mouth. Hare-lip Louis, the gendarme corporal, who'd been left in the house to guard Pete!

He plunged at me, swinging his rifle at my head, yelling. I shouted his name, and he struck at me again. The gun-butt sliced past my face. I hit at him with the shovel. Larruping downward, his rifle-stock whacked my hands, and the shovel went flying out of my fingers.

I screamed his name and jumped him, grabbing his arms, throwing him flat under a trampling morass of ankles and feet. I banged his head against the angel's pedestal. I screamed,

"Where's Pete! Where's Pete! Where's *ma'mselle?*" and let up on him for an answer.

He squalled, "*Ma'mselle* no more! *Zombie* come to house call Louis, tell Louis go 'long Cacos! Louis see *zombie! Zombie* boss Louis! Papa Proudfoot gran' *zombie*—"

I drove a knee in his stomach and banged his head. "Where's the girl?"

He kicked his heels, fighting like a cat. He screeched:

"*Ma'mselle* in château. *Ma'mselle* finish. *Zombie* tell Louis go away from door. *Zombie* go to door, finish *ma'mselle*—"

HIS EYES were white mirrors of terror, glaring shiny into mine. He got a thumb on my cheek, slid it over the bone and pressed on my eye. We rolled through a churn of legs. Something hit me a crack on the neck; driving me sideways. Louis wrenched away from my hands, planted a foot in my spine and shoved me smothering into the mound of soft clods. I got my fingers closed on something that felt like iron; rolled; bounded to my feet, the iron crowbar that had been the stake in the grave gripped in my hands. I saw the hare-lipped face, screamed, "What happened to the girl? Pete! Pete!" and swung the iron stake.

Louis dodged. I shouted at him, swinging the stake. That solid iron post seemed light as a feather and it must have weighed plenty. It missed a lot of heads, spun me in a futile twirl and spanked the granite angel a whack in the pants. Stone splinters spurted through the air. The blow tore the bar from my fingers. I staggered backward and had to windmill my arms to keep from flopping into the grave.

Louis towered over me. I perceived there was a knife in that upraised fist where the rifle had been. I saw the blade was aimed to stab me between the eyes. It didn't come. I seemed to be waiting. The knife seemed to be waiting. The blade wouldn't drop. The black man had jammed the joint of his elbow. The effort to bring down the knife wrung streams of ink from his forehead, started his eyes from their sockets.

Then I saw those goo-gooed eyes weren't looking at me, but

over my shoulder at something behind my back! The cry that blew from his rabbit lips would have waked the dead. And did!

"Stop!" The voice spoke out of the grave.

In a quiet so total and sudden the night seemed to have smashed, I spun and looked down.

The body in the coffin moved! The hands beneath the black cape stirred. The eye in the shroud was wide open, glassy, staring. The cloaked mouth moved in its cowl-like wrappings, and a voice came through the cloth in a muffled, toneless neigh—

"Cacos, I come—The King of all *Zombies* waits to lead you. Let the dead master rise from his tomb—"

The voice died out in a horse-like, whinnying sigh. The black-wrapped head lifted slowly from its pillow. The body in the coffin swayed to a stand. There was a hideous minute while I stared at the dark stain over the breast. A corresponding smear where the cape had been torn out the back. I could see where the stake, going through, had left a dent in the bottom of the coffin. Once more I was glaring at a streak of color across the toe of the left shoe. Dandelion yellow!

CHAPTER XIV

BURIED!

"VIVE LE MORT! King of all Zombies—"
"Vive le mort! King of all *Zombies*—"
"Exurgent mortui!"
"Exurgent mortui!"

The minute won't be clocked when I can efface the memory of that black, mummy-like body coming out of his grave after twenty-four hours interment in a coffin anchored by an iron stake and tons of angel; nor will I forget the look of that empty casket with the dent in its floor on the grave-bottom, while its rightful inhabitant stood beside the mound of sods that had covered him, arms spread out under the cloak, the one live eye showing in the black-muffled face like a gleaming fish-scale, the clammy voice doing things to that Caco mob.

The voice neighed through black cloth—that flabbergasting gibberish—and the woolly heads of the Negroes lifted and fell like cabbages on a sea. The hidden mouth spoke and the mob bayed a recitative chant. The fallen torches spluttered, shedding a salmon-colored light through nodding topknots and moonray slanting down through the bones of the silk cotton tree scarred the black-wrapped head with blue striping.

Picture that silhouetted figure on the dirt mound, that blue-striped shadow-blob face with its single glazed eye. Listen to that talk from the tomb, and look at one white man, one-eyed himself, paralyzed on the fringe of the scene.

The grave yawned between me and that thing on the mound;

from what source I drew the power of locomotion I don't know; but I made a backward fumble to find my coat, and picked my pocket for the gun. My hand on that gun was like a leaf of lettuce, but I got it somehow.

"You've been in the house!" I bawled. "What have you done with the girl—"

The cry tore a cartilage in my throat; broke shrill as a child's above that gobbling Caco chant. God knows what answer I expected; certainly not the one that came

The mob choked silent, and the thing on the clod pile wheeled and impaled me with a glance from that fish-scale eye. All the venom in the world was concentrated in that stare. It went through my head and came out the back and pinched the skin on my neck-nape. The hate in that eye would have poisoned a rattlesnake.

"Fool!" came the muffled malediction. "Would you speak thus rudely to a *zombie?*"

"*Zombie* be damned," I croaked. "The girl—what have you done to her—"

The lidless, mica-bright eye seemed to kindle green in its socket. The cataleptic voice gave a heathenish sort of giggle. "I have taken care of the girl," neighed the thing across the grave, "hee hee hee! The ungrateful little wench has been paid for her thanklessness. I shot her through both her little eyes at eleven o'clock tonight—"

"God—"

I swung the pistol, working the trigger. The trigger labored and the black gun chattered like a typewriter. The black thing, monstrous across the grave, screamed out in its cape; but it wasn't shot. Those bullets had been used up on Toadstool.

MY VISUAL impressions went blind, but I heard that cloth-drugged mouth screaming, "Blackguard, would you try to murder the dead?" and the black mob came in two hollering rivers around the ends of the grave and crashed on top of me. Hare-lip Louis hit me like a falling oak; I was thrown like a calf;

ropes sailed over my head; thongs pinned my hands behind my back; I was trussed before I could excavate my face from the mud.

I was picked up, thrown from hand to hand, shuttled, whirled like wheat rushed through a binder, and my next impression was total paralysis in a monstrous ball of twine, bound neck to foot like a stick wrapped with kite-string.

Tottering like an invalid, the black-cloaked figure came down off its rostrum, and moved at me, cawing like a witch. It might have been an old woman in mourning gowns shrilling senile imprecations at a vandal in her cemetery lot. Only—

"How would you like," came the crow-like voice, "to try my coffin for your own?"

I could only stare.

The black cape swished the mud, as the dark figure whirled. *"Cacos, ici!* To the grave with him!"

Black hands shot out to grab me. I was lifted like a sack of meat, held horizontally over the grave, dropped. If I hadn't been spun in a cocoon of rope, that ten-foot drop into a coffin would have broken my spine and killed me then and there. A moment was coming when I was going to wish it had.

My head walloped the pillow; the jolt whacked my breath out; then I could see my own boots pointed at their end of the rosewood retainer, earthen walls sheared up on either side, and far above my face the sky was a rectangle of yeasty clouds streaking a dome of night. Far above my feet the black-shrouded figure in its cape was crucified against the moon, arms widespread like wings, chin on stained bosom, that one ulcerous eyeball of frosted hate glittering down at me.

A melancholy cold invaded the grave. A Negro with the face of an Egyptian looked down at me with a shovel in his hands.

The crucified silhouette dropped its arms. "Bury him!"

That was my requiem. I suppose I was hollering and kicking, for little cascades of pebbles came slithering down the grave walls and rattled on my rosewood frame. Then a black shadow hovered like an airplane wing over the foot of the grave. The lid was thrown down with a stunning crash, and I shouted in total darkness.

The dead was burying me alive!

WHANG! IN all the good world I will never hear again a sound as appalling as that first coffin nail going into the lid. I'd waited in mortal suspense for that sound, and when it came I must have glowed with terror. *Whang-bang-whang-bang!* It didn't take those spikes long to travel around the lid-rim. Feet that had scuffled on the lid stopped scuffling. A little cone of gray light sifted down through the coffin cover where a foot standing over the stake-hole had been removed.

Light! Flat in that house of darkness I watched a misty and miserable little funnel of foggy light the way one might watch Hope balanced on a sobbing abyss. That light was the mother of the world. Down in that sunken coffin it was like the sun. I could crank up my neck, crane my head from its corrosive pillow and stare down my nose at the fainting little ray; and I wept while it was there. I'd been extravagant with the sun, before. I'd blown out matches. I'd complained at electric signs. I know better manners, now. I know one could almost do without air if there was light for the seeing of the end. How I breathed at that stingy handful of illumination, sprained my neck to stare at it, begged it to stay. .

Thud! It was gone. Now there was another sound on the coffin lid. *Thud-thud-thud.* I howled to keep the echo out of my ears, but the thudding was louder in my black prison. The thudding of clods raining down on a casket—more particularly, *my* casket! I didn't stop screaming, but my throat did, and I had to lie there flat on my back and listen to that earth blizzarding down. It was loud at first. Too damnably loud.

Then it receded, was muffled, faint. Too damnably faint.

Now my ears were begging to hear those clods the way my eyeball had entreated at the light. And now, like the light, the sound was extinguished, and the only echo in the coffin was the constricted rustling of my movements, little scratchings in the dark, blood pounding in my ears.

I could hear my bootheels rattling on the floor at their end of the box, the breath pumping in and out of my lungs. The low altitude had affected my respiration. The darkness was playing on my nerves. Dark? Mix all the blacks together—Black Tom and Black Friday and black plague and black mass—and compound them with India ink, and the color would have shone like radium in that rosewood casket buried on a hilltop in Haiti.

The air was too black, too foul and thick-black to breathe! The clod that had plugged the lid-hole had dropped a spoonful of earth on my chest and the weight was like a soft foot pressing down. I rolled on my side to rid my chest of the earth, but the weight persisted. Then I hitched along the coffin floor until my toes touched end. Then I hitched back into the head-end until my scalp bumped. Craftily I figured the coffin was about seven by two and a half, and frantically I tried to remember about cubic inches of air, but the only thing I could, remember was that black-cloaked figure swooping out of the grave and the fiendish voice neighing, "I shot her through the eyes—"

I rolled from side to side. I tried desperately to lie still, and then I could feel that dent in the floor under my left shoulderblade, and I had to move. Pete had been killed! Pete had been killed! The words banged back and forth in my mind. Lord! Killed by that thing! And I was dying, now. Dying in that suffocating blackness deep underground—

I BEGAN to yell and thrash, roll and drum my heels, crying Pete's name, shouting, cursing. The acoustics in a coffin are bad. My voice was stifled in the airless confinement. My cries were like lead, loud but without color or resonance in that coagulated underground dark. I couldn't tell whether I shouted or thought I shouted. I lay gasping on my back and wondered if the grave was half filled, three quarters filled, filled. A queer half stupor was stuffing up my head like a bad cold, and ideas jittered around in my brain like comatose dreams.

Suddenly I was remembering a news story I'd once read in the *Trib* about two mechanics asphyxiated by gasoline fumes. Revived by serum injections, they were told by astonished doctors that their hearts had stopped twelve minutes. One died when the heart stopped, whereupon the curious physicians wondered how it felt to be dead; but the garage men replied uneasily that they hadn't felt anything. Down there in my own tomb, I recalled having remarked about this article to Pete.

"Then death's like that," I had pointed. "Like fainting, and gets half a column on the second page. A blank. There isn't any heaven."

"Who wants to believe in the old fashioned heaven?" Pete had demurred. (Her voice came out of memory so distinctly I could almost hear it. I could remember the scene of the incident. We'd blown ourselves to the Grand Central Oyster Bar, and she was perched on a stool and smiling over the newspaper—) "Who wants Saint Peter to pin 'em with a lot of dusty medals for good deeds long since forgotten that should've been done anyway? But that newspaper doesn't prove death is a blank. Religious people would say those men hadn't died. Spiritualists would say they came back and lost any memory of what happened on the other side. I'd say—let's worry about living and when the time comes I can take it. I'm dying for some of those clams—"

Good God! I lay dying in a coffin in Haiti and thinking of the Grand Central Oyster Bar in New York. And Pete was dead. Pete, who'd said she could take it. Hot tears made scalding red flashes in the black that blindfolded my eyes. My fault she'd come to this cursed island. I had it coming to me for leaving her in that château. Fate was a leper with a grinning tongue—to turn loose on her that twenty-four hours of abomination. If I could only have plunged my hands into the folds of that black cape; ripped the shroud off that fish-eyed creature out of the coffin. Who? What manner of fiendish bogle had resurrected itself from Uncle Eli's grave? With yellow oil paint on his shoe—

"Oh, God—Get me out of here—"

THERE WAS a time, down in that midnight-dank, airless coffin, when I wanted to pray; when I had to dig my teeth in my underlip to keep from shouting for celestial mercy that might have been inclined not to recognize my voice. Comfort is the reward of the steadfast in faith; not for the last-minute convert frightened by a showdown.

"Besides, you've got to die sometime," I bellowed at myself. "Everybody does!"

The only difference being that most people weren't buried beforehand and didn't have to watch it coming. Most people thought they were never going to die. Crowds in cities rushing pell-mell past the undertakers, laughing and singing and cursing, mobbing for theaters and restaurants and stock markets and assignations—dying every one of them—condemned by every clock-tick—never knowing—

"Hoo-hoo-hoo—"

I had to laugh. I suppose the hearse-black confinement, the ground-cold, the evil staling of the air was making me a little morbid. Laughter dried my throat to a herring. Tightened a tourniquet of pressure around my chest. A sort of redness that wasn't color swam behind my eyelids. I could hear myself panting like a thirsty spaniel. I could hear the involuntary drumming of my heels on the hard floor. I heard myself say out loud, "Those two mechanics didn't feel anything—" I shouted, fought to sit up, mashed my forehead against the invisible roof, tossed from elbow to elbow. God! How many feet of earth were over me now? Was the grave filled? Were they patting the mound flat with shovels? The Marines! Didn't they know I was down there in Haiti, smothering? *Down* there in Haiti, was right! Get me out of that darkness! Just give me a chance, one more chance at that thing who'd shot a helpless girl—Lord! All this struggling made me drink up the air. Why couldn't I lie still?

"Take it like a man!" I screamed at myself.

"There's no such a thing as a *zombie!*" I shrieked.

"Quit bawling," I howled at myself. "The heart just stops—"

"But there was a stake through Uncle Eli's heart," I howled. "That thing—stained cloak—came out alive—shot Pete, Pete, Pete—"

I remember the smothering as of a great muff of feathers held over my mouth and nose, a giddy slowing up of the heart, a ballooning of the head. A lot of little doors in my brain blew open and a kaleidoscope of words, sensations, mental pictures, catcalls and colors callioped around in my mind as I fought and shouted. My heart was a ball of terror, my lungs chugging engines that seemed to turn a pinwheel—a wild flashing jumble like one of those Russian films showing buildings at angles and things coming every which way. Ambrose, Sir Duffin, the En-sign, Widow Gladys, Manfred, Toadstool, Ti Pedro—faces in the pin-wheel. A doctor staggering across the lawn by an iron dog. A little old darky with a face of crêpe reading a will. A mulatto officer brandishing a saber.

The pinwheel was whirling furiously against a nightmare-gray hill, against an old house dripping with vines; and Pete was a shadow with a picture hat in hand frozen before a black and headless silhouette that stood in a coffin and reached at her with wing-like arms. I was trying to kill him with a pistol that only chattered in my hand, and something from behind was choking me. Pete was calling my name, calling my name—

Darkness smashed around me into a million confetti colors. The pinwheel burst. The bottom dropped out of everything.

CHAPTER XV

DEAD OR ALIVE!

IT WAS QUEER how the voice persisted; how it came through a vacuum-like, foggish, swimming barrier that had neither color nor form, like a lost messenger running in misty corridors, paging me in emptiness. A called name hunting through nebulous vacancy. An echo trying to find the place where echoes go. "Cart—Oh, Cart—"

I'd dreamed this dream before; only this time it wasn't a dream because I was dead. But the dream persisted with the voice and a misty shine was penetrating the fog. The little echo carrying a candle, running about this way and that, trying to find its way home. "Cart—Cart—"

The gray mist brightened to pale yellow, like the shine of the sun on the bottom of a thunderhead. Fog wreathed and swam, and through its vapors came the recollection of a face; a memory that blurred and retreated, swam into focus like something seen through tears, steadied and was there. Something in me tried to sit up. I thought, "Pete, is that you?"

The echo was getting nearer, nearer. "Cart—can you hear me—please answer—please—"

I thought, "Sure, I can hear you, Pete. Those mechanics were wrong—"

The echo and the yellow shine and the face merged together, sound, form and color in a point of saffron behind smoke. "Please come on—Please don't lie here, Cart—Please don't fall again—There now—Stand up—" I was sleepy, dreaming I heard Pete's voice, saw her face in mist. Mist that fluttered and whispered, the yellow shine moving ahead of me and Pete's dim features just beyond the shine. Somehow she was reaching out her arms to me, and I was struggling to move after them through the dream. Just as I would touch them, the dream would end. Then the voice would come paging me; I would see the light; fight to my feet and move on.

"A little farther—just a little farther, Cart—I can't drag you—please!"

I laughed idiotically; banged my head hard against something; dragged to my feet and opened one eye. Pete seemed to be there with a candle in one hand, propping me up against a black wall with the other. Tears were running down her face. She was shaking me angrily. She was teasing at me to move, to come on, to stand up and get going, like the Widow Gladys taunting Toadstool up the staircase. For a minute I thought we were on the staircase. Pete said very clearly, "Come down these steps—"

But the dream washed into darkness and I thought we were moving in a tunnel. Close walls on either side and a heaviness of dust, black as coal, and I seemed to be stumbling and colliding, fumbling with Pete and the light. I thought I said, "Raisin bread down here!" and I thought I could hear Pete saying, "Yes, Cart. Yes—Please come on—"

In the dream I stumbled dizzily, on and on, and Pete was towing me by the hand, begging me to follow. I thought I heard her say, "Take slow, deep breaths." Then I thought I was taking slow, deep breaths. Immediately her voice spoke out of memory so clearly I thought it wasn't a dream. I thought I opened one eye and stared at a blazing candle and Pete was there clear as day.

"Thank God!" she cried. "We're there now. There's some whisky will fix you. Can you hear me?"

"Where are we?" My voice was as loud as reality.

"The house," came the words, distinct as speech. "Slowly here. Steps. You take the candle and I'll go first—"

I seemed to reach out and take the candle. Then I fell on steps

I couldn't see with the candle, smashed the diminutive flame under a clumsy sprawl, inhaled a mouthful of cobweb, faded into oblivion. In oblivion I was choking. Coughing and choking. I threw my head back to stop it. Something cracked on the back of my head. I woke up.

I WOKE up sitting against the roll-top desk in the office under the stairs, my legs outstretched in front of me on the floor, my back propped against the desk; and Pete had a hand under my chin and was pouring whisky from a square brown bottle into my teeth. A wax candle blinked atop the desk, directing a shadow-dance along the inverted stairway of the ceiling. I could hear rain throwing itself in gusts against the dim blue shine of the little church window. I stared, swallowing fire, at the panel in the wall near the squat iron safe; and made out a vague inner flight of steps that must be the passage up to Uncle Eli's wardrobe. I had a fuddled impression I'd just taken a fall down those shadowy steps. I swallowed another gulp, and heard a sound outside somewhere, a sort of mass meeting babble muffled by closed doors.

"I'm alive," I whispered tentatively, and hearing my own voice brought me around with a bang. *"Pete! I'm alive!"*

Kneeling against me, she put a wrist over her eyes and began to cry. We *were* in that office! The stairway, the rain, the candle-glimmer, the babble beyond the hall door, Pete—I threw a hand to my face. A cauliflowered eye. No wonder my vision was addled. Lord, what a headache! I grabbed Pete's arm, electrified.

"I'm all right, Pete. You—*you*—"

"It was awful," she said faintly. "No water. I couldn't bring you out of it. Then I heard you breathe. You did get to your feet. Then just as you'd come around you'd faint again."

I clapped a hand to my blinded eye; sent my good eye darting. "Pete, I was knocked cold. It must have been this blow in the eye—"

"Cart, I thought you were gone—"

"Gone?" I panted. "I dreamed I was dead. Good Lord! I

dreamed—I dreamed we'd dug up Uncle Eli. Something—a thing black and alive—came out of the coffin. Paint on the side of his shoe and—" Memory bombed in my head. "He said he'd killed you. Shot you dead. Yes! There was a fight. Cacos. That hare-lipped gendarme came at me. Said you'd been finished. Good God! it must have been then I was hit! No, but I saw the black body in the grave before the Cacos came and—" I clutched my forehead. "That crack on the head has me all twisted up—"

"Drink the rest of this," Pete whispered. "We mustn't stay any longer. I—I haven't a gun—"

I swallowed another gulp. Pete balled up her handkerchief and scrubbed grime and dried blood off my mouth and nose.

"Wow, what a dream!" I panted out. "It seemed they buried me in the coffin. The Cacos—up there in that graveyard. Nailed on the lid. Why—it was real, Pete, real as the devil and I—I can't seem to figure where the reality ended and the dream began."

Her lips were white, her mouth tensed. "Cart, can you stand?"

I put my hands on the floor and pushed myself upright. Pete held me against the desk. My head was splitting, but my one available eye had cleared.

"A whole mess of bad dreams," I gasped on. "First I thought you and I—on the staircase—only somehow we were Widow Gladys and Toadstool—and then I thought we were in the tunnel where—" Heat flowed up from my stomach; another thought bombed through my brain. "Where's Tousellines?" I caught Pete's shoulder. "And Narcisse?"

"I—"

"What's that *sound?*"

"Quiet!" She turned from me swiftly and sent a glance of fear at the door to the hall. Beyond the door, the hall was filling with noise, as if a crowd was pouring in from the veranda, tramping and stamping and clapping hands. The door was closed, and the uproar rattled the knob. I took a breath to speak. Pete whirled; put her fingers over my mouth.

"They're in the hall—"

I WASN'T punch drunk now. The house was echoing to a bedlamite clamor, a thumping and drumming, an undertone sifting of rumba gourds, sticks clacking together and beating time to a weird off-key singsong—*do-re-mi*—*do-re-mi*—that was nerved faster and faster, louder and louder in a din that shook the office door, tremored the floor under me, vibrated the ceiling.

I snatched the chunky bottle and tried to drain sense down my throat. Fingers gripped icy on my wrist, Pete stood, wide-eyed, watching the door. Bodies seemed to be rushing pell-mell in the hall, trampling like an elephant herd, trumpeting that three-note chant. Then a drum boomed out a tremendous rata-plan, the rushing and chanting dropped into a well of quiet, and telephoned through the office door came a thin-piped, whinny-ing echo like a voice heard from a rooming-house speaking tube.

"Silence, Cacos—The King of all *Zombies* speaks—"

Liquor, dizziness, headache, everything went out of me in one single shock. I remembered that voice coming from the lobby of the hall. I knew that neighing whinny beyond the door. Raw-nerved, I made a convulsive grab at Pete's arm.

"It's *him!*"

Before she could realize my meaning, the voice was going again.

"The King of all *Zombies,* the White Master of the Dead, would tell the living black that those who follow him can never die! The dead who fall with him shall be raised again. Behold, Cacos, the master of life and death, the un-dead come to rule from the tomb beyond—Speak, Tousellines, and tell them what I say—"

I could have sworn a subterranean hand was rocking the floor. Quivering, one-eyed, panting in the candle-lit stuffiness of that office under the stairs, I had to catch the edge of the desk and glare at the door beyond which a speaker, undeniably Tousellines, had started a mewling stream of Creole in a tone so soprano with terror it almost whistled. The parroted jitter was answered by a cannonade of cheers. Once more the drum boomed for silence; the horse-like whinny echoed down the hall.

"Behold the dead from the grave, risen to lead you! Behold the white *zombie* came to show you the way. Attend, Cacos! Arm! Send word through the *mornes*. Let your brothers answer the call. Say no harm can befall the black who follows in the service of the *zombie* king. Say no evil can come to him who joins forces with the un-dead dead—Tell them, Tousellines, tell them—"

"Pete," I whispered, "it's him—*him*—"

Tousellines squealed; sound broke in surf waves that shook through the door to alarm the candle and rattle the rain-hammered window; the drum outside brought a smash of silence, the neighing went on—

"Cacos, the army of your country comes to bring you harm. Tomorrow the brothers of your race will come to wrest victory from your hands. But the hills are yours for the taking. The land, the rivers, fields, all shall be yours. Call your friends to a day of conquest. Call the blacks to the army of the King of the Dead. Spread word the *zombie* master has come from his grave to lead. Behold him standing in his palace before you to lead you again as last night, from victory to victory. Remember the gold of yesterday; arise, conquer for the gold of tomorrow. Cacos, the Dead King calls. Tell them, Tousellines! Speak!"

TRANSLATING THIS rhapsodic jargon into Creole did not seem to agree with the oratorical powers of Master Tousellines. His frantic caterwauling shrilled like the language of a terri-fied monkey. The ensuing din filled the house with a rumpus of echoes, a pipe-organ percussion that shook a dust-cloud from the office walls. "Papa Proudfoot! Papa Proudfoot!" That name blasted from a jungle of throats and whitened my hair.

Robbed of animation, I could only hang to the desk, knees shaking; stare one-eyed at the door, at Pete, at the door.

I had been in that coffin! Pete—Pete, who had been killed—

She was purple-eyed. Illuminated with candle-shine, her face was colorless porcelain. She stood with a distracted hand in the glinty thicket of her hair, staring at the door, whispering. "Mad," her voice just came to me. "Stark, raving mad—"

Silence gushed again from the hall. Rain at the office window seemed real enough; but that midnight deluge was the only reality in that cataclysmic moment; never before or since have I heard a voice as unworldly as the whinnying farrago out there in the hall, or known a scene as unnatural as the two of us with the candle listening there in that closed office.

"Cacos, the King of the *Zombies* has spoken!" The neigh ascended to a raucous, cold-in-the-chest scream. "Behold the white dead man who lives with the heart torn from his body. Behold the corpse upright from his tomb. Arise and salute! Follow and conquer! Behold Papa Proudfoot, King of the *Zombies,* new Emperor of Haiti—"

I don't know whether the cheered blast opened the door, or whether Pete opened it. I know she had stepped forward to put a hand on the knob. Her fingers, drawn from her hair, had loosed a gleaming shawl about her shoulders; her face was marble; and she had moved with a hypnotic fixity, a somnambulant effort that I couldn't have stopped. My hands shaking the desk had brought the rolltop slamming down on my fingers (I never saw them bleeding until afterwards) and I could not have stopped her. Not I, fresh out of my coffin ten feet underground, my wits gone kiting, my left eye a cabbage and my fingers caught in a desk and my right eye staring at that picture framed by the opened door.

I know one picture I'll never pass off with a secret (if envious) feeling that I could do a better. The picture of that hall, framed by the office door. Pen and ink sketch, black and white.

Black for the swooped-up shadows, the murky corners, the balcony's overhang, the cloudy loft of the ceiling. Black for the massed heads piled before the black front door, shiny black for bald spots, blue-black for cheekbones, upthrown fists, knots of muscle. Tar for the statue of Tousellines petrified near the library door; and blackest of all, the figure silhouetted against the charcoal smudge of the opened library, arms wide, cape-wings spread in bat-like profile.

And white for the candles that gleamed pale in burnt-cork hands, the outshooting pinpoints of light sketched through the dark, the eggs of Negroid eyes, the ivory grins of piano-key teeth. Blue-white for the shine on gun barrel and machete; gray-white for the bandaged head of Lieutenant Narcisse, dimly visible between two baleful Nubians. White shadows for the sheet-wound row seen regimented on the library floor; and whitest of all for the torso of the black-winged thing in that doorway, the face like a plaster death mask, the hands like talons of bone at the tip of each wing, the body to the belt like a skinny, blue, butcher-shop chicken, ribs and wishbone poking through.

ONE SPLASH of ruby had dropped in that pen sketch, and the smear glowed like a badge on that naked chicken-breast. The thing turned its head in the library door and stood like the Prussian eagle. I saw two eyes like fish scales, the mouth a blue trap under the blade-hooked nose, the strip of adhesive on the tall, bald forehead. And then it wasn't the Prussian eagle, but a horrible and perverted Blue Eagle, for I saw a carpenter's hammer in one fist of talons, in the other a shiny handful of spikes.

A corpse holding a mass meeting! A dead man making a speech! No wonder an eerie gale was blowing through the hall, fluttering the drapes on his skinny arms, stirring the cobweb hairs on his skull.

He lifted the hammer in a sort of dictator's salute—

"Papa Proudfoot, King of all *Zombies*—"

The black and white hall shook with the response, the shouting of white-fringed mouths, drums knuckled, rumba-rattles going like applause in a night club. A palsy seemed to infect the timbers of the house. Wind rushed through the surging, massed heads and flattened the candle-flames on their wicks. Narcisse's ashen countenance, dimly visible between the shoulders of the Nubians supporting him, was distorted and wet. He was moaning like a sick man. The thing in the library door lifted its fistful of spikes and screamed.

"Papa Proudfoot, Emperor of Haiti—Tomorrow, Cacos! Tomorrow we strike! Put flame to the enemy! Pillage and burn! Haiti is ours! Tell them," the blue mouth raved at Tousellines, "that Papa Proudfoot leaves them a moment for an errand with the *Culte des Morts*. Bid them execute this traitor Narcisse and the body is theirs for the sport. Say I go to my office for consultation with the dead. Send the black Louis upstairs to bring down the body of the dead *Ma'mselle* Dale, and then—"

"Uncle Eli!"

In memory to this day that name, as Pete cried it then, puts a creep in the part of my hair. Every egg in that black basket of white eyes rolled at the frail shade in the office door. The thing in the library door whipped its isinglass stare straight at the office where Pete moved.

I yanked my fingers out of the desk and the top came down with a little report.

"Uncle Eli!"

Pete moved into the candle-gloom of the hall. Her arm seemed to float up from her side, finger pointed at the Dracula-face of the exhumed in front of her. The bat couldn't budge. The hammer fell from one bunch of claws and banged on the floor like a shot. The nails showered down like a ringing rain.

"Uncle Eli, I condemn you as my murderer. I condemn you for the deaths of those in your household. Tell them, Tousellines," she cried, "that the Princess of the Dead has come to claim the throne. Shot through the eyes, I was, but I rise from death to accuse my assassin and break the evil spell he would put on these Cacos and their country. Speak my command, Tousellines—the Queen of the *Zombies*—has come—"

THE WORLD, as far as I was concerned, came to a stop. Only shadows in the stopped world swayed, as Pete pointed at Uncle Eli. For a year of sixty seconds, you could have heard a spider's thoughts in that hall; then the lawyer's lower lip broke into piercing squeals; the mob in the front door moaned, shouted, surged backwards; Pete stood in a wind of fear that seemed to pour from those cringing egg-eyes.

I guess my own eyes were doing some bulging; but the eyes of Uncle Eli! The eyes of that cadaver with that red gouge on his chicken-breast were bulbs of un-socketed terror, straining at the girl like frogs trying to escape a leash, wider and wider until it seemed they must break in that face. Something broke in that plaster death mask! The adhesive-taped forehead wouldn't hold. Under the spell of the girl's pointed finger that face appeared to crumple, fall inward, collapse.

A single blue vein ran from temple to temple like a zigzag of lightning. The eyeballs turned upward and stuck. The blue mouth yawned open and gave vent to an exorcised devil in sound.

"Aaaaaaaaaa—"

One hand clutched the wattled throat. The knees buckled, the stomach bent. He fell like an "S," corkscrewing slowly on the way down, the black cloak slipping down off his shoulders like an evening wrap. There was a second when I glimpsed a livid smear in the middle of his pallid spine. A little swirl of black cloth, and he was down.

"Let the Cacos return to their homes!" Pete gave the cry. "The King of the Zombies is dead!"

The sound of Tousellines shrieking. The sound of Narcisse, released from his captors, falling as if his ankles were broken and hitting the floor. The sound of the Cacos going home. I've an idea those black Haitian brigands are running yet, for they funneled through the door like racing buffalos, and the night sped them on with whistles and screams. Their departure left a hurricane in the house. Things were falling in upstairs rooms and dishes were dropping with a sound like shot clay pigeons in the pantry.

I rocked out of the office; stood goggling the dead thing in the library door. There was a rumble under my feet.

"Cart! Tousellines!" Pete's cry penetrated the sawdust in my

The eyes of Uncle Eli were bulbs of unsocketed terror

brain cavity. "Wake up, both of you! Narcisse is hurt! We've got to get out of here and carry him! Quick—before they come back—"

"Ma'mselle! Mon Dieu!" The old darky could only weep and wring his monkey-hands. I couldn't even wring my hands.

"Don't stand there!" Pete whirled at me.

"Hurry! Cart, I'm going upstairs after the picture—"

Picture! Lord! There she was halfway up the staircase. Her running feet seemed to shudder the balustrade. A rain squall slapped the front door, set it banging on its hinges. A cloud of water entered the hall. In the library where a shutter must have blown open, books were tumbling from shelves, and a paper volume flew around in the morguish gloom like a gull trying to get out. Sheets flagged on the dead in their mute line-up; doors slammed up and down the hall; candles were going out all over the place; it was the debacle at the end of Alice in Wonderland.

Pete was Alice flying down the stairs with her traveling bag and a big scroll of canvas clasped in her arms. Somehow I was picking up the cavalry boots at one end of Lieutenant Narcisse, and Tousellines was tugging manfully to raise the shoulders.

"Oh, dear," Pete was crying. "Hurry—"

WE STAGGERED through the door, wobbled over the veranda and plunged into a cataract. Over my shoulder I had a last look at the château's hall. Candlelight was licking at the wan, green face of Uncle Eli with its ruptured eyes, adhesive-taped forehead, and the blue mouth set like a trap. Naked to the hips, the black cape billowing and lashing about his legs, he lay on his side, face toward the door, the red smear glowing on his breast—like a picked chicken blown down off its hook.

One last time I looked back. Not until we'd cleared the end of the valley, running through Noah's rain, and left a mile between us and the house. The deluge had blown itself into fulminating wind, and a prong of yellow moon had torn a hole in the sky.

The valley was a flooded blue bowl; the château a silver-striped animal crouching shadowy on the slope below the cemetery bluff. Angel and tree stood high in the moon-pallored dark like two little crests on a beetling crown.

Sighting them there, I thought I saw them move down the sky. Black blocks of thunder tumbled across the windy valley; left a tremor in the air. Pete dropped her suitcase to catch at my arm; and Tousellines lowered his end of Narcisse with a strangled shout. I shouted, too. That angel *was* moving! The tree was chasing after it. Far to the west the *mornes* echoed to a chorus of Lilliputian screams. The valley gave a roar to drown out the wails of the fleeing Cacos; and I watched graveyard and hillcrest come tumbling and bumbling, sliding and booming down the far escarpment like warm chocolate down the side of a cake; a glacier of storm-loosened mud that buried half the valley in its avalanche.

Whoom! Like that. The black hill fell across the bowl. Haiti trembled. Château Morne Noir was gone.

"*M'sieu* Proudfoot! *M'sieu* Proudfoot!" That was Narcisse, wakened by the thunder, lifting a lethargic head to look around. "*M'sieu* Proudfoot—Zombie—"

"Zombie nothing," was Pete's low-throated answer. "This time Uncle Eli is buried to stay."

We moved on up the leafy wet path in a mystery of quieting darkness.

CHAPTER XVI

PETE'S WORD

I QUOTE THE following from *Moment*—that racy little magazine that gossips its way through the news of the world for the quick digestion of the breakfast reader—and if the cited excerpt missed the scoop of a lifetime for the thinnest skim of the story, it is more due the close-mouthed conservatism of a considerate American consul than lack of reportorial acumen on the part of *Moment's* sharp-shooting staff:

> Haiti—Buried Corpse Leaves Grave—Later Found in Buried House. Perhaps the strangest story of the year comes from the little island Republic of Haiti (French-speaking Negro population) where belief in zombies (corpses brought to life by witchcraft) was stirred to fever pitch during queer seismic antic last week. Some kilometers inland from Cap Haitien, scene of Christophe's Citadel, rise series of forbidding mountains and mornes; a certain district known as Morne Noir overseered by château privately owned by American, Eli Proudfoot, cane planter, one time millionaire, whose recent suicide provoked police investigation and reminded local authorities of unsolved murder of Coast Guard Captain Browninshields killed in Haiti last year (see *Moment*, Sept. 5, 1933).
>
> Death of landowner Proudfoot caused ghost story during brief Caco (bandit) uprising during which local bank blown up, countryside terrorized. Police detachment and army battalion arriving from Port au Prince found revolt extinguished by night of storm after avalasse (tropical rainstorm, landslide) buried Morne Noir château under avalanche. (*Moment*, Apr. 3,

'34.) Digging through ruins Haitian soldiers find entire household including local physician crushed, unrecognizable, identified only by clothing, in pulverized house. Landslide tearing
old structure to pieces played gruesome tricks on victims. Two
found wrapped in bed sheets. Body discovered in swimming
pool. Boy has splintered billiard cue jammed through ribs, ivory
ball crushed into mouth.

Grimmest trick of tropical violence was throwing of grave
over roof of house. Monument of angel crashes through dining
room. Coffin that was buried on hilltop lands in front yard.
Strangest of all is body of Proudfoot, twenty-four hours buried,
lying in wreckage of main hall, practically unmutilated, clearly
identified. Police discover chest of corpse crushed by fallen
planking from roof, but autopsy reveals cerebral hemorrhage,
and one doctor claims death caused by heart trouble. Secret
Service following trail of party said to have attended funeral
night before. Police investigating.

But *Moment* never printed the half of it till later, and not quite
all of it, then. The quoted item did not appear until the day of
our arrival in New York, hours after the last chapter had been
told down there in Haiti....

I THINK it was called the Hotel Merveilleux. Only a shanty in
old shanty town might have been a vision of heaven by comparison (there was a perfume or a goat somewhere that reminded me
of that song) but that hotel with its little blue sun-filled patios
and a lime tree brilliant with birds, was a marvel as far as I was
concerned. There was wash water and soap. Soup and rum. There
was a sandy-haired American consular agent with a cynical grin,
named Drupievsky, and a meal of something swell called *escar-
got* which I thoroughly enjoyed until I found it meant snails.

Lieutenant Nemo Narcisse, Inspector Chief of the Garde
d'Haiti, was on hand with his former pride and punctilio only a
little tarnished; and Maître Pierre Valentin Bonjean Tousellines,
LL.B., Comte de Limonade, arrived from somewhere with his
cheeks returned to their normal licorice, his Mother Goose
umbrella on his arm, and a portmanteau bristling with red tape.

There was a white-haired Haitian general with more medals than a Bowery pawn shop window, and more manners than a lot of Aryans I can think of. And Pete, in a white linen traveling ensemble with a hat at a jaunt and a little red feather.

She shook the hat from her brown-gold head, balanced it on one knee, and soberly tidied up the feather. She could knock me over with it any minute now.

She was saying, "Whether he shot Browninshields, himself, or hired it done, we don't know; but we do know he was directly responsible for the deaths of those others. It was the marksmanship gave me my first inkling—but, good heavens! I just couldn't believe—"

"He must have been a honey," the consular agent chuckled. "Say, how about letting me in on the beginning?" He thrust out long, flanneled legs and wriggled the toes in his open air sandals. His face was pleased with Pete. "Start with Act One. How'd the show open?"

"Exactly," urged the white-headed general. "I would, myself, like to hear it in—what shall we say?—chronological order, if you will forgive my deplorable English." He smiled and fingered a notebook from a tunic pocket under a Croix de Guerre. He jotted with a pencil. *"Alors, ma'mselle? M'sieu?"*

"This is Miss Dale's story," I said. "I'm still lost."

PETE GAVE me a strained smile. "So was I, Cart, up to the moment you told about seeing that half loaf of raisin bread. But—from the very first that will sounded fishy. I mean all those codicils or stipulations or whatever you call them," she directed at Tousellines. "That part about the heirs remaining in the château twenty-four hours, forced to attend the funeral and all. Just the sort of thing to have the household in conniptions, yet keep them on hand. And the way it was devised—down the list. Calculated to start any sort of a free-for-all. And that eccentric business of the grave-plot marked out, the monument prepared, the exacting instructions to dig the grave just ten feet deep, and that ghastly stake to be driven into the coffin. Every detail had something to do with the murderer's trap for us. I—I might have guessed—"

"Guessed?" I snapped. "Why? Lots of old people are fussy about their funerals, their coffins. I can't see how—"

"I thought it was just an old man's morbid streak," Pete lifted her shoulders. "And when Maître Tousellines told us about *zombies* it—well, it seemed logical a lonely old man might do something of the sort."

The general nodded. "The post in the grave, it is old Haitian superstition."

"And the whole plan hinged on that stake in the coffin," Pete breathed. "Right away it was an alibi and an ace in the game. A stake in the grave, a monument planted on top, a body buried ten feet underground and a mile from the house—and yet when we walked back downhill after the funeral and retired to our rooms and Dr. Sevestre stayed outside for a stroll on the lawn, *the murderer was there in the château to meet him!*"

I had a mental picture of that black-shrouded body in the coffin; I could feel again that dent in the casket floor under my left shoulder blade; once more I saw that chicken-breasted thing in the black hall with that stab-red smear under its wishbone. It put dampness on my forehead and I was glad to hear the consul or agent give a whistle of consternation.

"Whew, Miss Dale! I can't figure the answer to this." Tousellines agitated his features into raisin-wrinkles; Narcisse made an audible swallow; the general scratched in his notebook; I waited for Pete.

"He must've been on the front veranda concealed in the vines. Anyway, he hit the doctor with two quick shots."

"Why knock off Sevestre?"

"As Lieutenant Narcisse later suggested, the doctor knew too much," Pete declared. "A great deal was known by Dr. Sevestre. That was why the others in that household were killed, too."

I fuddled, "but, Pete, what did they know?"

SHE REMINDED me, "You told me the answer to that. Just after the police had left the château. Don't you remember telling me about Browninshields and rum runners, and how you thought Uncle Eli had been murdered because he knew who'd killed the Coast Guard captain? Well, that's the reason those seven others were killed. They were the ones who knew. About Browninshields. And they were murdered because the killer was afraid they might expose him."

"We were spending every effort to run down the Browninshields assassin," the Haitian general advised. "Morne Noir Château had long been under suspicion, and was also under surveillance for smuggling."

"Old Proudfoot had been bootlegging rum to the States," the consular agent suspected. "He used up an awful lot of cane and his boats were always off somewhere. He seemed to have more money than your ordinary planter."

"Of this smuggling business," Tousellines put in mournfully, "I was never aware. I knew my client had agents in New York with whom he was communicating, but I thought always it was sugar."

"The household was on the death list because they knew who killed, or was behind the killing of Browninshields," Pete went on. "The will called them together to their—their deaths. Dr. Sevestre was slain because he knew about the plan. He was double crossed."

"But why were *you* summoned to Morne Noir?" I gaped at Pete. "You weren't any murder witness to be put on the spot."

"I wasn't supposed to be put on the spot," Pete explained with a little shudder. "That was a slip in the plan, for I—I was intended for something else. Another slip was when you, Cart, arrived on the scene. And the killer never expected the police so soon on the job. I think it spoiled his scheme when he knew the Haitian gendarmes and Lieutenant Narcisse were on hand at the doctor's shooting."

NARCISSE'S FOREHEAD was doleful. "I? Name of a thousand pipes, but as a police detective I am the most blind. I still do not see."

"But you forced the hand," Pete rewarded him with a smile. "If you hadn't been there I don't think the Caco uprising would have come so soon. That was the deepest-laid part of the plot. If it had come later—but the killer had to play it fast, and he wasn't ready. He had to do something to get the police out of the château. What time was the doctor shot?"

Narcisse consulted a pad from his tunic. "Two o'clock."

"And Sir Duffin, the Englishman?"

"A moment or so before six."

"Then while the lieutenant was interrogating the household right after the doctor's murder," Pete explained to the general, "the killer was off in the night—he must have had a horse hidden down the compound—riding like mad to start the Cacos attacking Cap Haitien, and start the story that a *zombie* was on the loose. Some time between two and six he returned, entered the château and hid somewhere—probably the office, maybe the tunnel behind the desk. Meantime, with all of us in the library, he had a chance to cut off the telephone.

"And then he heard the Englishman go sneaking up the passage to the wardrobe in the upstairs room."

"That *cochon!*" Narcisse spat. "He was playing the ghost, *mon general,* to frighten those others away, to have the will for himself."

"The killer trailed him upstairs to the wardrobe and shot him in the back," Pete recounted.

The agent said, as if it didn't matter, "I knew that British beggar. He was a louse."

"I think," Pete surmised, "the murderer had expected his companions to do away with Sir Duffin. First on the will, you see. But the police had disarmed the household and that left the whole massacre up to the murderer. *He* wasn't disarmed, by any means. He could open the safe at first chance and take all the guns he wanted."

"*Bon sang de Dieu!* what a terror!" Tousellines shook out.

"Madman's cunning," the girl whispered huskily. "If he hadn't dropped one accidental clue he—he might have carried out his entire plan. But he killed Sir Duffin, and darted back to the office. Perhaps that's when he took that old duelling pistol from the safe. Everybody is up in Uncle Eli's room; the terror has started. Now the killer can sneak into any room he pleases and wait for his next victim. While we're in the dining room, then, he's in the billiard room."

"Waiting for Ambrose," Narcisse gulped.

"He knows, too, that Ti Pedro is locked in the storeroom next door, and he wants to terrify the household. That's why he cut himself a lance from a billiard cue and staged that ghastly scene with the albino. Meantime suspicion would be on everybody but him."

Narcisse mourned, "The will made it seem so, and with those vipers all telling lies, each on the other—what would you have?"

The general raised genial gabled eyebrows. "*Enfin, ma'mselle?*"

HER TIRED eyes darkened with memory. "After breakfast Ambrose, going to the billiard room, did not see the murderer. Perhaps he was out on the veranda, lurking behind the window shutters. Then the boy was called to the office under the stairs for questioning. When he was returned to the billiard room the lights blew out. The storm played hand and glove with murder all the way. The killer stepped through the shutters; Ambrose saw him, perhaps in a flash of lightning, and screamed. He was dead in a second. And then there was a single shot."

"*Eh bien, mais oui, alors!*" Lieutenant Narcisse clapped a dramatic hand to his bandaged brow. "But this pistol afterwards found on the staircase across that hall?"

"Planted," Pete determined. "Everybody was milling and shouting in the dark of the hall; then crowding the door of the storeroom where Ti Pedro lay dead. Meanwhile the killer, leaving the billiard room by a window, could circle the house on the veranda, open the front door unnoticed, and throw the pistol on

that staircase without being heard. We were all petrified, looking at Ti Pedro—"

"With a bullet most exactly in the top of his black skull," the
police officer blattered. "And the storeroom was locked. The door
to the billiard room had not been opened. The bullet down into
the head. And who set on fire the grass carpet? Does an assassin in the next room with solid wall and locked door between
do that? There was a window, too, that had not been opened.
C'est incroyable!"

"There's only one way I can explain that," Pete said. She leaned
forward on the white bench and searched our variety-show
expressions as if for confirmation. The white-haired general
frowned amazement and the consul looked amused. She sighed.
"This is what happened, I think. In fact, it's the only way it could
have happened. Ambrose screamed in the billiard room and was
stabbed. Ti Pedro heard that scream, same as we all did. Licked
in a dark room next door, he did the thing any person would do
under like circumstances. He made a light."

"A light?" Narcisse let his mouth come open.

"Only a little one," was the answer. "You couldn't see it in the
hall, even if the transom in that door was open. Can't you picture
it? Why, Ti Pedro lit a match and tried to peek into the billiard
room to see what in Heaven's name had happened to Ambrose!"

"Peek into the billiard room?" It was my turn to miss.

She made a little gesture of exasperation. "The precise thing
anybody would have done. The door between the two rooms.
Those old doors all have big keyholes. Of course! Ti Pedro struck
a match, stooped to put an eye to the keyhole.

"There must have been a flash of lightning outside, and the
poor Dominican saw Ambrose on the floor with that cue in his
chest: Horrified, Ti Pedro let the burning match drop from his
fingers. Then he reached down to pick it up—"

"By the goat-horned soul of Faustin the First!" the general
swore gallantly. "I believe *ma'mselle* is one superior detective."

"And the murderer on the other side of the door saw the

match-light at the keyhole," Pete hurried on, "and jumped at the door with the gun, put the muzzle at the keyhole and fired! Ti Pedro's head was down—bending to pick up the match like that—right in line to catch the bullet where—where it did. The blow threw him backwards and the rug was—on fire."

"By George," Drupievsky grinned. "I guess that taught him a lesson."

Narcisse stammered, "But why did you not accuse me of stupidity, *ma'mselle*."

"I wasn't sure," Pete said. "I'm only guessing now. I did try to say something, but we'd discovered Ambrose by that time. The killer had stuffed that pool ball in Ambrose's teeth to make it look as if the albino was third and—anyway I didn't know *who* had done it. That was what had me—had me frightened."

"Good riddance, so far," the consular agent chuckled, taking an apple from his pocket to gnaw an unbashful bite. "Ti Pedro and Ambrose weren't any loss to anybody except the hangman. Who's next?"

"Well, next Lieutenant Narcisse ordered Mr. Cartershall and me upstairs and—then Cart had to paint on a picture—and suddenly word came about the Caco attack at Cap Haitien, and the police had to leave."

TOUSELLINES SWALLOWED a quaver and took up the story. "I was left in charge and it was like hearing my own death sentence. That house of scorpions! When Widow Gladys came out of her room with a pistol, *bleu!*—"

I cried, "That's how she got that pistol! The murderer, out on the veranda, he tossed it into her window."

"And this Jamaican woman, she was killed?" the general grunted.

I described the gun battle on the staircase, the precipitous death of the Toadstool and his mamma.

It was not too credible, out there in that sun-filled courtyard with birds in a lime tree and the consul crunching a red apple. He finished with a magnificent bite, shied the core at a guinea hen fussing along the blue wall, grinned at me with one fruit-mumped cheek and said, wiping his hands on his pockets, "Fella, you had a nerve playing around with that gang. As for your lady friend, Miss Dale here, I take my hat off. Howdja keep from running out over the horizon?"

"With a bandit uprising? And that afternoon storm and not knowing the country or anything?" I shook my head.

Pete said gravely, "And the rest of them were as scared of us by that time as we were of them. I mean Manfred and the En-sign."

"So the widow and her kid blasted each other off the waiting list," smiled the consul. "How about the next two?"

I described Pete's disappearance, my chase around the house, the En-sign and Manfred stalking each other in the rain, the sailor's timely end. "And Manfred went out of his head; fled down the terrace like a runaway elephant. Blinded by the storm, he ran smack into that swimming pool, stumbled in and drowned."

The consular agent grinned. "If you keep this up I'll think crime doesn't pay and go back home and get a job. Seven of those rats in twenty-four hours!"

"And Mr. Cartershall and I were the only ones left," Pete paled. "I—I was the last name on the will, you see." She made an apprehensive gesture.

It brought a squeak of dismay out of Tousellines. Brows gathered in a troubled frown, the old darky waved his portmanteau at Pete. *"Ma'mselle,* forgive me for not speaking of this at once. The will of your uncle—it appears there are complications. It is not, I find, valid, and—"

I broke him off with an angry, "You mean to say Miss Dale won't get the estate after all this gosh-awful—"

"I don't want anything," Pete protested vehemently.

"But there is no estate," the little black lawyer blabbed regretfully. "I am this morning advised by cable that *M'sieu* Proudfoot's holdings on the New York Exchange are completely nothing. A matter of unpaid margins. Château Morne Noir has not paid the taxes and faces confiscation, and the plantation was heavily mortgaged only last month and—

"And repeal wiped out the bootlegging business," Pete cried, "and that's what lay behind this whole desperate plot. The rum runners were under pressure from the police on the Browninshields murder. The gang was broke. Uncle Eli was penniless, facing bankruptcy—"

"*Un moment,*" the general interposed with a Colonial bow. "*Ma'mselle* is not penniless. I do not know if the good American consul, *M'sieu* Drupievsky, has yet informed you, but there is a posted reward of ten thousand dollars for the dead or alive capture of the gunman responsible for the Browninshields murder."

"Yeah," the consular agent stood up. "And it goes to Miss Dale."

PETE STOOD up. "Then half of it belongs to Mr. Cartershall."

I stood up. "The dickens it does. I don't even know, yet, how that corpse got out of its grave or who the real—I mean, how it—"

Narcisse stood up. "It looked like *M'sieu* Proudfoot—"

Pete insisted, "Mr. Cartershall gets half because he—" she looped an arm through my wooden one, "because you spied that half loaf of raisin bread and I'd never of noticed it. I was too rattled to see it, Cart, down in that tunnel room, and if you'd missed it we—we wouldn't be hearing about earthly rewards, anyway."

"Pete," I mumbled, "what in the world!"

"Afterwards, back in the house, alone with Corporal Louis, I began to be sure about it. Raisin bread down in that tunnel. On a kitchen table. Somebody was—hungry. Corpses don't—don't eat. How did it get down there. Why? And that fugitive you'd chased *had* to be somewhere."

"But we pounded all over the walls and floor of that room!"

Pete said quietly, "And never thought about the ceiling."

"The ceiling?"

"Yes, and alone in the house with the rest of you gone up the *morne* to exhume Uncle Eli, it—it came to me. Honestly, I wanted to die with fear. I knew right then the killer might be there in the château. The gendarme stood guard outside my closed door; I was just on the point of calling to him when—I heard the murderer speaking out there on the balcony. The corporal fled in terror, and I don't blame him a bit. Then there were two shots—in *Cart's* room—and I heard the gunman go racing downstairs, and then for a long time I didn't hear anything."

Perspiration watered my collar. "He fired two shots in my room?"

"Your door must have been open a little way. He stepped over the threshold, fired twice, then ran. Then I guessed where he'd gone—the raisin bread—everything came clear in every detail— I knew who it was!"

"I saw the paint on his shoe," I whispered. "The tube I dropped up there. He must've stepped on it."

"He meant to kill me," Pete said tightly. "He'd got me down here in Haiti—his first plan was to keep me here. Then he heard Cart and me—talking together—he thought we were engaged—it maddened him, I suppose. So he tried to shoot me. It took me a long time to get up courage to leave my room. Finally I took a candle and started—down to the office—down the tunnel. Nobody was in the cave at its end when I got there, but I—I heard a terrible sound above the ceiling. Shouting and calling. Right over my head. Like a delirium in the air. Cart's voice!"

"The tunnel!" I guess I hollered. "It led from the house out to that grave on the hill!"

"And I could hear you in the grave," she put a hand over her eyes. "I stood on the table and pounded with my fists on the ceiling. I pounded and pounded. Finally I struck something and the wooden ceiling—a big piece of it—swung down like a sort of trap door. There was a foot of space above the opening and—and I was looking up at the bottom of the rosewood coffin!"

"Say!" Mr. Drupievsky's face was wry with incredulity.

"I didn't know how to get through. You see, the sides and ends of the casket were resting on ledges of hard earth. Anyone looking down into the grave from above wouldn't see any hole under the coffin. Looking up at the thing from underneath I could only see a patch of rosewood about the size of a—a big washboard. Just big enough to let a body pass through. Remember, how the casket was especially constructed and kept hidden in the storeroom? Well—it has a trap door, too."

SHE PUT her hands on my arm. "That's how the runner vanished in the tunnel ahead of you, Cart. In the pitch dark, he jumped up on that table. You ran straight across the room and bumped into me. We rolled and fought on the floor and that beast opened the trap in the ceiling and the trap in the coffin and crawled up into the grave. That's when he dropped that bread on the table."

"Ye gods!" Only I didn't say ye gods.

"I didn't know how to open the door in the coffin's bottom. A hidden spring built in the casket somewhere. I suppose there was a release inside where a man could work that false bottom, too. Anyway, I had to smash off a table leg, and finally with that I pounded the rosewood to pieces. Cart tumbled out and I thought he was smothered. I had a terrible time dragging him back through the tunnel, he kept fainting and groaning—"

I gagged, "But if Uncle Eli was—"

"He was never dead in the first place," Pete said, tight-lipped. "His suicide was a fake. Dr. Sevestre, in on the scheme, simply palmed a bullet from his head and pretended an autopsy. The adhesive tape merely hid the fact there wasn't any bullet hole. That's what the doctor knew, and that's why Uncle Eli killed him first. We know why he slaughtered the rest of his gangmen. And he planned to make himself dictator of Haiti."

"He called himself the Emperor," Tousellines blurted.

"As a *zombie*," Pete nodded, "he could play on the superstitions of these people and bring the Cacos under his control. He'd lost his estate, now he wanted the island. Mad, yes. He planned to seize all of Haiti. He would have made me—his slave or something, and, playing the living dead—"

"But the stake in the grave!" I groaned. "And when the grave was dug there wasn't any hole down through because I saw the bottom, earth, puddles—"

"Plenty of room in Uncle Eli's casket," Pete whispered. "He could hug against one side and the stake would miss him entirely. And then it sprung the trap in the bottom of the coffin. Don't you see? The grave-diggers were instructed to go down exactly ten feet. Which left a foot or so of earth between the grave bottom and the roof of that underground room. You remember the floor of that dugout was scattered with dirt. That's where it came from. The stake pounded through the coffin lid, drove open the trap in the floor of the coffin, broke through the floor of the grave and forced open the door in the ceiling underneath. The dirt in the space between poured through and Uncle Eli dropped out of the coffin into the tunnel. Easy enough to paint those horrible smears on his chest and back. And when he heard the police were going to exhume his body it gave him a chance to play *zombie* better than ever—"

"He," said the consular agent, "was a nice guy."

"At the last he was going back under the coffin to nail it up—with Cart inside."

Pete sat down. "To think he should have died of heart trouble, then. He thought he'd shot me, and when I walked out of the office, playing his own game—well, I wouldn't have imagined he had any heart to have trouble with—"

BUT E.E. Cartershall (that's me) had a heart to have trouble with. I sat staring at Pete so long the afternoon mellowed into twilight. I heard the consular agent chuckle, "Well, Miss Dale gets the reward," and, "That plane will stop for you both tomorrow." I heard people bidding us *"Bon soir,"* and *"Mille merci,"* as we departed the courtyard of the Hotel Merveilleux. I sat staring at Pete and having heart trouble.

Finally I had to light a cigarette for nonchalance.

I resigned. "Send me to the foot of the class, Pete. Why should Uncle Eli fire twice in my room and think he'd killed you when—"

"Wait." She disengaged a hand from mine; ran through a screen door into the nice hotel.

I fingered a slab of beefsteak lashed to my black eye, and waited. Presently Pete returned with an oil painting in her hand. "Southern Hospitality, by E.E. Cartershall, '34." Life size, Patricia Dale in afternoon frock with a straw hat swinging at her side. I glared like Richard Coeur de Lion.

"It was tacked to the closet door." Pete held up the canvas, tears shining in her eyes.

There were no tears in the portrait's eyes. The portrait had no eyes. Two little holes had been burned through the canvas where the painted eyes had been.

"Pete," I smiled, "do you remember promising you'd give me your word on something when this painting was finished?"

"Yes," Pete said.

"Well," I smiled, "it's finished now, all right. How about you and I—and a pent house. I insist on a pent house. We can't get too far above ground to suit me."

"Yes," Pete said.

ABOUT THE AUTHOR

AS A GUEST speaker at Pulpcon in Dayton, Ohio in July, 1986, I played the old Q. and A. game. I believe the opening of that game makes a good beginning for the present discussion of my fiction writing for the pulps.

Q. How and when did my fiction writing begin?

A. I have in my files the initial effort—a book entitled *The Devul and the Knight* [sic] written age five, hand-printed, hand-illustrated and hand-bound, price one cent (two copies, one remainder). The "K" circumflexed over the "night" was inserted by a brother ten years my senior. From the penny profit (from a sale within the family), I purchased a Mary Jane—taffy wrapped around a glob of peanut butter. Um.

Q. Then?

A. Shortly thereafter, I wrote, hand-printed, hand illustrated and hand-bound *Hawk Eye the Indian Boy* (two copies, price one cent, one remainder) which bought me another Mary Jane.

Q. And?

A. There followed a production entitled *The Sheriff of Red Roach Ranch*. ("Roach" was the spelling of my wicked older brother when I asked him if "Rock" was spelled with two "Ks." No matter.) I copied the spelling "Sheriff and "Ranch" from a book I was reading. Again, the one cent sale (leaving one remainder) paid for another Mary Jane.

Thus I conceived a notion.

Born was the idea that by writing I could eat.

That idea served as an apothegm for my subsequent career as a writer— a ruling not invariably a truism. As it eventuated there were times when I had Thanksgiving dinner at bottom of the totem pole at a hot dog stand.

However, I wrote many yarns for my high school magazine-an effort that caused an English teacher to suggest I submit a fiction effort to a magazine. Not overly optimistic, I knew I couldn't compete in a try for that day's top, the *Saturday Evening Post.* So I picked

Theodore Roscoe

a pulp—*NorthWest Stories.* Luck! A check for $40.00! And a request for another story. This first story, "The Duel," would appear in the September 1926 issue.

That did it.

It was summertime, and I'd been a temporary P.O. employee peddling mail on a route on Long Island. With a high school buddy similarly employed, who shared room and board. And I had just carried a very heavy parcel-post package addressed to a "Tillie Tisswisser," 8,001 some local avenue at the end of the line. After lugging it an extra half mile, I discovered there was no such address. Belatedly suspicious, I pried open one corner of the package and exposed a cinder block. Which my pal had wrapped and mailed with a slew of cancelled stamps.

That would have done it if my check hadn't come that day with $40.00. "I quit! I just made a fortune!" I told them at the P.O. where I dumped the cinder block. (And I got even with my buddy by ducking out of our boarding house by letting my suitcase out of our bedroom window on a clothes line and leaving him stuck with the rent.)

Anyway, the $40.00 check started me on what eventuated as a career, writing for *Action Stories, Argosy, Short Stories* and *Adventure,* for such astute editors as Jack Byrne, Don Moore and, after the war (World War II), Burroughs Mitchell and Bud Hart. Of whom I still see Bud Hart—the others no longer among those present.

World War II pretty much killed most of the now extinct pulps. From paper shortage? I can't say. But many pulp writers faded away during the war. Among them, one of the best. Frederick Faust ("Max Brand"). I'm not certain, but I believe he may have been killed at Anzio.

If one finds some astonishing names among the early pulp editors some of the writers are equally surprising. In the early *Argosy-All Story.* Mary Roberts Rinehart, Octavus Roy Cohen, Zane Gray, E. Phillips Oppenheim, John Buchan. (Buchan, who wrote "The Thirty-Nine Steps," became Governor-General of Canada.)

ONE OF the questions often asked me is how did I happen to write about an old veteran yarn-spinner who spun yarns about his service in the French Foreign Legion. In North Africa back in the early '30s I encountered on a street in Casablanca this old-time Legionnaire with hashmarks up to his elbow. He agreed to talk over wine at a *brasserie.*

He didn't wear the classic old-time Legion uniform-the button-back blue overcoat, white trousers, blue cummerbund, heavy desert-boots called *brodequins.* He wore an old artillery-man's outfit. But the square-brim *kepi* with the gold torch insignia was Legion.

Questioning him in my limping French, and struggling to comprehend his metaphors, I got a *formidable* story. Aside from obvious hyperbole and manifest adjectives, some of it was perhaps true.

Here was my prototype for Thibaut Corday. Which, of course, wouldn't be his right name. You could enlist in the Legion under any name you chose, and since his right name was Hyacinth Rastagouch, he chose Corday for what is called a *nom de guerre.* Which became your official name as a "Stepson of France." Meaning you couldn't be extradited for a crime committed elsewhere—a fact, it was said contributed to the enlistment of numerous criminals using an alias. Who knows?

Because Frenchmen can't enlist in the French Legion, I had Corday say he was a Belgian. Or was it a Swiss? Anyway, the teller of my story attributed to Corday good English, partly translated.

Since his yarns were obviously mixtures of fact and fiction, I never presumed they would be taken seriously by the reader. And was surprised when several critics wrote to tell me the military tactics in this or that Corday tale were hokum. They were so intended to sound.

Incidentally, some Legion veterans in New York voted me an honorary member of the Veterans of the French Foreign Legion.

Actually, I never saw the Legion in combat. At a Legion H.Q. back in Sidi Bel Abbes, I was querying one of the officers. Apparently he thought I was planning to enlist. He shook his head at me with the comment: *"Discipline terrible!"* They followed the old rule, *"March qu creve."* "March or die." If a Legionnaire fell out, exhausted, in a Sahara march, they sent a sharpshooter back to kill him, and spare him from torture by desert tribesmen. But the Legionnaires I saw in action weren't risking their lives.

In Europe back then there was a saying. When the English conquer a country they build a custom house. The Germans build a fort. The French build a road. Back then (the '30s) the Legionnaires I saw in action were covered with not-very-glamorous dust, wielding picks and shovels building a road. Some of them in barracks slept in cots with the cot-legs in cans filled with water, to defeat scorpions. Their pay, if I recall correctly, afforded them a daily bottle of *pinard* (cheap red wine). Nothing so intriguing, colorful and lively as in such novels as *Beau Geste*.

So don't join the French Foreign Legion today. You'd get a plain khaki uniform, and risk only being bored to death.

Still, you'd learn one thing. Watch them, if chance occurs, on parade in France or on TV. There's no military outfit anywhere that can out-march their particular step.

ASIDE FROM the Foreign Legion, I most enjoyed writing for *Action Stories* a series about an adventurer named Peter Scarlet. There were at least 14 Peter Scarlet stories, beginning with "Jungle Joker" in the May 1927 issue of *Action Stories*. Other favorites were a tale entitled "On Account of a Woman" (*Adventure*, January 1936) and a tale for *Argosy*, "The Voodoo Express" (October 10, 1931).

On another tack, I enjoyed writing a series for *Argosy* titled "Four Corners," which began with "He Took Richmond" in the June 5, 1937 issue of *Argosy*. These were adventures experienced by a youngster whose uncle was Sheriff in a small town about 100 miles from New York. One of the early Four Corners stories was "I Was the Kid With the Drum" (October 30, 1937)—a murder mystery. They used to have a kid aid the drummer by carrying in a parade the front end of a big base drum (guess where the body was concealed in a hurry by the murderer in this case). Of course, the drum seemed heavier than usual. And the drum-beat seemed more of a thump than the usual vibratory boom. The kid in the story didn't get it. But anyway the murderous drummer discovered he'd killed the wrong person.

In another "Four Corners" tale, I had a thief change his money into coins—loot he could bury in a well. Okay? But when he went back to safely get and spend this big bag of coins, he was trapped by the fact the silver dollars all bore the same date—the date of the robbery.

In one of my favorite Four Corners stories, "Frivolous Sal" (*Argosy*, July 17, 1937), the small town gentry were worried because it was rumored the young woman, so named (after a popular song), kept a diary. Fruitless efforts were made to get hold of it. In the end? Try to guess it.

I had a lot of fun writing "The Head," which appeared in *Short Stories*, December 10, 1932. As a stringer reporter, I had gone to Panama to investigate rumors of "White Indians" in the remote interior near the Colombian border. At a bar in Cristobal I asked the bar-keep if he'd heard of these Indians. Overhearing my query, a bar-fly character asked if I was interred in Jiboro Indians—the tribe that, through a mysterious process, boned, cured and somehow shrank human heads to the size of a base-ball. (Origin of the term "head-shrinker" for a psychologist.) The bar-fly said he had one to sell, and produced what appeared to be a much-shrunken human head. As the Jiboro Indians actu-ally beheaded their enemies and with incredible artsy-crafty skill created such curiosities, I was interested in the specimen handed me by the bar-fly. Ah! Only $300.00.

But the bartender, behind his hand, winked at me a negative signal. I didn't buy the head.

When the bar-fly indignantly took off with his allegedly shrunken head, the bartender advised me it was a fake, a monkey head fixed up to look human.

Later I saw an authentic shrunken head on display in another bar.

When World War II put an end to my pulp efforts, by good luck I sold *Only in New England*—a novel I'd intended for *Argosy*—to Scribner's. Surprisingly, it made the Literary Guild Book of the Month.

Thereafter, I wrote two Navy histories—*U.S. Submarine Oper-ations, World War II* (1949) and *U.S. Destroyer Operations, World War II* (1953) which were published by the Naval Institute at Annapolis (and are still on the market). I also wrote *This is Your Navy* (1950) for service reading. This was followed by *The Web of Conspiracy* (1959), about the Lincoln assassination, which became a *DuPont Show of the Month* on TV in 1961. Of which, with a great deal of help from my devoted wife, Rosamond, got me going again in fiction.

Today I can't recall what some of these tall tales written 50 years ago were about. Maybe I should have written some of them under an assumed name. But when I wrote them I felt I should take my lumps if, compared to many of early *Argosy's* great writers, my efforts proved mediocre. And on the other hand, if some drew plaudits, I'd like to take a bow in person.

Brave, no?

THE ARGOSY LIBRARY ™

SERIES 5 INCLUDES:

* WORTS * SHEEHAN * SERVISS *

* BRAND * PERRY * ROSCOE *

* BEECHAM *

* WIRT * FORSYTH *

* ROUSSEAU *

THE BEST FICTION
FROM THE FRANK
A. MUNSEY LINE